D0475952

'Captives are rarely in a position to bargain about their future, and you're no different, princess or not. You *are* my slave. Better get used to it.'

'Then it would have been better to let me die at Eboracum with my maid, Roman. That way I would have been free.' Throwing off the blanket, she stood up in one swift unbending of her body, intending to put more distance between them.

The soft mattress hampered her feet—the curve of the canvas was not designed for her height—and the long reach of Quintus's arm caught her wrist in an iron grip, pulling her off-balance. Furiously she tried to throw him off, her eyes blazing with green fire. 'No man may *touch* me!' she yelled, competing with the roar outside.

'Then that's another thing you'd better get used to, Princess High and Mighty.'

Author Note

For many years I longed to set a story in Bath, one of England's most ancient and beautiful cities in the West Country, developed by the Romans for its famous natural hot springs. Like other natural phenomena, the springs were venerated by earlier Celtic tribes, but after the Roman invasion the place became known as Aquae Sulis (Waters of Sulis, the presiding Celtic god). Excavations have revealed exactly how the Romans built temples and healing pools to channel the waters, creating a spa for visitors from far and wide to bathe and make offerings in return for all kinds of help. It must have been an early example of a tourist town, with all amenities. The name of Minerva, the Roman goddess of healing, was then linked to that of Sulis (as Sulis Minerva) so as not to offend the local deities, of whom the northern goddess Brigantia is yet another counterpart.

Tracing the history of places back through the ages—like Bath, Lincoln and York, for instance—can be both fascinating and rewarding when so much has been discovered through archaeology to show us how people lived. The social history is what I find most interesting—particularly the various ways in which ordinary people sought cures for their ills through nature, in discoveries that reveal how closely their daily needs and hopes resembled our own. I hope that my story of how Romans and Celts co-existed during those difficult times of occupation will be the beginning of deeper research by the reader.

The Roman army packed up and left England two hundred years after this story, leaving our island with Latinised place-names that have since changed to the ones we know today. So Eboracum is now York, Danum is Doncaster, Lindum is Lincoln, Corinium Dobunnorum is Cirencester, Aquae Sulis is Bath, and Corieltauvorum is Leicester. Other places mentioned, like Margidunum, have now disappeared, being little more than staging-posts along the main highway.

SLAVE PRINCESS

Juliet Landon

All the characters in this book have no existence outside the imagination of the author, and have no relation whatsoever to anyone bearing the same name or names. They are not even distantly inspired by any individual known or unknown to the author, and all the incidents are pure invention.

First published in Great Britain 2011
by Mills & Boon, an imprint of Harlequin (UK) Limited.
Large Print edition 2011
Harlequin (UK) Limited, Eton House, 18-24 Paradise Road,
Richmond, Surrey TW9 1SR

ISB

Harlequin (UK) policy is to use papers that are natural, renewable and recyclable products and made from wood grown in sustainable forests. The logging and manufacturing process conform to the legal environmental regulations of the country of origin.

Printed and bound in Great Britain
by CPI Antony Rowe, Chippenham, Wiltshire

Juliet Landon's keen interest in art and history, both of which she used to teach, combined with a fertile imagination, make writing historical novels a favourite occupation. She is particularly interested in researching the early medieval and Regency periods, and the problems encountered by women in a man's world. Her heart's home is in her native North Yorkshire, but now she lives happily in a Hampshire village close to her family. Her first books, which were on embroidery and design, were published under her own name of Jan Messent.

Previous novels by the same author:

ONE NIGHT IN PARADISE**
THE WIDOW'S BARGAIN
THE BOUGHT BRIDE
HIS DUTY, HER DESTINY
THE WARLORD'S MISTRESS
A SCANDALOUS MISTRESS*
DISHONOUR AND DESIRE*
THE RAKE'S UNCONVENTIONAL MISTRESS*
MARRYING THE MISTRESS
SCANDALOUS INNOCENT
(collaboration with the National Trust)

**Ladies of Paradise Road*
**linked to *Ladies of Paradise Road* trilogy

Praise for
Juliet Landon

THE RAKE'S UNCONVENTIONAL MISTRESS

'Landon's understanding of the social mores and language of the era flows through the pages…'
—*RT Book Reviews*

A SCANDALOUS MISTRESS

'…sensual and emotion-filled read…'
—*RT Book Reviews*

HIS DUTY, HER DESTINY

'Landon has written a titillating and entertaining battle of the sexes, one in which readers cannot help but take sides—both of them.'
—*RT Book Reviews*

THE BOUGHT BRIDE

'Landon carefully creates the atmosphere of the eleventh century, incorporating intriguing historical details…'
—*RT Book Reviews*

THE KNIGHT'S CONQUEST

'A feisty heroine, a heroic knight, an entertaining battle of wills and plenty of colourful history flavour this tale, making it a delightful one-night read.'
—*RT Book Reviews*

Chapter One

Eboracum—A.D. *208*

The slapping of cupped hands on oiled skin echoed off the stone walls of the gymnasium like lukewarm applause. It was interrupted, however, by a bad-tempered grunt. 'Steady, man! That's still sore.'

Fingertips explored a pink scar streaking diagonally like a ribbon across the muscled shoulder. It was healing well. 'Where, sir? Just there?' The fingers fondled.

'Ouch! Yes, you imbecile!'

The slave grinned and continued his kneading.

'If you were not such a good masseur, I'd have you flogged,' the deep voice grumbled into the towelled pillow.

'Yes, sir,' the slave replied, hearing a smile in the empty threat. Quintus Tiberius Martial was not a soft touch in any sense, but nor was he given to floggings and beatings. Florian had been in the Tribune's service since he was twelve years old and so far had only suffered tongue-lashings for his misdemeanours.

The Tribune's back was long, tapering and sculpted, divided by a valley with hills and mounds of hard muscle rising on each side, the Titanic shoulders extending to arms as strong as tree branches.

His dice-playing towel-wrapped companions looked up from their game to smile at the tetchiness. 'Time you had some exercise,' one of them volunteered, softly.

From the slab, Quintus opened one dark eye to glare at his friend. 'I've been exercising all morning, if you recall. Where were you?'

'Not that kind,' the friend said, winking at his partner.

The partner moved one of the pieces on the board and shuffled himself deeper into his towel. 'Horizontal, he means,' he said, helpfully.

'Yes…well…this is probably as horizontal as I'm going to get until I'm properly mended,' Quintus mumbled, crossly.

'Rubbish!' said the friend, wiping the sweat

from his face with one forearm. 'You *are* mended. Isn't he, Florian?'

'Indeed, sir. I believe our forthcoming trip to the hot springs in the south will complete the cure, but I see no reason why the Tribune should not take—'

'Oh, spare me the lecture and get on with your pummelling, lad,' Quintus returned sharply. 'One punishment at a time, for pity's sake.'

'Yes, sir,' said Florian, lifting the towel from his master's brawny thighs. 'Will you turn, sir, if you please?'

Quintus obliged, staring up at the thick cloud of steam that hung in the curve of the vaulted ceiling. There were sounds of splashing and the deep bellow of men's voices, the grunts of effort as heavy weights hit the floor, a distant laugh, the patter of bare feet on stone and the accompanying pants as two men wrestled over on the other side of the steaming pool. He caught the whiff of almond and lavender oil as Florian set to work on his chest. He closed his eyes, knowing that his two companions, Tullus and Lucan, would not let the matter rest there. His shoulder had responded well to treatment, but the damage to his knee was more serious, and it was that which had concluded his brilliant career as a military tribune and steered him instead towards administration. His abilities as an expert in the imperial system of record-keeping, accounting and taxes had been recognised even before he was fully recovered, and in record time the Emperor Severus had placed him in his personal service as Provincial Procurator directly responsible to him, not to the Governor of the northern provinces whose hospitality they were at present both using and abusing.

As a respected and successful cavalry officer, Quintus had wanted nothing more than a soldier's life, and although his new position was both challenging and demanding, and lucrative, it could never compare to the heady excitement of command, continuous movement and brotherhood.

'We have your best interests at heart, Quintus my friend,' said Lucan. 'This expedition down to Aquae Sulis will take quite a few days, and you know what will happen every time we're offered a night's hospitality.'

'I've never known you to protest at an excess of hospitality,' Quintus said, gruffly. 'The girls you're offered are never refused, if my memory serves me. What's the problem?'

'You are,' Lucan said. 'How many ways do you know of refusing? No, thank you. Not tonight. Too tired. My leg hurts. My shoulder is sore.'

'You're bound to give some offence,' said Tullus, nodding.

The two friends were Assistant Procurators, junior administrators in Quintus's office of scribes, secretaries and accountants. Younger by a few years than his thirty, they had no plans for marriage, mainly due to the roving nature of the job, but their experience of women from the countries through which they had passed in the Emperor's service was, to say the least, extensive. No one understood better than they how hospitality worked on long journeys, how it was always assumed that a single male guest would need a companion for the night. Slaves were an ever-present commodity to be used at the master's discretion, and for Quintus to be continually plied with this amenity while he was away could become something of a nuisance.

In his army days, he would have thought nothing of it, but these last few months had been physically hampered by pain and some anger at the turn of events, and though his recuperation had involved a punishing regime of exercises to tone his body, he had allowed himself no rewards. Not even the trip to Aquae Sulis was solely for his health; there was some investigating to be done, too.

'Giving offence,' he responded, 'has never kept

me awake at night.' Flinging aside the hip-covering towel, he sat up and swung his legs over the side of the slab, causing Florian to skip to one side. He ran a hand through his damp dark hair and scowled at his feet. 'I'll take a woman when I'm ready,' he said. 'I shall not be stuck for excuses.'

Lucan was tall and as lithe as a panther, his nose handsomely hooked, his mouth wide and often smiling, his Greek ancestry enchantingly obvious. Unwinding himself from his towel, he stood up to face his friend, giving the towel a kick, his eyes laughing with a distinct lack of sympathy. 'You won't need any excuses if you take a woman with you,' he said. 'She doesn't have to be anyone in particular. Just for show. A slave will do, as long as she's well bred. One you can pass off as your woman. A companion. She needn't sleep with you if you don't wish it. You just let it be known that you're provided for, thank you very much. No more offers. No refusals. No offence. Everyone happy.'

Ready to dismiss the suggestion out of hand, Quintus held his tongue, recognising an element of good advice. Apart from a few romantic encounters, the hospitality to which Lucan referred had never been an issue in the army where women were taken, paid for and left on a more business-like basis than in civilian life. Outside the barracks, any single, wealthy, good-looking man of equestrian rank with the personal friendship of the Emperor, injured or not, was quickly regarded as husband material for the daughters, nieces and widows of good family. Already Quintus Tiberius Martial had attracted some attention from the women of the royal court surrounding Julia Domna, wife of the Emperor Severus. Clearly his two friends were beginning to think he was using his injuries as an excuse, though the fact was that his knee gave him more trouble than he would admit, and when the prestigious office had been offered, he had taken it immediately rather than see it given to someone else. The demands of such a high position were of a different order from the demands of making love, and Quintus had no wish to start making a fool of himself in a department at which he had always excelled.

Tullus pushed the game-board aside in disgust and stood up, vigorously tousling his nut-brown hair with the towel, emerging red-faced and serious. 'He's right,' he said, eyeing his superior's long limbs, noting how he sidled off the slab, gingerly testing the knee with the swollen joint. This man, Tullus thought, was a prime specimen, almost in the peak of fitness, with an intellect as bright as any he'd ever worked with, darkly good looking with a heavy-lidded insolence and steady eyes that made women blush and stammer. He would not be chaste for much longer, thought Tullus. 'The Empress has some high-class slaves in her service,' he said. 'You have only to ask her. Just for the trip to Aquae Sulis and back. We shall be off tomorrow.'

'I shan't have time,' Quintus said, dismissing Florian with a nod. 'The Emperor wants to see me this afternoon. More instructions.'

'More? I thought everything was arranged,' said Tullus over his shoulder. He was poised on the edge of the pool, studying the ripples and reflections.

'So did I,' said Quintus, joining him. 'He was pleased to be mysterious, but I believe he wants someone else to join the party.'

Standing between them, Lucan groaned. 'Oh, Jupiter! Not another aged cripple with wobbly knees who needs spa treatment. We'll never get there if we're on escort duty to—' His protest was cut short by a bellow as he was shoved unceremoniously into the water, hitting it with a loud smack and having no time to surface before two hefty male bodies landed on top of him, sending a tidal wave over the floor to wash Florian's toes. Steam swirled around flailing limbs, engulfing them.

'The Tribune Quintus Tiberius Martial,' snapped the guard, opening the door of the Emperor's newly whitewashed office.

Quintus stepped forward, his nose wrinkling at the pungent smell of medication that clung to the soldierly white-haired man who, despite the warmth of the April day, wore a fur-lined cloak and a pair of white-and-brown striped socks. 'Your Excellency,' Quintus said, bowing and waiting for the Emperor's attention to lift from the scroll he was reading.

The tube of papyrus sprang upwards with a rattle. 'Ah, Quintus! All prepared? Right,' he went on, not waiting for any denial, 'so I've had funds set aside for you in that box over there…' he pointed with the scroll to a wooden brass-bound chest '…and there'll be a two-man guard on it while you're in transit. That's for expenses. And here's the final list of names and residences for the journey. They're expecting you all the way from here to Lindum, Corinium, Aquae Sulis and all points in between, but it's for you to decide the pace and where to pitch camp for the night.'

'Thank you, my lord.'

Quintus had been in the Emperor's inner sanctum many times since their arrival at Eboracum earlier in the year and was used to the sparse functional surroundings favoured by him and his two sons. As a Lybian, Severus found the harsh British climate not at all to his liking, but since his recent visit to Hadrian's Wall, even further north, his chest complaint had been responding to treatment. Something, thought Quintus, must have agreed with him, apart from victory.

'How's the knee today?'

'Bearable, sir, I thank you.'

'Good. So you won't mind taking along an extra passenger tomorrow, I take it.'

As if the entourage was not big enough already with attendants and aides, servants and slaves, bodyguards and bald Greek lawyers. 'Just the one, sir?'

'Ah…no. She'll probably want to take her maid along with her, too.'

Inwardly, Quintus groaned. 'A woman, sir? Not the Lady Julia Domna, surely?'

Severus sighed and rested his behind on a white marble table with gilded lions' legs, his dark eyes straying briefly to the door and back to his sandals. 'No, not my wife.' His voice was subdued. The Empress would not have approved of his plan.

Quintus wondered whether there would be any point in objecting, but suspected not. Women always slowed a journey down, one reason why he'd been disinclined to accept his friends' suggestion.

The Emperor wriggled his toes. 'That battle last week,' he said. 'Remember?'

'Indeed I do, sir. You killed the chieftain. It was well done.'

'And if he'd been the *only* chieftain, Quintus, it would have been even better. But as you know, the Brigantes are the biggest and most powerful collection of tribes in Britain, even scrapping amongst themselves for dominance, and as soon as we remove one chieftain, another springs up in his place like bloody mushrooms. This time we have two of them. Sons of the last one. But we took the daughter captive.'

'I didn't know that, sir.'

The Governor of the northern province where the massive Brigantian tribes made such a nuisance of themselves had sent to the Emperor of Rome for help to put them in their place, once and for all. Severus, his sons, wife and a huge army had come post-haste from victories in Gaul and had already achieved some success.

'I kept it quiet,' Severus replied. 'On the night

the chieftain was killed, a party of our men sneaked up to their hill-fort to torch it while their backs were turned. They came back with the daughter and her maid. But I can't keep them here indefinitely, Quintus. My eldest son is eager to bait them in the arena, but that would be asking for more trouble than they're worth. I'd have the whole of the Brigantes united against us like a pack of ravening wolves. Subduing them one at a time is enough without provoking them still further. I wish he'd understand that.'

Imprisonment, Quintus knew only too well, was not an alternative form of punishment generally favoured by the Romans. Captives were either sold as slaves or killed. To keep them was an unnecessary burden on the state. High-status captives were sometimes taken in chains to Rome, displayed as trophies, but there was rarely a role for women in all this.

'Would the two brothers not search for her, sir?'

'Perhaps. But they'll have a good idea of where she is, and anyway they'll have their hands full sorting things out after their father's death. I have reliable spies in Eboracum. Nothing has been seen of them after the battle. But I have to get rid of her, now, immediately.' He leaned back, taking a deep breath. 'Besides, there's another reason.'

'Sir?'

'This woman's tribe recently received a deputation from the Dobunni tribe down in the south. The spa Aquae Sulis is in their territory.'

Quintus was already beginning to understand. 'Ah,' he said.

'A chieftain's son, apparently. I'm told that it's his father who favours an alliance with the local Brigantes, sending his son up here to make an offer for the daughter. I'm told she's been promised.'

'To the Dobunnii.'

'Yes. It's the kind of alliance that would give him some clout in the south.'

'So he needs the Brigantes's help. Is this the same troublemaker who's building up a resistance army down there, sir?'

'I believe it is. These impetuous young things take on all the advantages we've offered over the best part of two hundred years, all the trappings of Roman citizenship, but the one thing they can't accept is that they're expected to pay for our protection. One of these days they're going to get a shock when we all go back to Rome and leave them to it, Quintus. But it always boils down to the tax problem. And this young renegade, so

I'm told, has been recruiting young rebels to be trained for his resistance army.'

'Jupiter!'

'Quite. If he's not stopped very soon, we'll have more to do here in Britain than we thought. I don't want to be stuck up here for years and have no wish to die here, either. We have to find this ringleader and put him out of action.'

'So he's disappeared, sir?'

'Yes. We believe he was up here a week ago to make his offer, but now he's fled, leaving the intended bride to eat her heart out in captivity. Not a very committed type. He obviously saw no reason to stay after the father was lost and the village destroyed. Perhaps the two sons are not so keen on an alliance. I don't know.'

'We're sure he's gone, then? Not in hiding? Waiting for a chance?'

'Can't be sure. But what I believe is that, if the woman is taken down to his neck of the woods, she'll surely try to make contact with him. My hope is that she'll lead you to him.'

'Or he'll learn of her whereabouts and try for a rescue.'

'Then it's up to you to watch and take him. Bring him back here with you or, if you have to, kill him. We'd have taken him earlier if we'd thought he'd abandon the mission. We thought he'd stay and fight with them, but he didn't.'

'And the woman?'

'Oh, do whatever you like with her, lad. Just keep her from under my feet.'

'Willing or not,' murmured Quintus.

But Severus heard and threw back his head in a bark of laughter that was not wholly solicitous. 'Hah! She'll not be willing, I can promise you that. She's the most unwilling wench I've ever… no…I should not say any more. I can see the idea of carting her off down to Aquae Sulis doesn't exactly thrill you to the core, does it?'

'I would rather convey a raging bullock, sir, if you wouldn't mind.'

'Unfortunately, that would not be quite so effective, Quintus. You going down there tomorrow happens to fill the bill perfectly. Besides, between you and me, I would rather my son was denied access to her. His manner of dispatching captives lacks finesse, I find.'

Quintus nodded, being too diplomatic to speak out loud on the sensitive issue of Caracalla's disgraceful behaviour, even towards his own brother. 'And the other business, sir? The tax fraud?'

'That must be investigated thoroughly, once you reach the spa,' said Severus. 'The tax officials are expecting you, and they'll give you all the assistance you need. You'll have plenty of time for the healing and rest. No hurry. I want you to come back refreshed and ready for duty.'

Privately, Quintus saw his recuperation being gnawed away by a package of extra duties he'd hoped to be spared, the notion of being refreshed growing dimmer by the hour. 'Thank you, sir,' he said. 'Any instructions about the woman?'

'Oh, her! Well, she's apparently known as a princess, according to the maid, so she'll certainly regard you as an inferior, Quintus. Very high status.'

'Hmm! Does she understand our tongue, sir?'

'So far, we haven't had a word from her in any tongue, but I think she has a fair understanding of what's being said. You can take her along as your slave, if you wish, or you may prefer to sell her to a merchant when she's fulfilled her purpose. It's up to you. You'd get a good price. She'll have knowledge of cures and such. These tribal women often do, you know. She might even be quite useful to you, but just get her away from here. Far away.'

Quintus was puzzled. Where was the catch? There had to be one. 'Would she be of no use to the Lady Julia Domna?' he said, grasping at straws.

'No,' said Severus, irritably. 'None at all.'

'Does she ride, sir?'

The frown disappeared as the Emperor passed the scroll to Quintus and scratched into his curling beard. His white bushy brows, stark against the dark skin, lifted and lowered in time to the opening and closing of his mouth; Quintus saw that he'd been about to say something else about the captive before thinking better of it. He began to shuffle through a pile of scrolls, quickly losing interest. 'On that score I have no suggestions to offer,' he said, callously. 'You may have to drag her there by the hair. Have you ever had the pleasure of trying to make one of these tribal women do something they don't want to?'

'No, sir. Not yet.'

'Well, then, I have high hopes of you, lad. If a Tribune of equestrian rank can't do it, I shall eat one of my socks.'

'Only one, sir?'

Severus kept on shuffling. 'Only one.' He smiled. 'Get somebody to take you down there. And don't let me hear the rumpus.'

Quintus bowed. 'Do we know her name, sir?'

The Emperor looked up with an unusually blank stare. 'Damned if I know,' he said. 'See if the maid will tell you.'

No matter what standard of accommodation the captive had been given, it would not have found favour with her, for the heavy door was locked, confining her to four walls and depriving her of every Brigantian woman's right: freedom. The room was, in fact, generous as prisons go, plastered walls, red-tiled floor, a barred window above head height, a low wooden sleeping-bench with a few blankets. That was all, apart from heaps of broken earthenware in the corners and one whole pottery beaker towards which one skinny arm was waving in the hope of attracting attention.

'Please,' a faint voice whispered. 'Please?'

The bench had been pulled up below the window with the curled-up body of a young maid lying motionless at one end, covered with a rich cloak. Trying not to stand on her, her regal mistress of the Briganti tribe balanced on the tips of her toes to see out of the window where the spring sun beamed between scudding clouds, showing her that she was facing home, miles away to the north of Eboracum. The princess, a tall slender woman of twenty-two summers, swayed dangerously as she let go of the bar with one hand to look down at the poor waif. 'Wait,' she whispered.

The movement made her dizzy and faint, her legs trembling with the effort of reaching up, her usual robust energy sapped by hunger. Warily, she began her descent, clenching her teeth, commanding her feet to tread where they would do no further damage. In mid-step, she let go of the window-bar as the echoing rattle of a key in the door held her, poised and swaying like a reed, narrowing her eyes in anger at the intrusion. Every time the guard brought food, she was aware of the room's appalling smell of unwashed bodies, rats, sickness and despair, the very idea of eating almost turning her stomach.

But this time, the armour-plated guard stood back to allow a stranger to enter, a tall white-clad man, obviously an official, who frowned at the sight of the young woman in the belted green tunic with a head of bright copper-coloured hair some way above his, glowing like a halo with the sun behind it. Her lips parted, then closed again quickly. The angry expression remained.

Years of discipline held Quintus's initial reaction where it would not show, yet his eyes faced the sun and the captive Brigantian caught that first fleeting glimpse of shock before the haughty lids came down like shutters. Clearly, he would have preferred it if she'd been on his level, or even lower, but he took the opportunity her position afforded him to take in the intricately woven green-and-heather plaid, the borders of gold-thread embroidery, the tooled leather shoes and patterned girdle. There was heavy gold on her wrists and neck, a wink of red garnets through the hair, and the cords that wrapped her thick plait were twisted with glass beads from the Norse countries, cornelians and lapis from the other side of the world.

Pretending to ignore her perilous position, Quintus glanced round the room. 'What's been happening here?' he said to the guard, indicating the broken pottery.

'Her food, sir,' said the man, expressionless. 'Everything I bring in gets thrown against the wall. The rats like it well enough.'

'How long?'

'Since she set foot in the place, sir. The maid's ready to pack it in, by the look of things. All she gets is water. Tyrannical, I call it, sir.'

'Seven…eight days?'

'Aye, sir. Look 'ere.' The guard pointed to his bruised cheek. 'She threw a bowl at me. They can starve for all I care.'

'That's what you get if you don't wear your helmet,' Quintus said, dismissively. No wonder the Emperor wants rid of her, he thought. He'd not want her death here in Eboracum. Miles away, perhaps, but not here under his roof. Another glance up at the captive's face, however, alerted him to the probability of that fate if something was not done immediately to reverse it. She was swaying dangerously, her eyes half-closed in pain.

'Come down,' he said, sternly. 'Take my arm. Come on.'

The guard looked dubious. 'She'll not let you touch her, sir.'

But the stern command had reached through a cold haze as if from a long way away, and the hand she put out to steady herself touched something firm and warm that supported her, keeping her from falling. Not for the world would she willingly have allowed any Roman to touch her, nor would she have touched one, but now she found herself being placed carefully upon the floor and helped to sit unsteadily beside her maid's feet that stuck out from beneath the gold fringe of a cloak. Seated on the edge of the bed, she felt her head being pushed slowly down between her knees in a most undignified manner.

'Let me up!' she gasped. 'I'm all right.'

The guard let out a yelp. 'Ye gods! That's the first time she's said a word, sir. Honest. We all thought she was word-struck!'

'There's something to be said for it, in a woman,' Quintus remarked, removing his hand from her head, 'but I have a suspicion we shall hear a lot more of it before we're much older.' Bending, he picked up the beaker of water from the floor and placed it in the woman's hand. 'Take a sip of that,' he said. 'Then you'd better listen to me.'

She refused his command, preferring instead to place a hand under her maid's head and offer the water to her parched lips. With closed eyes sunk deep into brown sockets, the girl could take only a sip before bubbling the rest of it away down her chin, coughing weakly.

'Are you going to let her die, then?' said Quintus. 'Can you not see she has no strength? *You* may be able to last out a few more weeks, but *she* won't. Do you want her death on your hands? No one regards your protest, woman. You're wasting life for no good reason.'

The captive pulled herself up straight, her back like a ramrod, a token of inflexibility. Her hands trembled around the beaker of water, her mouth panting.

'Listen to me,' Quintus said. 'I've come to offer

you a choice. Either you come with me and give your maid a chance to recover, or you allow her to die through your own neglect. No good mistress would do that to her maid.'

'It is not how you think, Roman,' the captive whispered. 'That fool knows nothing. My maid is not neglected. She is mine.' Her hand rested tenderly on the maid's hip, then slid down to take the claw-like fingers in her own. She was close to desperation, knowing that although her voice was weak, the hard edge of physical effort had been mistaken for a mistress's authority and ownership. Already she had decided that the death of her maid would coincide with her own, using the window-bars and her tablet-woven girdle to speed her into the next world. Tears in her proud eyes sparkled in the sunlight, tears that had been suppressed during days and nights of isolation, unwelcome, shaming tears to be brushed away impatiently with one flick of the wrist.

Quintus kept up the pressure. 'Correction!' he snapped. 'She is *not* yours. She is mine, as you both are. You belong to me now. Yes, you, too.'

The woman's gasp was audible as she jerked her head up to look him full in the face, her eyes blazing with furious tears like watery blue-green gems. The very notion of being owned by a Roman was impossible for her even to contemplate. 'Never! *Never!*' she growled, her voice raw with fury. 'I belong to no one except my father, the chieftain of our tribe. Leave me, Roman. *Get out!*' With an astonishing resurgence of energy, she glared at Quintus with all the contempt she could summon, not having the slightest notion, in her trembling rage, what a picture of sheer animal loveliness she presented as the sun caught the edges of the blazing red hair surrounding her face. Like the sheen on water, her skin was almost translucent, her mouth wide and pale, her eyes dark-lashed. Too large, and too full of rage.

A frail hand caught at her sleeve, tugging gently. 'Please, mistress,' the maid whispered, her voice almost too low to hear. 'We should go, for your father's sake.'

'Don't *shame* me,' the woman whispered back, angrily. 'Where is your pride? You think my father would want us to belong to a *Roman*? Rather we should die first.'

The little hand fell away. 'It could not be worse than this,' the girl said on a sigh of resignation. 'Accept his offer.'

'Well?' said Quintus. 'I'm not going to carry you out of here kicking and screaming. If you're determined to stay…' He turned towards the door, signalling the guard to go.

'No…*wait*!' The woman held out a hand to him. 'Save her. Take her with you. She can go. There's just a chance…?'

'It's both of you, or neither. Make up your mind.'

'You don't understand,' she replied, trying not to plead. 'I cannot be owned. I cannot be so shamed. I am a chieftain's only daughter.'

'And I'm not ecstatic about having to take you where I'm going either, if you must know. I have neither the time nor the inclination to act as nursemaid to two women intent on self-harm when there are thousands out there trying to find cures and enough food to keep themselves alive. I suppose you think your deaths would be an heroic gesture, do you? Well, I think it'd be a bit of a waste when you could help others to stay alive, but the decision is yours. Either you accompany me down to the south, or you stay here and—'

'What? *South*, did you say?'

'That's what I said. Tomorrow I'm off down to the healing spa at Aquae Sulis. Not exactly in your direction, is it?'

The captive princess stood up. Too quickly. Unfocused, her eyes swam, fighting the sudden pain in her head. 'I'll come,' she whispered, swaying.

'Then you'd better tell me your name. I cannot keep on calling you Woman.'

Her knees melted and the growing roar in her ears brought with it a cold blackness to envelop her in a drowning tide. 'Brighid,' she said.

Quickly, he caught up the sinking body in his arms, wincing at the twinge in his knee. 'What in the name of Hades have I let myself in for?' he asked of no one in particular. 'Go on,' he said to the guard. 'You carry the maid and I'll take this one.' Still frowning, he looked down at the limp figure in his arms, at the mass of red hair on his shoulder and the angelic face deep into her swoon, and briefly he wondered why they could not have captured some worn-out old crone who would not last out the journey instead of this high-flown goddess.

Chapter Two

The wagon swayed and jolted without mercy as Brighid tried once more to pack another sheepskin beneath her aching limbs, falling back against the pile of cushions as the effort took its toll of her, reminding her yet again of her weakness.

Her obvious discomfort alerted her travelling companion, who sat easily on a pile of skins at the open end of the wagon, jauntily riding out each bump without a care. He turned, reaching her on his hands and knees over the blankets, flopping by her side without ceremony. Then, taking a cushion, he thumped it and placed it behind her head, lifting her shoulders with his other arm. He was a slave. His touch did not matter. 'Better?' he said, cheekily. 'Ready for some more milk?'

Brighid shook her head. 'I can't keep it down,' she said.

'It doesn't matter,' he said. 'Some of it stays.

There now. That's better. Try to sleep again.' Pulling the blanket over her, he tucked her feet in and continued his role as the nurse his master had declared, quite loudly, that *he* had no intention of being. To which Florian had replied, well out of range, that the Tribune would probably be as bad a nurse as he was a patient.

The departure from Eboracum had been delayed for an hour while the body of the little maid was hastily buried and flowers found to adorn her favourite shrine. There were prayers to be said, and small rituals to observe. After that they could spare no more time, because the Tribune had said, impatiently, they'd never reach their first stop before nightfall. Now, lying in the well-padded wagon while staring up at the flapping canvas cover, Brighid knew that the lass would never have survived the first mile.

Her conscience was not troubling her on that score. Death had been a release longed for by the maid since the birth of her baby only a few weeks ago. Fathered on the fourteen-year-old slave by Brighid's own father, the baby had been a girl and of no use to the tribe; even before the maid had begun to recover from her fever, the village elders had taken it away to be exposed. It had broken the maid's heart, but the chieftain preferred to sire males and his word was law. The mother had pined and weakened, and was barely starting to recover when a band of Roman soldiers attacked the village while the warriors were away fighting, setting fire to the thatches, killing those who fled and capturing Brighid and the maid as saleable goods for the Emperor's delight.

He was not delighted, for the high-status woman was a liability and her maid was sick, and the rough capture had done her no good at all. Brighid had more than the usual knowledge of remedies for all kinds of ills, but with no access to her herbs and a maid determined to go to her ancestors, what kind of protest could any woman make except to refuse to eat? At the very least it gave her some control over her own life. And death. In charge of their welfare, the guard had at first tried to bully them into eating, but had soon discovered how aggressively defensive his prisoner could be. After that, there was nothing to be done—the barrack-block at Eboracum was not designed to house women.

Shapes moved across the wagon's tail-board, horses tossing heads, riders crossing, a blur of buildings with red roof tops, the white town walls and the great arch of the gate. A mounted man rode up close to take a long look inside, his cloak thrown over one shoulder, his bare arms brown against a white tunic. His eyes narrowed against the dimness. Thick straight hair lifted in the wind, grown longer since leaving the army, his mouth unsmiling as his gaze met that of his new charge. For a space of time they tried to read however much, or little, the other would reveal, then he nodded and moved away, his cheeks tightening, accepting the inevitable with undisguised sourness.

'Churl!' she whispered. 'I don't want to be here, either.'

But one good thing might yet come out of this, she thought, closing her eyes. They were heading south towards the territory of the Dobunni, the tribe to which Helm belonged, and though her knowledge of Britain's geography was very limited, the name Aquae Sulis had been spoken often enough, while Helm was negotiating with her father, to convince her that the spa was in Dobunni country. So if, in fact, Helm had returned home believing that all his plans had fallen through, she would surely be able to send him a message that she was nearby, not out of his reach. If she was allowed some freedom, she might even be able to find him herself.

Naturally, she had not been allowed to get to

know the young warrior at all well. Her thoughts on the matter were unimportant and of no consequence to the success of the agreement. Had she been an ordinary member of the tribe, she might have demanded some say in her future, might even have been allowed to live with a man of her choice for a trial year before taking the final step. Even then, she could divorce him if he proved disappointing. But Brighid was far from ordinary, more of a bargaining tool for her father, a woman of class who would bind tribes in mutual co-operation, and this she had always known. Nevertheless, that did not prevent her from taking an interest in the man who had travelled for days, even weeks, to buy her from her family and when on the few occasions she had been presented, always from a distance, she had taken in every detail as avidly as any woman on the verge of such a commitment.

She had been impresssed by what she saw, a brawny confident young man of her own height, clear of eye and tongue, bold of step and with a commanding manner that was always a sign of a future leader. There was little doubt that she could come to like him, eventually, though her two older brothers had reservations that counted for nothing. A young braggart, one of them had said in her hearing, and not the only fish in the sea for their high-born sister.

In the circumstances, it was disturbing to her that Helm had completely disappeared without getting a message of hope to her. Nor had her brothers made contact, or her father, either by direct representation or by more devious means. Slaves were open to bribery and a chieftain had his ways. The feeling of abandonment had grown daily, and now she was being left to her own devices with no inkling of what to expect from the man who thought he owned her, and not even a name to put to him. Yesterday, he had left her completely in the hands of women who were, apparently, the Empress's own slaves.

Yesterday had been a blur of helplessness. Between bouts of sickness and fainting, she had been too weak to say what she needed, too impotent to protest at being handled, undressed, bathed, combed and re-clothed as if she were an infant. She had ceased to care when the slave called Florian installed himself as her new maid, telling her with great disrespect that she had better come down off her high horse because they were all slaves together, including her, except that he was indispensable and she was quite the opposite.

Which did nothing for her peace of mind, however well meant.

They cleaned the little maid up, too, but she lapsed into a deep sleep and did not wake again, and by morning she was cold and still, and at peace with her loved ones. Brighid had wept bitterly for her, and again for the sweet infant they had both loved and lost. How many more losses would there be, she wondered, before a gain? Did she have anything more to lose?

She had slept, waking when the wagon bounced softly over grass and came to a halt with shouted commands all round and a dimness under the canvas that indicated dusk, overhanging trees and a stop for the night. Florian came to her, smiling as always. 'Good,' he said. 'Long sleep. No sickness. Now for something nourishing. Give me a few moments while they get the fires going. Need to make yourself comfortable? Right, here's a pot. I'll leave it to you. Keep it covered. Flies, you know.' He grinned, scrabbling away and vaulting over the tail-board like an athlete.

Her head was clear, and she felt hunger for the first time in days.

Instructions followed to the letter, she stood up to take stock of her surroundings. She noticed that she was wearing a long tunic of unbleached linen and that all her own clothes were nowhere to be seen. Her hair had been replaited tidily except for wisps loosened by sleep, yet her neck, arms and hair were bare of ornament, another loss that generated a tidal wave of indignation and a different kind of bereavement. Those precious pieces meant everything to her, made for her alone, never worn by anyone else, and never a day passed without her wearing them. The awful feeling of vulnerability hit her like a physical pain.

Throwing a woollen shawl around her shoulders, she took tottering steps to reach the tailboard, determined to find out where they had put her property, already reciting in her head the form her inquisition would take. But from the far end of the wagon, she had not seen the two-man guard who stood at each side of the opening, and now their shining helmets and broad metal-plated backs stopped her in her tracks, warning her that although Florian could come and go, she was still a prisoner.

Biting back the angry tears, she held the shawl tightly across her as a cool breeze lifted the underside of the oak leaves above them, lending a sense of urgency to the unloading and carrying, the pegging out of canvas, the tethering and feeding of horses, always the first to be tended. Fires were being kindled with the fuel they carried with them, every man to his task, working like cogs in a machine. Other wagons had been unhitched and arranged like a fortress, and she saw that they were loaded with baggage with no space inside for sleeping, like hers. She hoped it would be like this every night, with a view of the sky through the doorway.

From round one side of the wagon strode three men, a white-fringed cloak identifying the one who had released her at Eboracum, whose name she would not ask. Over his shoulder he glanced her way, then, pausing in his stride, he turned for a longer look with an expression that gave nothing away except that he had taken in every detail of her appearance. Nodding his approval to the two guards, he rejoined his two companions, their questions raising a deep laugh from all three, setting up Brighid's hackles for no good reason except guesswork. It had been her chance to demand the return of her possessions and she had not taken it.

Cursing herself, she turned her back on the scene and began to tidy her bed, folding the blankets and arranging the cushions the way the little maid had been used to doing. Some of the limited space was taken up by a stout wooden chest, locked, bolted and barred. She sat on it and waited, listening to the activities outside, her eyes darkening to grey-blue in the fading light.

It was the first time she had taken a good look at the man, their first meeting having been disadvantaged in every way. Now she had seen the full length of him wearing a short tunic instead of the longer purple-banded toga that had given her a hint of his rank. Only senators, tribunes and knights, and a few others, were allowed that privilege. She doubted if he was old enough to be a senator, nor did she think one of that rank would be camping out under rain-filled clouds, but rather in some luxurious villa with all the bowing and scraping of overwhelmed hosts and their wives. She judged him to be less than thirty, obviously a military man, going by his close leather breeches that clung to muscled calves and thighs, stopping short of his ankles. He looked as if the day's riding suited him well, for his thick hair was windswept across his forehead like an unruly mop of silk with the gloss of a raven's wing. He was, she admitted reluctantly, much better looking than Helm; had the two men changed places, she could quickly have learned to like him and to suffer his hands on her body. But now there was no room in her life for that kind of sentiment, nor had there ever been since she realised the political nature of her position.

If only she knew what the future held for her. If only her possessions had not been removed, then an attempt at escape might have been worth planning. But without shoes and only a linen tunic and a shawl to her name, no identifying ornaments, and no idea where she was, any plans would have to wait.

'Where are my clothes?' she said as soon as Florian climbed in, balancing a bowl of steaming broth in one hand.

His smile remained. 'You're sitting on them,' he said.

'What?' She swivelled on the chest. 'In here? And my ornaments, too?'

'In there, with your shoes and clothes. Yes.'

'I want to wear them.'

'I expect you will, when my master decides.' He took a spoon from inside his tunic, passed it to her and told her to eat while it was still warm. It was the first solid food she had eaten for over a week and, by its comforting warmth, the questions uppermost in her mind were released. Presumably to make sure she ate it, Florian stayed with her as the sky darkened ominously, the only source of light being the crackling fire outside that sent flickering shadows to dance across the canvas cover.

'Who is he, your master?' she said, passing the bowl back to him.

He spooned up the last leftover mouthful and fed it to her like a mother bird. 'He is Quintus Tiberius Martial,' he said, proudly rolling the words around his tongue. 'Tribune of Equestrian rank—that's quite high, you know—Provincial Procurator in the service of the Roman Emperor Septimus Severus. And before you ask me any more questions, young lady, you had better know that I am duty bound to report them to my master. I am the Tribune's masseur, and I've been told to offer you my services, should you wish it.'

'Thank you, Florian. It may be a little too soon for that.'

'An apple, then?' He pulled one out of his tunic where the spoon had come from, like a magician.

She shook her head, watching him unfurl, reminding her of a fern in spring.

'It will rain tonight. Don't worry about the canvas. It won't leak.' He looked round the wagon. 'I'm impressed. You've been tidying up. We'll make a handy slave out of you yet, I believe.'

'That is one thing I shall never be, believe me,' she said, severely.

'Then try convincing the Tribune,' he said, heading for the opening. 'I think he's rather set on the idea. But I told you that yesterday. Good-night, Princess.'

She would like to have hurled the apple at his head, but a sudden wave of tiredness swept over her and it was all she could do to fall on to her pile of sheepskins and close her eyes against the murmurs and laughter outside.

The roar of rain upon canvas woke her. That, and the dim yellow glow inside the wagon, and the feeling that she was not alone. Instantly awake, her hand searched for the dagger that was always beside her. The habit died hard. It was not there.

'Sit up,' said a deep voice. 'I need to talk to you.'

He was sitting on the chest, the smooth bronzed skin of his body almost aflame in the light from the lantern, his arms resting along his thighs, great shoulders hunched behind the head that hung low between them, his face turned in her direction. It was clear he'd been studying her for some time, for now he straightened up and stretched like a cat. He wore calf-length under-breeches of white linen, and his hair was damp-black as if the rain had caught him. And in the confined space of the wagon, he was much too close for comfort.

Grabbing at the blanket, Brighid pulled it to her chin and hauled herself up against the cushion. 'I don't wish to talk to you,' she retorted, breathlessly.

'I was hoping you wouldn't. *I* need to talk to *you*,' he repeated.

'Yes, you *do* have some explaining to do. How long does this journey last? And when can I have my possessions returned?'

'I don't need to explain myself to slaves,' he replied, looking her over again, measuring her up with his insolent eyes.

'I am *not* a slave!'

'Oh, don't let's hear all that again. Florian's had enough of it and I don't intend to hear it. The facts are, woman, that you have no choice in the matter. The Emperor has ordered me to take you off his hands and to do what I like with you; as far as I'm concerned, that means selling you on to the next slave merchant we meet on the way.'

'You wouldn't do that! No…you *couldn't*!' she cried.

'I assure you, lass, I would and I can. I don't have a place for high-and-mighty princesses in my line of work and I don't intend you to spoil my holiday, either. Lindum will be the end of the line for you. Our next stop down the road. We'll be there by this time tomorrow.'

The blood ran cold along Brighid's arms. He wanted rid of her. She had seen the slave merchants and their shocking filthy tricks, the humiliated women, the wealthy leering buyers. Of all fates, that would be the most shaming. Her teeth chattered as she tried desperately to keep a tight hold on her dignity, not to show her stark fear. She was a chieftain's daughter. She would not plead. Not even for this.

'If the Emperor wanted me off his hands, Roman, then why did he have me taken in the first place? Does your Emperor not know what he wants, these days? Could he not have ransomed me?'

'His men were too eager. It's common enough. They thought he'd have a use for you. He doesn't. Not for a woman of your rank whose death would be on his hands in a month or so, if you had your way. He's not come all the way to Britain to *make* trouble, but to stop it. Nor is he interested in ransoms. Of what worth is a woman?'

At one time, she thought, she was worth plenty. Now, very little. With pride, she was about to tell him how the Dobunni tribe had wanted to buy her and how Helm and her father had discussed deep into the night how much gold, how many cows, pigs and sheep must change hands for her. But that was pointless, and in the past, and the less this man knew about her, the better. But she must do something, *say* something to make him keep her with him until they reached the south. 'I would have thought, Roman, that as soon as my disappearance was discovered, the trouble the Emperor wishes to avoid will double or treble in the next week or two. Does that not concern you?'

'Why should it? All the more reason why you should be out of the way as fast as possible. Has anyone come to find you? No messages?'

She did not need to answer when her face reflected her despair.

'Tell me something,' he said, leaning forwards again, glancing up at the sound of thunder. 'Do all chieftains have their daughters taught to speak as the Romans do? You have a good accent. You'd fetch a good price as a noblewoman's maid.'

'The Briganti know that high-born women are most sought after by other tribes if they speak in the Roman tongue. It's useful to them. We are not the barbarians you think us to be, Roman. My brothers and I were taught well.'

'And have *you* been sought after?' he asked, softly.

'Yes.'

'By whom? Are you married to him?'

'No. You ask me too many questions, sir,' she said, holding her burning cheek.

'You may think so, but the question a slave merchant will ask *me* is whether you are a maid or not. Are you?'

Subconsciously, in a gesture of crushing fear, she drew her knees up to her chin and laid her cheek upon them, turning her burning face away from his scrutiny. 'No one except my kin may ask me that,' she whispered.

'I can soon find out,' he said.

'No…no, please! I've had nothing to do with a man. It was never allowed. Other girls of the village, other women, but not me. I would be worthless, otherwise. Besides, there was no one.' Her voice tailed away, her mind turning somersaults over the hurdles of pride versus safety. He needed to know how much she'd fetch on the market, not how much use she'd be to him personally, which is what she'd thought earlier. And now she would have to change his mind, offer him something to keep her with him all the way to the Dobunni territory. She would have to plead, if necessary. It was something she was unused to, except to the gods. 'Give me more time,' she said, 'until I'm stronger. Until we get to wherever we're going. I'll keep well out of your way. I shall cause you no trouble.'

The rain drummed on the canvas as he said nothing in reply, until he straightened up again as if he'd come to a decision. 'I wonder what you'd look like in Roman dress,' he said, thoughtfully.

Hope flared briefly in Brighid's breast. 'I'd look like a Roman citizen,' she said. 'And I'd behave like one, if I thought my life depended on it. Is that what concerns you? My clothes? My appearance?'

'*Would* you behave like one? I have my doubts.'

Her head lifted, poised elegantly upon the long neck, while her hands fell away from her knees and rested in graceful curves upon the blanket. 'Try me,' she said. 'Give me a chance. I don't want to be sold. I'm not ready to be anyone's slave. Whatever else you wish, but not that.'

'Your readiness is not my concern, lass,' he said, yawning as he stood up. 'Captives are rarely in a position to bargain about their future, and you're no different, princess or not. You *are* my slave. Better get used to it. I'm tired. We'll decide on this in the morning.'

'Then it would have been better to let me die at Eboracum with my maid, Roman. That way, I would have been free.' Throwing off the blanket, she stood up in one swift unbend of her body, intending to put more distance between them. Earlier that day she had felt a reason to stay alive, to seek the help of the man who had wanted her, even though he would never have been her choice if she'd been less high born. Now, the tables were turned, and it looked as if her flimsy plan had all but vanished.

The soft mattress hampered her feet, the curve of the canvas was not designed for her height, and the long reach of Quintus's arm caught her wrist in an iron grip, pulling her off balance. Furiously, she tried to throw him off, her eyes blazing with green fire. 'No man may *touch* me!' she yelled, competing with the roar outside.

'Then that's another thing you'd better get used to, Princess High and Mighty. And if this show of temper is meant to convince me that you can behave in a civilised manner, then you've fallen at the first jump, haven't you? And mind that lamp, for Jove's sake!' His swinging her round sent her sprawling against the chest. 'Any more nonsense, woman, and you'll find yourself shackled to a slave-merchant's line-up at Lindum. If you doubt me, just try it. I have no taste for ill-tempered barbarian women.'

She knew it was a mistake. Righting herself, she pulled her legs under her, covering them with the linen tunic that was not quite long enough, bowing her head submissively. 'Forgive me,' she whispered. 'I feel my losses deeply. If I lost my freedom once more, permanently, I would take my own life and forfeit the protection of the goddess Brigantia, after whom I am named. She is angered that I no longer wear her gifts, nor have I offered at her shrine since my capture. I am not the bad-tempered barbarian you think me. I grieve for my maid, her lost child and for my family, but I have no way to relieve it, Roman.' With downcast eyes, she could only feel the pad of his bare feet as he took a stride across the mattress to lower himself between her and the side of the wagon, only a hand's reach away. Thunder still crashed overhead. 'She's angry,' she whispered. 'Very angry.'

'I thought goddesses were more understanding than that. Your Brigantia must be a very vengeful dame. They mean so much to you, do they? Your ornaments?'

'She gave them to me when I was born. I began to wear them when I became a woman,' she said, plying and unplying the fringe of the blanket. 'They are a part of me. If I lose them, I lose who I am. That's the reason, I suppose.'

'The reason?'

'The reason why I'm losing myself. I shall be someone else's property, not my own woman. I do not know if my spirit can rise above it. I have yet to find out.'

'So what if you were to wear them again?'

Her head lifted at that. 'You would allow it?'

Quintus blinked at the gaze she fixed on him, moved by the strange unearthly power of blue-green waters that shimmered off the coastline of his beloved home, Hispania. He saw the sun and sea, vineyards and villas, warmth and good friends who asked for nothing but friendship. He saw it all in her eyes, felt her grief, as if her losses were his losses also. 'Tomorrow morning you shall have them. Meanwhile, they're in there and you're sleeping next to them. Your goddess surely won't mind that so much.'

'Thank you, Roman. Oh…thank you!' Her fists clenched over the fringe. 'I must not weep,' she whispered. 'I must *not* weep. I am strong.'

'And perhaps we'll find a way of making a portable shrine to Brigantia. Wait till we reach Lindum. There's sure to be something on the market. 'Tis a terrible thing to lose touch with your own deity.'

'Then you'll allow me to stay with you? Not sell me?'

'For the moment.' He yawned again, covering his white teeth with the back of his hand. 'But let's get one thing straight, shall we? Whether you wear Brigantia's gifts or not, whether you think of yourself as your own woman or not, that fact is that you remain *my* property. I have orders to get rid of you, and that's what I shall do. It's all a matter of how and when. I doubt whether your goddess will approve, but that's how things are. Understand that from the beginning and your chances of staying alive will improve. You'll have to learn to adapt, Princess. You're not very good at that, are you?'

'I will try,' she said. 'I can learn. Truly, I *will* learn, Roman.'

'So learn to address me with respect, if you will. To you, I am Tribune.'

'Yes. And I am known as Brighid, sir.' She pronounced it 'Bridget'.

Quintus, however, did not. 'To me, you'll be known as Princess. It suits my purposes,' he said, curtly.

Ah, she thought. More saleable. As with the gold

ornaments. These Romans so love display, don't they? Especially on a woman.

Bending across to where the lantern stood in one corner, he opened the shutter and nipped the wick, plunging the wagon into complete darkness that seemed to intensify the rattling of the rain on all sides. The blanket was pulled out of her hands as he held it to open the bed, and his sharp command, 'Lie down!' took her completely by surprise as his legs burrowed downwards and a cushion was pulled from behind her.

'What!' she yelped. 'No…no, sir! You cannot stay here!'

His arm came heavily across her, but the chest was at her side and there was no way out of the predicament. 'Listen, woman,' he said. 'Either I sleep in here, or I get those two guards to take my place. They'll be warm and dry at the moment, and I doubt they'll be too honoured to spend the night cramped up in here. You choose.'

'You don't understand, sir,' she said, trying to prise his arm away. 'I have never slept with a man.'

'Then don't sleep. Stay awake, if you prefer. This will be another new experience for you to learn. Come on. Wriggle down. You'll be quite safe.'

The notion of keeping her distance had to be

abandoned as she slid down beside the warm bulk that took up more than half the mattress, the only room for protest being to turn her back on him. But he wrapped the blanket over her, pulling her into the bend of his body and resting his arm on the gentle swell of her hip, and though it was not an uncomfortable ordeal for her, her whole being was alive to his intimate closeness, his warmth along her back from neck to ankle, the disturbing male scent of him, his strange contours. She had seen the village men naked, half-naked and all stages in between for there was no privacy to speak of at home in the communal huts. But she had seen no man's body as beautifully crafted as this one's, honed to perfection, pampered by his personal masseur, probably adored and satisfied by countless women. He was unwilling to have a woman of her kind in tow, even for the novelty value of owning a Brigantian slave, yet she had neither seen nor heard any other woman in the cavalcade.

'Don't you have a woman to go to?' she muttered, resentfully.

'Yes,' said the voice, rumbling into the cushion. 'I'm with her. Go to sleep. We have to be away by dawn if we're to reach Lindum tomorrow.'

The beating of the rain lulled her to sleep long

before she heard the thunder pass on to disturb other miscreants. Once she woke to hear the gentle hiss of rain, when she reached out a hand to touch the chest where her treasures lay, and fell back into sleep. The next time, there was silence except for the soft breathing of the man behind her. She wanted to turn, but her tunic was caught under him and she could not free it without waking him.

'What is it?' he whispered.

'You're lying on my tunic. And my hair.'

There was a huff of amusement as his hand delved and freed her hair, then, before she knew what he meant to do, he hauled on the other side of her tunic, rolling her over to face him, to be enclosed in his arms, her mouth against his firm jaw, her legs pressed against him. Her breasts lay upon the great mound of his chest, taking the heat of him through the linen, and when he laid her thick plait across his own neck like a winter muffler, she knew he intended her to stay and to sleep again, safe in his arms.

But sleep was hard to recapture when her head was being held in the crook of his neck, his mouth only inches away from hers, his arm cradling the soft red mass of her hair. Carefully, to ease it, she laid her leg over his, thus unwittingly inviting his free hand to slide gently over the roundness of her buttock and along her thigh, eventually sliding under the linen to find her silken skin.

She made a grab at his hand. 'Please…Tribune… no!' she said, fiercely. 'I cannot…will not…do this with you. You told me I was safe.'

She felt his smile on her forehead as his lips brushed against it. 'Then what was all that about learning to adapt?' he said.

'For pity's sake, give me more time,' she said, clinging to his hand.

'Let go, lass. Time enough.'

But would there be time enough? she wondered, as she listened to the camp begin to stir outside. Would she still be a maid when she found Helm, or would he reject the used goods she had travelled all that way to offer him, all at the Tribune's whim?

Chapter Three

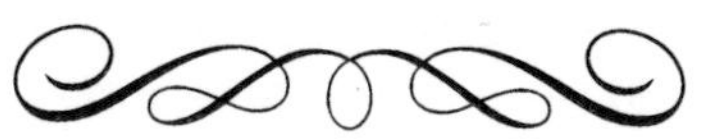

'So, my friend,' said Tullus, rather smugly, 'you took our advice, I see.' His cheek bulged as he chewed hungrily on his loaf while he searched in the pan for another piece of bacon to follow it.

'You see nothing of the sort,' Quintus replied, holding out his beaker to be filled. 'If I had not slept there, who would?'

That was too much for Lucan. His loud laugh turned heads in their direction. 'Oho, the martyr!' he chortled. 'You had only to ask us. One of us would have obliged, to save you the discomfort.'

'Well, save yourselves any more speculation. She has to stay virginal for the Dobunni lad to want her still. If she's not, she'll be of no use either to him or us, will she? That's the first thing he'll want to know.'

Tullus nodded agreement. He was the more serious of the two juniors, with an attractive contemplative quality that intrigued his female friends, especially when his deep grey eyes studied them with a flattering intensity. Unlike the feline grace of his friend, Tullus was built more like a wrestler who tones his body with weights, swimming and riding as much as his office work would allow. Quintus liked them both for their superior accounting skills and for their loyalty to him, putting up with their banter as an elder brother with his siblings. 'Does she know about her father yet?' said Tullus, licking his fingers.

'No,' said Quintus, sharply. 'It's not a good time to tell her when she's just lost her maid.'

Lucan looked at him and waited. None of this was good timing when they were looking forward to some time off. 'She's accepted the situation, then?' he said, hoping for some clarification.

'Far from it. I've told her I'll sell her before we reach Aquae Sulis if she doesn't toe the line.'

'But you wouldn't, would you?'

'Of course not. But she doesn't know that,' Quintus said, wiping a finger round his pewter dish. 'But nor can we cart her through our hosts' houses looking like something from the back woods. That would take more explaining than it's worth. She's going to have to dress up.'

'Like a Roman citizen? That should be interesting.'

'It will be. This is where I need your support.'

'Go ahead,' said Tullus.

'Except for one, our hosts don't know us. I just happen to own a slave who's a Brigantian princess. Right?'

'Unusual, but I don't see why not,' said Lucan. 'Go on.'

'Well, that's it, really. I shall not present her. She'll stay in the background in my room with Florian. She'll be safe enough with him.'

Lucan and Tullus nodded, smiling in unison. 'And how long has this…er…relationship been going on? In case we're asked?' said Lucan, innocently.

Quintus stood, brushing the crumbs from his lap. 'Since a few days ago, I suppose. But I don't see why anyone needs to know. I'll get some proper clothes for her at the next market.' He stood still for a moment with a pensive look in his eye.

'What?' said Tullus. 'You doubt she'll accept them?'

'Nothing more certain. Find a barber before we reach Lindum, both of you. Now let's get this lot moving. Come on.' He strode away, shouting orders.

Lucan released his grin at last. 'Halfway there,' he whispered.

'Oh, I think that's rather too optimistic, my friend,' Tullus replied. 'From what I've seen of her, I'd say she'll keep him on the hop for a while yet. What's going to happen when she hears about her father?'

'Expect all Hades to be let loose. Do I really need a barber?' Lucan wiped a hand round his blue jaw.

'If the boss says shave, we shave. We owe it to our hostess. D'ye know, I'm looking forward to a decent bed.'

'As will our boss be. He's pretending, you know, that she's a bit of a nuisance—I believe he's quite taken with her.'

'That's the impression I'm getting too. There's a new spring in his step.'

'As there would be in yours, young Tullus, after a night with the Princess.'

Brighid was shaken out of her sleep by a gentle hand on her arm. 'It's late,' Florian was saying in her ear. 'The camp is already packing up. Wake, or you'll get no food. Did the Tribune keep you awake all night?'

She rolled herself upright, pushing away her

loose hair. 'Mind your own business,' she said. 'What's all that din?'

'We're almost ready to leave. What do Brigantian princesses eat for breakfast these days?' he said with a knowing grin.

'Porridge, and a thin slice of masseur's tongue, if you'd be so kind.'

'Tongue's off,' he quipped, 'but I'll find you some stodge, if you insist.'

'Clear off while I get dressed. Where can I go and bathe?'

Florian paused at the tail-board. 'Bathe, *domina*? I would not recommend it. Not here. Not unless you want an audience.'

'Then how am I ever going to get cleaned up?'

'Better do it in here until we reach our lodgings. Wait. I'll bring some water.'

The extraordinary events of the night came back to her as she unravelled the blankets and saw the pillow with the dent in it close to her own. He had left without disturbing her, she who always woke at the slightest sound. Even more remarkable was his opening of the chest beside her where now her treasures lay in a row on top of her folded clothes, set out for inspection like a soldier's kit.

Even by Roman standards, the pieces were of the highest craftsmanship, technically perfect.

The most impressive was a flat crescent-shaped neck-collar with a raised pattern of sinuous spirals studded with cornelians and lapis lazuli, and inlaid with coloured champleve enamel. One bracelet was a wide band of beaten gold with triskeles, sun discs and lunar crescents in relief, the other was fashioned like a coiled serpent with rock crystals for eyes. Her earrings were the delicate heads of birds with garnet eyes, spheres hanging from their beaks chased with spirals, as intricate as man could devise. There was a pile of anklets of twisted gold, a belt with a gold enamelled buckle, several brooches and long hairpins with gemstone tops. Gathering them on to her lap, she fondled them lovingly.

The horses were being hitched to her wagon by the time Florian brought her the porridge and a bucket of water in which to wash, and by the time the wheels were back on the road she had sluiced away the scents of the night that clung to her skin, leaving her only partly refreshed and longing to bathe at leisure. However, her clothes were clean; she could only assume that someone had washed them and laid them out to dry overnight, ready for her to use.

She dressed, clothes and ornaments alternately,

ears, ankles and wrists, brooches fastening front to back, the belt buckled in a tighter notch. Without a mirror, she could not know how the starving had hollowed her cheeks, or how the violent events of the past week had diluted the girlish bloom given her by sun, breeze and ice-cold stream. Unable to see the fastening beneath her chin, she found it impossible to manage the hinge of the neck-plate at the front. But as she held it, the canvas flap was lifted to admit a leather-covered leg, then the other, then wide shoulders ducking underneath.

She turned her face away, suddenly unnerved as her body responded to his nearness, recalling his bold searching hands and the male warmth of his skin. Guiltily, she realised that the memory had scarcely left her since waking, sneaking into every thought, relevant or not, just to taunt her.

'You slept late,' he said, poking upwards at the puddles of rainwater on the canvas, tipping the last drops away.

'I hardly slept at all.'

'You'll get used to it.'

'I don't intend to.'

He chuckled, a deep throaty murmur as meaningful as any argument. 'Here, give that to me. Turn round this way.'

She stood up to face him, lifting her hair for him to place it round her neck and to bring the broad edges together. 'The rivet?' he said, softly.

She held it up for him to slip through the precise dovetails, aware of his fingers upon her skin. Quickly, she stepped back, almost losing her balance as the wagon jolted over a rut. 'Thank you,' she said. 'For these, too. Where are we?'

Like a colossus, he braced himself against one of the wooden ribs. 'Next stop will be a small place called Danum. I shall send Florian out to purchase some stuff to make you something after the Roman fashion, and, before you start to protest, let me remind you that you promised to adapt.'

'I didn't promise to apply for Roman citizenship, Tribune.'

'You won't *be* a Roman, will you, wearing Brigantia's wealth round your neck and arms? How could anyone possibly mistake you for a Roman citizen, woman?'

'So what's wrong with my own clothes? Are we out to confuse everybody?'

'Sit down before you fall over. Now listen. We shall be staying at the home of a retired legionary commander and his wife in Lindum, and I don't intend to spend my evening explaining the presence of a wild red-headed Brigantian captive in my baggage when they know I'm on my way to a health spa for treatment. It will save me much tedium if it's simply known that I have a Brigantian princess with me whose appearance will cause no comment.'

'Except, of course, that I am quite obviously the only female in your party and I wear my own adornments. You really believe that will cause no comment, do you?'

'Very well,' he said, taking a step towards the exit, 'if you don't like the sound of that, the solution is simple.'

She knew what he meant. 'No…stop…Tribune! Please. I didn't mean to…' Leaping to her feet, she staggered across the wobbling floor, intending to catch him before it was too late. 'I *will* adapt. I *will* go along with you. Whatever it looks like.'

He took an arm to steady her, steeling himself against the deep luminous green of her eyes that would have made any mortal man forget his own name. At that moment, she was the fierce tribal princess to whom he was suggesting a change of identity, which, naturally, she resented. 'I'm not about to change who you are,' he replied, hoping to convince her. 'I doubt anyone could do that just by having you dress the Roman way. But I would rather our host and hostess regarded you as my woman than a barbarian captive I'm dragging along for some mysterious reason of my own. The choice is yours, Princess. Take it or leave it.'

'As your woman? But I'm not….'

'Then pretend! Adapt. You told me you could do it.'

The moss-green eyes blazed with fear, stirring him to a recklessness he'd intended never to show. But she needed to be convinced, an incentive to play the part, for he had nothing genuine with which to threaten her, and the safety he had promised her last night was already wearing thin. As if to hold her against the rocking of the wagon, he grasped her shoulders before she could tell danger from safety, pulling her hard against him with a groan of sudden desire. 'Then this may help,' he said, taking a handful of the red hair, tilting her face to his own.

Brighid felt his kiss flood through her, melting her limbs, reaching her thighs. She ought to have fought him. But when it ended, instead of railing at him that a woman like her must not be treated in that manner, she stood silent, swaying to the wagon's motion, her hand over her lips, watching him disappear in one leap through the canvas flaps.

'Divine Brigantia,' she whispered behind her fingers, 'don't let it happen to me, or I shall be worthless. I am promised, goddess. You know that I am.' Even so, her body did not share in the same high-mindedness, for although the Tribune would probably think nothing of this kind of thing, she had been taken one step deeper into the forbidden dream that had haunted her throughout the night. It would be difficult enough for her to escape from captivity, but even more so to run from the bondage of her newest emotions.

Unplaiting her hair, fingers and thoughts working furiously together, realising too late that she lacked a comb, she finger-raked it back into a bunch and fixed it on top of her head with her pins. But help was not far away, for the small town of Danum was only a few miles down the road and already bustling with market traders and all the chaos of early morning preparations. The clamour reached her as the wagon came to a standstill, bringing her to the tail-board where Florian's black curly head was coming up to her level.

'We're stopping on the edge of a marketplace,' he told her. 'and I have to go and find you something to wear. I doubt if they'll have much to offer, so no point in telling me what colour you want.

I'll have to take what I can get. What size sandals do I buy?'

With resignation, she placed her foot on the edge of the tail-board. 'There. Take a look. Buy whatever you like, Florian. Size, colour, shape, fabric—anything. But I need a comb. And the Tribune said I might have a small shrine. The small portable kind for travellers. Brigantia is the one to look for, though we may have passed out of the Brigantes territory by now, for all I know.'

Florian's eyes followed her as she turned away, his eyes showing some surprise. 'Oh dear,' he said, sympathetically. 'Still not quite yourself, are you? Go and lie down a while, *domina*. I'll do my best for you.'

Florian did his best, and more, although it took him longer than the alloted time, for which he received the sharp end of his master's tongue. Throwing his purchases up into the wagon even as it was moving off, he passed the last package more carefully into Brighid's hands. 'Careful with that. Hope it's the right one. Too late to change it,' he panted.

She felt its weight and saw the bright metallic gleam before recognising the hand-high figurine of Brigantia, a helmet-wearing version symbolising her warrior-wisdom, a wise owl on one arm, a spear in the crook of the other. The goddess stood proudly inside an arched niche, her name inscribed in Roman capitals on the pedestal.

'Polished pewter,' said Florian. 'And here are the scented candles to set at each side of her, and a garland of flowers I begged from the temple flower-girl.' He took these from his black curls and passed them to her. 'Sweet violet, borage and crocus. There. You can set her up wherever we are. Feel better now?'

'You did well, Florian. Thank you. Much better. I'll set her over here where she'll not fall over.' Her thanks were genuine. The solace of having her deity close at hand was something she had missed greatly since her capture as much as the loss of her family. Brighid had not had a mother since she was eleven, so it had always been to her goddess she had turned more than to the older village women who would have claimed an intimacy more for status than genuine fondness. Friendships and rivalries were thickly intertwined in her incestuous society, and to stay on the edge was often safer.

Florian was setting out his other purchases for her inspection, delighting in each item as much as if they were for himself. He shook out lengths of linen much finer than anything Brighid had ever worn, soft, sumptuous, flowing rivers of fabric in white and cream, blue-green and palest madder-dyed pink. Draping them over her shoulders to judge them against her hair, he tilted his head to one side, then threw a heap of scarves over them to add sparkle, a deeper tone, a texture of fringes and tassels. 'Do you know, *domina*,' he said, 'with that jewellery, this is going to look amazing. Quite unique. Nobody will be able to copy this look. Nobody.'

At last, Brighid began to see what the Tribune had seen from the start. At her father's insistence, she had adopted other aspects of the Roman life, the language and learning, but never the appearance. Not until now, when nothing of her woollen plaid showed under the shimmer of fine linen, had she realised what the effect would be. As Florian continued to ply her with ribbons and braids, goat-kid purses and pairs of soft openwork sandals, the Tribune himself climbed aboard to see how his *denarii* had been spent, making Brighid's heart leap to see his admiration, quickly concealed, and to hear his restrained compliment that she would surely raise a few eyebrows at Lindum.

'Is that what you aim for, Tribune? To raise a

few eyebrows?' she asked, striking a graceful pose with arms full of cloth.

'Yes, Princess. Why not? Better to be unique.'

Florian agreed. 'But that's exactly what I said, sir. Unique.'

Lazily, Quintus glanced at him without a smile. 'Yes, my lad. And when you've finished in here, you can come and tell me what you've spent and how many extras you purchased while you were about it.'

'Yes, sir.'

'Including that lad you brought back with you. He seems to think he's a fixture. What's he for, exactly?'

Florian coloured up, his eyes darting over the fabrics. 'He's…er…for me, sir. He helped me to choose the *domina*'s shrine and explained to me which one was Brigantia. And then we found that…well…that we liked each other. Sir. He's very well spoken. Travelling down to Aquae Sulis, like us. I didn't think you'd mind.' His expression seemed to turn inwards. 'And I don't like sharing my mattress with people I don't like. And if you're going to be with…' He glanced at Brighid.

'Enough! You're a rascal, Florian. I ought to beat you.'

'Yes, sir.'

'Give him something to do. I don't want hangers-on in my party. He can stay as far as there and no further, so don't get too attached to him. He'll have to work his passage.'

'Thank you, sir.'

'Now you and the Princess had better cobble something together before we reach Lindum. Use the green. Did you buy threads?'

'I bought a workbox for the *domina*, sir. She has nothing.'

'Hmmm! Right.'

It appeared, after Quintus's departure, that Florian's purchases were rather more extensive than he had implied, for the workbox contained several extras for Brighid's personal use: scissors and tweezers, hanks of threads and needles, two brass mirrors, one large and one small for her purse, combs of bone and ivory, a pair of coloured glass bottles with stoppers, a pot of lip salve, two horn spoons and a bone-handled knife, two pewter dishes and bowls, a silk cushion, and her own Samian-ware beaker with hares chasing round the sides. And a basket-woven stool with a lid, to keep things in.

For her under- and over-gowns, no shaping was needed, each piece being little more than an oblong fastened together along shoulders and arms with small clasps, gathered into the waist with long ribbons that crossed over and under the breasts in a most seductive fashion. It being so different from her usual baggy shapeless garment, Brighid felt compelled to conceal various personal assets under the casual drape of a scarf. But Florian pulled it away, insisting that she need not be so coy when every fashionable matron would gladly show off what Brighid had, and more. 'They bind themselves up,' he said, admiring Brighid's beautiful firm bosom, 'to keep them from falling all over the place.'

'Florian...*please*!'

'It's true. You go in and come out in all the right places. Why hide it?'

The notion was not unfamiliar. There had been women in the village who hid very little, women taken noisily to her father's bed by night and condemned by day for their whores' tricks. Yet his daughter he had always kept close and safe from all censure. Here, well away from his influence, he could neither approve or disapprove of how she looked. Here, she could be a woman at last. Now, it would be what the Tribune wanted, and secretly what she wanted too. The admission shocked her.

Taking the largest mirror of polished brass, which must have cost a good deal, she studied the transformation, the blue-green reflected in her eyes, the poised and shapely figure swathed in clinging folds, the gold-edged bands outlining her form, the fine white *palla* draped over her shoulder. 'Good, Florian,' she said, with a shy smile.

'Like it?'

'Except for the hair. That won't do, will it?'

'No. Sit over here by the light. We can soon fix it. Hold the mirror.'

With the heaps of cast-off clothes, fabrics and accessories piled around her feet, she sat and watched how he combed her waist-length hair, taking two fine plaits away from her temples to join the rest which he pulled into a large thick braid twined with ribbons. His hands were deft, and it was obvious that the art of dressing a woman's hair was well known to him, and soon the braid was being coiled and pinned on top of her head in a sleek bun that accentuated the length of her neck. More than ever, the exquisite structure of her face and head were revealed, adding another layer of refinement to what was already graceful.

She knew without being told that, as a slave, she would not be dining with the Tribune or taking any part in the socialising. But from a distance she would be recognised as his woman, and she had agreed to play the part, whatever the cost to her pride. She would not shame herself by forgetting that she was a high-born Brigantian, for that was what he wanted her to be. A Princess. A prize worth having. Owned by him. Envied by others. Unique and rare. It was a compromise she never thought she might have to make when the man from the Dobunni had sought her for his wife only a few weeks ago.

Once she was alone again and the clutter of dressmaking packed away, Brighid turned her attention to her shrine, devoting the next slow mile to the one whose grace she felt had been forfeited for too long. In this, she exaggerated the situation, for Brigantia's attributes were not only great wisdom but also the gentle arts of healing, culture, poetry and all things domestic, and surely there was no goddess better placed to look with pity upon her subjects than this northern deity whose Roman counterpart was the esteemed Minerva. Brighid herself knew of this exalted connection, but in the hill-fort beyond Eboracum, it had meant little to her. She had been born on her goddess's feast day, Imbolc, the first day of February, when any kind of Roman connection had been too far away to contemplate. Then, the goddess had been offered prestigious sacrifices as thanks. Now, Brighid had nothing to offer except the flowers and her devotion.

It seemed to be enough, for the peace that came with the goddess's approval brought both tears and smiles to Brighid's eyes as she blew out the candles for safety's sake and then sat to consider her immediate future as well as possible uses for the tweezers. There was a limit to which this Romanising fiasco could go, she told herself, placing them at the bottom of her drawstring purse.

As mile after mile of flat land and vast skies flowed sluggishly past, putting time and space between everything that was dear to her, Brighid regretted the loss of the high tors, the fells and ghylls, and the wild moorland that was her home. So she was surprised to find that, as the sun began to dip into an orange-and-purple horizon, the wagon was rumbling slowly uphill towards a sizeable town spreading over a spur set high above the plain. This, Florian told her, was Lindum.

'You've been here before, have you?'

'We came this way to York, *domina*. I expect we'll be staying at the legate's house again. He's quite a harmless old thing.' Legates were not known for being harmless; they were of senatorial rank and very powerful. Florian saw the blank expression and laughed. 'We shall not see much of him or his wife, I don't suppose,' he said, kindly. 'We'll stay behind the scenes until we're needed.'

'Is Lindum like Eboracum?' Brighid said, trying to push away the thought that she might be needed.

'Not now. There used to be a legionary fortress here, but that's gone. They've re-used the buildings for retired army officers, so now they sit over their dining tables, reminiscing about their battles and showing off their scars and appointing themselves as local governors. All veterans, the lot of them. Quite harmless unless you happen to own a bit of land they want to build a basilica or a bath house on. Then they're not.' There was a distinctly bitter tone to Florian's profile of Lindum's senior citizens that Brighid chose not to enquire into. She did not intend to stay longer than she must with either Florian or his master, so there was little point in being curious, she told herself. Most slaves harboured some resentments.

Seated at the back of the wagon, she was herself an object of curiosity, at first from those following who were intrigued by the transformation, then by those they passed on the busy road into the town. Quintus was also fascinated by the elegant young woman whose combination of tribal and Roman was not only unusual but rather more sensational than even he had anticipated, and Brighid could hardly help but notice how he and his two friends rode immediately behind the guards where they could keep her in view as they passed under the great arch of the north gate. The Tribune had expressed no opinion of Florian's handiwork, but both slaves had recognised in his eyes a lingering approval as every detail was noted, though his curt nod was the only tangible sign he gave.

Florian had been accurate in his assessment of the elderly legate at whose mansion they arrived after a laborious jostle through the crowds. He had not, however, passed a similar opinion about the legate's wife who, just as elderly as her husband, had striven for many hours to remove the years from her well-worn face and figure. Sadly, her attempts had not had the desired effect, worst of all being the elaborate black wig that sat too far down on her brow, the knots of which were clearly visible. Left alone, her age-wrinkles would have made a fascinating map of emotion and experience, but the Lady Aurelia's decision to fill them in with lead-based powder made Brighid pity her and Florian to mutter under his breath that it looked as if she'd fallen into the flour bin again. It was beyond funny, Brighid thought, standing well back behind the Tribune's two personal slaves, noting at the first glance how the lady's eyes dwelt greedily upon his handsome face, caressing him with melting looks.

'Welcome, Tribune,' she said. 'Restored to health, I see. You were far from well when we saw you last. The Emperor has looked after you. And Tullus and Lucan, welcome.'

They went to stand in the atrium of the legate's mansion, now expanded and made more beautiful with painted columns and a tiled floor. A fountain caught the late afternoon sun before sparkling into the green pool; it was the cool lure of water that held Brighid's attention as Florian nudged her into awareness. 'Follow,' he whispered. 'Keep up. And keep your eyes lowered.'

'She's staring at me.'

'So's the old man, but you know better than to stare back.'

Gliding ahead in a swirl of orange-and-yellow silks, the Lady Aurelia led her guests along cool corridors, past doorways that had once been offices and round to the far side of the block where rooms had been set aside for Quintus's retinue. Brighid tried hard to make herself invisible against the green-painted walls, but the high-pitched voice of their hostess was meant to reach her ears as well as the Tribune's. 'There's a room upstairs for your slaves,' she said. 'There'll be food for them in the kitchen after we've eaten. We shall be ready to dine as soon as you've bathed, Tribune, and I can find a task for the girl, if you've finished with her for the day.'

'Thank you, my lady,' said Quintus, 'but I shall be keeping her with me.' There was an authority in his voice with which even the Lady Aurelia chose not to argue and, with a lift of her eyebrows and a stony stare sent like a dart in Brighid's direction, she left the room with Tullus and Lucan, leaving a faint vinegary smell in her wake. Quintus put the back of his hand to his nose, but whether to cover a smile or to stifle the smell no one could tell. He did, however, glance at Brighid, his dark brooding expression making her wonder what thoughts were passing through his mind, and whether his sigh was one of relief or annoyance.

Since he appeared to have all the assistance he needed, she decided to sit out of the way on a small day-bed by the wall and to take out her sewing, of which there was still plenty. It had not been easy to ply a needle in a jolting wagon, and here was a chance to make use of the last daylight hour. The Tribune's order to one of his slaves took her by surprise. 'Find your way to the kitchen and request a tray of food for the Princess. She's not going to wait till midnight before she gets a bite to eat. And fresh milk, not wine. I want it in here by the time I've bathed. See to it.'

'Yes, sir.'

'Florian, you stay here with the Princess and prepare my clothes. You come with me, lad,' he said to the other one. 'You, Princess, will stay in this room. No exploring.' She knew he must have read her mind, for the baths would be abandoned when the guests went in to dine. She doubted if Florian would stay here all that time, with a new friend waiting for him.

The new friend had not been inclined to wait, and he found a way to the Tribune's room soon after the guests had assembled and the sound of laughter had floated away into the spacious triclinium where the aroma of food mingled with the perfumed hems of robes. Brighid was eating ravenously, hardly bothering to look up as the discreet knock on the door broke the silence. Florian was on his feet immediately, as if that was what he'd been hoping for.

'Come inside quickly,' he whispered. 'You can't stay.'

'I know.'

At the sound of the voice, Brighid almost cried out and, had her mouth not been full of food, she might well have done so at the secretive half-smile sent over Florian's shoulder. So, she had not been abandoned after all. Her prayers had been answered.

Math, she whispered. *Dearest brother. You came for me.*

But Math frowned her to silence as Florian turned to introduce him and her smile had to be reined in before the joy and relief showed in her eyes.

Chapter Four

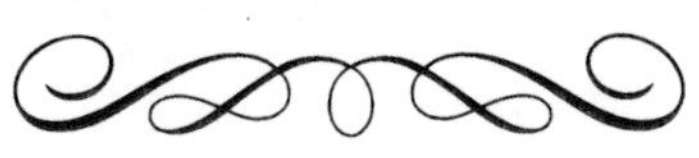

Brighid's tray of food, which was much better than slaves' fare and had been tasty a moment ago, now lost all flavour in the excitement of seeing her brother again after all the terrible heartache of separation. Older than her by only eighteen moons, Math was the younger of the two brothers, though all three siblings had different mothers. It was a custom taken to its limits by their father, the chieftain. Consequently Math bore no resemblance to his sister, and so little did he resemble his father in all the ways that mattered that beatings and scorn were daily fodder to the gentle young man who had felt that life without his sister would be unbearable.

From beneath her lashes, Brighid observed Math and Florian together and wondered why in twenty years she had never reached the same conclusion about her brother as she had about Florian in one day. Here in the company of Roman citizens, Florian's gentle tendencies were appreciated and utilised, not ridiculed, whereas at home in the hill-fort Math's ineptitude in all manly pursuits was seen as a disgrace. Was coming to find his sister and return her to her people Math's way of redeeming himself in his father's eyes? If there was a way, he would surely find it.

She could understand the brevity of their introduction, with Florian providing no more than a name. 'Princess, allow me to present my friend Max. Max, this is the Princess. She's the one I was purchasing the shrine for.'

Math bowed politely. 'I hope you were happy with our choice, *domina*,' he said.

'Perfect,' said Brighid, smiling into his large brown eyes. He was putting on a Roman face, she thought. Like her. The natural linen tunic suited him better than woollen plaids and leather. His hair was short and clean, dark brown like chestnut skins and free of that awful lime that men used to make it spiky. In spite of the broken nose, Math was still a comely young man, more so than his ferocious parent had ever been. 'I appreciate your help,' she said.

She would like to have said more, but Florian was impatient to claim him, and she knew they would have little enough time to make arrangements for the night. She put her tray aside and wiped her hands on the napkin, tempted to risk the Tribune's displeasure, and the threat that would surely follow, to find the bath-house and take a dip. With Math nearby to help her escape, her defiance doubled.

She was still dwelling on the possibility when one of the Tribune's slaves entered, addressing himself to her as one who merely recites the message but takes no responsibility for its content. 'The Tribune commands you to come to him, Princess,' he said with a sideways glance at the two friends. 'I am to escort you.'

'Now?' said Brighid, putting down the sewing she had just picked up. 'Whatever for?'

Florian helped the messenger out. '*Now, domina.* When the Tribune sends for you, you go. You don't ask why.' He came to her and helped her up, looking her over like a maid, tweaking at the folds of her gown and throwing the ends of her *palla* to hang down her back. 'Go quickly,' he said.

Filled with concern, her eyes met those of her brother. Without words, he was telling her to stand tall, to hold her head up like a high-born princess, not to act the humble slave, but to keep her dignity. Fortunately, it was an exchange that neither of the other two saw as she left the quiet room and headed for the triclinium where a steady stream of slaves carried salvers and bowls, urns and glasses as if for a feast of fifty instead of half that.

Frescoes decorated the walls; her sandalled feet slapped upon the patterned floor, past marble busts in niches, past the tables of rare woods and the dark fountain in the centre of the atrium, its droplets caught in the light of a dozen lamps. Sounds of laughter and the buzz of conversation reached her with the rich aroma of food, and she knew even before she arrived that this was to be some kind of demonstration of her docility. The newly tamed barbarian. Like the Tribune himself, their preconceived ideas about tribal people would be sadly out of date, and she wondered how much the Tribune had said about her, and who it was who wanted her there. She thought she could guess.

She had heard that Romans preferred to recline on couches to eat, but she had never quite understood how this could be done without taking up much space. So it was difficult for her to find the Tribune's face amongst so many white-clad men until she was edged past several pairs of slippered feet and brought to a stop at the end of one couch. By this time, the chatter had ceased and faces on the opposite side of the piled table were following her progress, watching like hawks for the submissiveness they expected, their hands groping blindly for the next mouthful of food.

It was the Lady Aurelia, just before Quintus turned, whose piercing voice began what she intended to be Brighid's humiliation, for she had been denied one chance already and the girl was obviously giving herself airs. 'Ah, here she is, Tribune. What does she call herself? Princess, is it? Well, we *are* honoured.'

From the head of the table, Quintus answered for her. 'It is I who calls her that, my lady. As the daughter of a chieftain, that is her title.'

'I see. So that's why you allow her to deck herself with all that tribal clutter. Does she do anything to earn her keep?'

That raised a laugh, as Aurelia knew it would, and Brighid could feel their intrusive stares taking in every detail of her appearance. She felt her anger rise, wondering how much of this she would have to take without responding.

'I should think she's worth her weight in gold, eh, Quintus?' called out one of the men facing him, looking round to see who saw the joke.

'Does she read to you?' called another.

'Does she speak?'

'Does she *need* to?'

Bellows of laughter. Tullus and Lucan looked uncomfortable. The guests were mostly ex-soldiers, not diplomats.

Quintus took it all in his stride. 'I've told you,' he said. 'The Princess's father had his offspring well educated. These people are not all as uncultured as you seem to believe. The idea is not new.'

Brighid could hold her tongue no longer. 'Your historian Tacitus recommended it,' she called out, rashly.

Mouths gaped at her effrontery. Here was a slave speaking without permission.

'Not *women*,' one man said, loudly. 'He was talking about men.'

'But the poet Martial was not,' she retorted. 'He actually approved of the British woman Claudia Rufina. She was taken for an Italian by the women of Rome, sir.'

'Nobody will ever take *you* for one,' snapped the Lady Aurelia, 'wearing *that* stuff round your neck. And with *that* hair.'

'I should hope not, my lady,' said Brighid, hotly. 'But perhaps we should not discuss hair. *Mine* is my own, at least.'

The silence was almost tangible.

Quintus moved fast, leaping to his feet to take

Brighid's arm as the shocked amusement rippled round the room, hands hiding smiles, heads ducking, eyes peeping towards their white-faced hostess. By his stillness, her husband seemed to imply that she had brought it on herself.

But having burned her bridges so soon, Brighid was sure to be in deep trouble unless she could escape in time to avoid it. In which case, she might as well have her last say. 'And *my* people, lady,' she called out, dodging under Quintus's arm, 'have better manners than to send for a woman in order to insult her for the amusement of guests.'

'Enough!' Quintus said with one hand in the small of her back.

'Not tamed yet then, Tribune?' called a voice on the edge of laughter.

With a distinct lack of ceremony she was propelled towards her waiting escort. 'Take her back. I'll deal with her later. And watch her,' Quintus growled.

'Yes, sir.'

But Brighid was already striding away from the subdued guests where the grating voice of the outraged hostess could be heard telling them all what *she* would do with an impertinent slave girl, princess or not. Without a look back, Brighid dodged around kitchen slaves like quicksilver, her rage at boiling point, the blazing green of her eyes awash with tears. This was just the kind of thing her father had protected her from amongst people of their own sort. Here, in Roman guise, she was a target for more abuse than before. She ought never to have dressed up like this, for she had suspected all along that the mixture of styles would provoke the wrong kind of interest. A hybrid to be made fun of. A circus freak.

Furiously, her fingers clawed at the ties that bound her gown, at the floating *palla* that had concealed very little, after all, and at the brooch on her shoulder. Her sense of direction registered nothing of turns to right or left, of doorways and steps, the night air and garden scents.

'No, *domina*! No, not that way!' called her young escort.

Blinded by tears and rage, Brighid paid no attention, stepping out of her blue-green gown and hurling it at the poor lad's head. He crashed into a column, yelped, and tried again. 'Come back, Princess! It's the other way, not…' His protest faded as she rounded a corner where the floor was warm and the faint aroma of water and steam lured her on. A trio of small oil lamps cast a light from the steaming pool to ripple upon the curved ceiling above, inviting her to wash away the coarse remarks that clung to her like grime. Her escort had not followed. She was alone.

Without a pause in her stride she ran down the shallow steps into the water, pulling the white undergarment over her head to let it float away while she plunged deep into the comforting cleansing bath that closed over her head, as kindly as sleep. With hands together, she cut through the warmth, surfacing at the far end dressed only in her collar, bracelets and anklets, the plaits and braids of her hair already darkening. After all the deprivations and discomforts, the lack of freedom and exercise, the warm flow of water over her naked body was more blissful than a plunge into an icy stream, and because the experience was likely never to be repeated, she would make the most of the luxury while it was still hers.

Completely lost in her new liberty and of the ease of swimming in still water, she explored all the possibilities of acrobatics, rolling and tumbling, floating and diving like a dolphin, and only when she surfaced upon the watery steps, panting and laughing, did she see the two large bare feet just beyond her head. They belonged, quite obviously, to a man, for only a few inches above them was the hem of a toga. Purple-banded. He was bending, holding out a hand.

'Come on,' he said, sternly. 'Come out now.'

Her fun was over. Now would come the reckoning. But she was not ready to give up her freedom so soon. Remembering the way he had said and done so little to take her side against the opposition, Brighid cupped her hand under the water and flung it at him, hoping to make him step back. Then, as fast as a fish, she turned and fled, only facing him again from the middle of the pool where she had to tread water to stay afloat. To her horror, she saw that he was unwinding his toga like a bandage, preparing to join her.

'You've been watching, haven't you? Go away!' she yelled.

He came to stand on the steps, naked, magnificent. 'If you want the rest of them to come in here,' he said, quietly, 'keep shouting.' Then, without warning, he plunged, heading straight for her in one arrow-sharp trajectory that might have caught her in two seconds had she not dived deeply beneath him, hiding under the surface as he scanned the pool and blinked water out of his eyes. She surfaced yards away, facing him angrily, and again he speared himself at her, only to see her become a shadow underneath him, crossing his path.

The pool had been built for soldiers as part of the barracks complex with space enough for manoeuvre, and if Brighid had not already tired herself with diving, she would have been confident about staying out of his reach. But her water-logged hair and the gold around her neck and limbs added to the effort of surfacing, and now her lungs had begun to ache. She dared not risk another breathtaking plunge.

Gasping for air, she saw through the haze of steam how his face and hair glistened, how his wide shoulders shone like armour, polished and hard. His arms lay outstretched upon the water, his narrowed eyes watching to see which way she would turn. 'Go away,' she panted. 'You may not see me like this. Don't come any nearer.'

'It was always a risk, Princess,' he said. 'Wasn't it?'

'If you intend to punish me, then wait till I'm clothed. You said little in my defence in there, Roman, but I'd not have thought your lack of manners was equal to theirs.' Again, she flung a handful of water at him.

He moved closer, but without the derisory smile she'd half-expected. 'There was no need to defend you, lass. You did well enough without my aid.

And my manners don't enter into it. A man may look at his slave in any state he chooses.'

The objectionable word acted like a trigger upon Brighid's temper and she hurled herself aside with a splash, yelping the predictable reply, 'I am *not* your slave! Do what you like...sell me... drown me...leave me...*no*! Leave me!' Her last words were torn apart by the surging foam and by her frantic struggles against the expanse of muscled chest that bore down upon her. His hands reached out.

The water at her back would not give way, so she ducked deep once more to evade him, kicking him as she passed, knowing that he would not let her go, even if it took all night. But although he chased her to the far end of the pool and back, with some near-misses, it was the shallow water-lapped steps that claimed her like a stranded fish, face down, with Quintus hanging on to one ankle. Her head felt like a lead weight, her lungs were on fire, and she had no strength to object or retaliate when his hand moved up to rest on the deep curve of her waist.

'That's what you needed, isn't it, Princess? Eh? Some exercise after all that confinement,' he said. 'That should take the edge off your temper.'

'There's nothing wrong with my temper,'

she panted. 'That woman insulted me, and those men—'

'Are soldiers, lass. They don't come across too many educated female slaves. It was nothing personal. To them, one slave is as good as another.' He reached across her to collect her white undergown, and she felt the brief blanketing warmth of him before he sat up to wring the water out of the cloth. She would have moved away, but her limbs ached and, even when he rolled her on to her back, there was nothing she could do except to snatch the wet cloth from him to hide herself from his examination. It fell upon her lower half, and he would not let her spread it further, taking her wrist away up on to the next step while she clung to the fabric, feeling her panic rise at what he intended.

'This is how I shall be punished, is it?' she whispered. 'For a man to see me like this is shameful to me, sir. Please…let me up.'

It was an argument Quintus declined. 'Too late to go into all that, lass,' he said. 'It's enough that you've started to earn your keep.' His eyes, however, followed the path of his hand as he leaned over her, watching the water swirl softly over her breasts, leaving a silvery sheen over the glowing skin.

Her face moved sharply aside as he caressed

the exotic peaks, smoothed and supported by the water, while her mind clung to the last vestiges of shame and battled against the incredible sensations under the hand that owned her. Like a slow consuming fire, halting her breath, suspending time, melting her aching limbs, his possessive hand made its own sensuous journey over the exposed parts of her body, stroking and tenderly kneading where a masseur would never have ventured, touching and teasing until she writhed and cried out, drawing up her knees.

Turning to face him, she found that his dripping wet hair was near her lips and that it was his mouth she could feel over her nipple, licking and lapping between gently squeezing fingers. Her instinct told her she must forbid it, protest, fight for her virtue. But it was too late, for nothing could persuade her that it was not what she wanted, or that her body had not already begun its own urgent response, beyond her experience, beyond her permission. His hair made dagger-points upon his strong neck, and she could breathe his exertions, see the working of his smooth cheek, the spiked lashes and straight nose. The danger of her position flooded back to her as he raised his head and looked into her eyes, giving her the chance to take control. 'Well, Princess?' he said, huskily.

'Still shamed? Was that on sufferance, or do I detect a different note in that cry?'

Pulling at her captured wrist, she turned on him the full glare of her eyes that caught the nearest lamplight, green as the water. 'You will detect whatever you wish, Roman, I don't doubt it. Now you've had your pleasure at my expense, let me go. I was right—you are no better than them.'

'I could curb that sharp tongue of yours, barbarian. That I could do. Perhaps another time.' He placed his hands under her arms, levering her up, and it was then she saw the swelling on the inside of his knee and what looked like a wound less than a year old, but still inflamed and unhealthy. She was pulled to her feet, and there was more to be seen on one shoulder, a pink ribbon of scar tissue she'd not noticed before. So, that was why he needed to visit the healing spring at Aquae Sulis. He had been injured and had hidden it from her well, until now.

Trembling, and shaken as much by what had just happened as by what had gone before, she stood with her back to him, wrestling with the wet linen that was all she had to cover herself. But with an arm over her shoulder, he took it from her, wrapping her in a cocoon of dry toga, deftly winding it round and round before lifting her into his arms, helpless as a swaddled babe, and carrying her out of the bath-house into the night.

She kept her eyes closed, and although she heard voices, she chose not to see the outraged stare of the Lady Aurelia, or the way that her eyes, in one rapacious glance, took in the sight of the Tribune's glistening nakedness. Nor did she see the envious expressions of the male guests who had gathered in the corridor more out of curiosity than for social reasons. No, too much was occupying Brighid's mind for her to make any sense of the Tribune's remark about earning her keep. Her brother had appeared, but what would be his plan for her? Would she be sold before they could make a run for home? Or would the Tribune keep her as his unusual woman, and was that decision already known to Florian, who had begun calling her *domina*? Mistress.

Questions regarding her virtue hung in the balance, decisions that only a day or two ago she would have placed firmly at the Roman's door, but were now also hers. Wrapped in his toga, carried close to him, her body still held the touch of his hands and lips, challenging all the long-held rules about the sanctity of a princess. He had already violated those rules with very little regard for her feelings, which he knew. How long would it be before her plan to find Helm became pointless? And how much would it cost her, if it did? Would her brother believe that she was still a virgin, after this? Would anyone?

The change of air pressure made her aware of her surroundings, the lamplit room, her sewing on the day-bed, and no one except the Tribune's slave to scurry in with her cast-off clothes and to scurry back out again with the wet linen. There was no sign of Florian or Math, so no one to witness the way her parcelled body was placed on the edge of the sleeping-couch to sit helplessly upright while Quintus sat behind her, enclosing her with his long legs.

'What are you doing?' she whispered.

'Your hair.'

'I can do that.'

'Yes, so can I.'

Fuming, she suffered his fumbling fingers on her head and felt the fall of thick wet locks over her shoulders, the relief on her scalp as the loosening began. She was obliged to co-operate when he pulled her head round to look at him. 'Stop your mewing, barbarian,' he cried, 'and think yourself fortunate to suffer no worse than this. I knew the Lady Aurelia might send for you, and I knew what your reaction would be when she did. *Firebrand.*

I did not, however, expect you to hurl insults at her. Show off your learning, perhaps, but no slave insults a lady if she wants to keep the hide on her back. If you wish to get out of this house in one piece, lass, you'd better stay close and do as I bid you.'

'She would not persecute another man's slave, surely?'

'Accidentally, she could maim you for life, my innocent. Believe me.' His lips were only inches away, and she knew by his darkening eyes that he yearned for her mouth and that he was about to take advantage of her again. 'And that would be a pity,' he whispered.

'Would it? Why?'

'Because, Princess, we have several more stops ahead of us when your presence as my woman will serve its intended purpose. That's why.'

'What, to dress up like a mime artist and pretend…'

'To warm my bed at night. That's your purpose. Get used to it.' His mouth closed over hers before she could complete her scathing reply, and the strong arm across her back made her aware that it was time for his needs to be met, instead of hers.

Since that chastening kiss in the wagon, bestowed, she thought, with more annoyance than desire, the taste of his mouth was only a fleeting memory amongst all the other first-time experiences at which most women of her age would have been well versed. Even so, Brighid had begun to realise that more protests would count for nothing and that there was perhaps a limit to the fury she could maintain. Tribal rules were one thing, but her personal safety was another, and the latter was by no means a foregone conclusion. The Roman's purpose for her could, she knew, easily be satisfied by another woman, if she herself proved to be too troublesome. Until she and Math could devise a plan, she would do best to keep up the same frosty acceptance of her predicament.

But this was easier said than done when the Tribune's kiss swept her much further than she could have imagined. Having witnessed only the rough-and-tumble—and, frankly, unappetizing—slobberings of village lovers and her father's nightly coupling in the next partition to hers, she had never looked forward to this kind of intimacy. It took almost no time at all for her to revise this notion when the warm searching of his mouth over hers obliterated every other feeling, every qualm or protest, every discomfort of being imprisoned and unable to move. That she was being used was certain, but was there not something liberating about being helpless in this situation? Released from having to struggle, or from active participation, she could do no more than savour every sensation, drown in the warm scent of his skin, taste the sweetness of his breath while his lips drank from hers.

She was tipped and moved in the sea of her hair, glimpsing through half-closed eyes fragments of light and dark that blurred into blissful nothing at each kiss. He lay over her, enclosing her body with his, kissing her throat above the collar, her eyelids, sparing her nothing after the exertions of their watery chase. At last, he pulled her into the bend of his body, her back to his front, sighing noisily into the mass of her damp hair. She believed it was a sigh of exhaustion, but therein lay her innocence. Nevertheless, before she fell asleep, she gave a quick word of thanks to Brigantia for the presence of a very long toga that had kept her chaste for another night.

As before, she woke at intervals, once to discover that she was being kissed again, very thoroughly. Still, she could do little about it except to take what he offered, saying nothing, knowing nothing except that she had begun to follow his lead, to learn his moves, to anticipate him and to offer herself time and again for more. She doubted he would notice. Or care.

At one stage, he unwound her upper half in response to her plea for release. Her arms, she said, had pins and needles. He laughed, tussling with yards of the precious fabric in the dark, falling asleep while fondling her beautiful cool breasts. She heard the soft rhythm of his breathing and could easily have prised his hand away. But she did not, telling herself that if the Fates had decreed it, who was she to argue?

Preparations for their departure began at dawn with a short fierce argument about whether or not Brighid would wear her Roman costume or revert to her own. 'You have little choice, *domina*,' Florian whispered. 'Your other things are in the wagon. And you'd better let me sort your hair out. Rough night, was it?' He ducked, avoiding his master's badly aimed cuff at his head. He was not in the least abashed.

'Hold your tongue, wretch!' Quintus barked. 'I don't keep you to comment on the state of the Princess's hair. Who left this tray of food here?'

'It's come from the kitchen, sir,' Florian said. 'For the Princess, the lad said.'

'Take it back,' she said. 'I'll wait.'

'You cannot wait,' Quintus told her. 'It may be hours before we stop. Eat some of it, at least.'

'No, Tribune. I'd rather not. It's poisoned. I can smell the belladonna from here.'

Quintus and Florian stared. 'Are you sure? I can't smell anything.'

'You wouldn't, sir. But I'm used to dealing with herbs and, if you were to ask me, I'd say that there's enough in there to kill a cow. She must have used up her entire supply.'

'Princess?' said Quintus. 'Are you sure? What would she use it for?'

'Women with dark eyes use it to make them sparkle,' she said. 'That's why we call it belladonna.'

'Leave it over there,' he commanded, 'and don't let anyone touch it. They can collect it when we've gone. Florian, you'll find something for the Princess to eat on the road. Buy some milk before we leave the town.'

'Yes, sir. Will you sit, *domina*? Your hair…'

'We have no time for that,' said Quintus. 'Do it later. Let's get away from here. Women!'

Brighid might have wondered whether that was aimed at her or at the legate's jealous wife, but suspected the latter, especially when she was ordered to stay close to him until she reached the safety of her wagon. All the same, she wished her hair had been plaited, for the sidelong looks of the men, including the Tribune's two friends and her own brother, were loaded with meaning that she was well able to decipher. 'Men!' she muttered.

The titillating news soon circulated the Tribune's retinue that his new slave, not being satisfied with insulting the hostess, had also made free with her heated pool and that the master had not punished her, but had actually carried her off to his bed. One of these alone would have caused a buzz; together, they were the cause of a new kind of respect for the woman they had previously thought of as no more than a distraction from the purpose of the journey. Except for Tullus and Lucan, that is, who knew more than the rest of them the reasons for her presence.

'There you go,' said Lucan, wheeling his mount round to follow the wagon. 'I knew it wouldn't be long. Got his hands full at last, our boss.'

'Two swallows do not make a summer,' said Tullus, amiably. 'You know better than to jump to conclusions, my friend. And, personally, I have my doubts.'

'Why?'

'Why? Because he does not wear the expression of a satisfied man, and the lady doesn't have the expression…'

'Of a satisfied woman,' Lucan finished for him. 'But did you see the hair?'

'I saw the Lady Aurelia's,' said Tullus.

Their irreverent laughter eventually subsided, but when they heard later, via Florian, about the poisoned breakfast, the laughing stopped. 'That's serious,' said Tullus. 'I know the lady wanted him, but *really*.'

This time, Lucan agreed. 'Not exactly what we had in mind, is it, when we suggested the remedy?'

'We ought to have done more to help him out.'

'Stick closer.'

'Get to know the Princess better.'

'If he'll allow it.'

Their suggestion that Brighid might like to ride pillion behind one of them was not met with enthusiasm by Quintus, who unkindly suspected their motives. He also believed that Brighid would exploit any step towards laxity, given a fraction of a chance. He did agree, none the less, that if the two of them could not ensure a close watch on her, then no one could. 'We're happy to share the duties as well as the pleasures,' Lucan told him. 'You asked for our help. Now accept it.'

'Thank you. You can safely leave the pleasures to me,' said Quintus.

Although Brighid was grateful for the change, it also delayed her from speaking in private with her brother, something that was a matter of urgency, with so much to ask him and so many miles passing by. Once out of Lindum and on to the well-made road to the south-west, they were able to make better progress, and after two hours of continuous riding, they halted to rest the horses at a small settlement where the inhabitants were used to travellers. Several of them stopped to gawp as Brighid was lifted down from behind Lucan and escorted to the wagon, one old man spitting on the ground in disgust at her curious half-Roman, half-British combination, as if it had been her own decision.

'I hope you can see now, Tribune,' Brighid said, 'that it might have been more politic for me to wear my own clothes. It seems to please nobody but you.'

Impatiently, Quintus swung her round, holding her hard against the tail-board of the wagon where both guards could hear what was being said. 'Stop your nagging, woman. And stop deceiving yourself, too. When you start to care a damn about what people think of you, the moon will turn to green cheese. I know exactly why you're so peeved.'

'Tell me, Roman,' she retorted.

'Because you've lost their sympathy, dressed like that, and because it will make your attempt to escape that much more difficult. Deny it, if you can.'

Her lids fell as her gaze slid away to the guard's sandals. 'So that was your intention,' she said. 'I see.'

'No. It was not. Think again.'

Inside the wagon, Brighid realised she had allowed him to upset her by his surliness after the tenderness of the night, so when her brother climbed in between the canvas flaps, her emotional sob was taken for delight as she fell into his arms and clung like a limpet.

'Hey,' he said, holding her at arm's length, 'it's all right, little sister. You knew I'd find you.'

'I didn't,' she said, gulping. 'I didn't know anything. It was dreadful.'

'Nothing? Didn't they tell you? About...?'

'About what?'

'Father. He didn't…well…return home. He was killed that night. They took his body back home on a chariot.'

Brighid's eyes widened, her mouth forming a perfect O. 'Dead?' she whispered. 'Is it true? Then we're free of him at last? Oh, Math! I never dared hope.'

Math nodded, his dark eyes sparkling with amusement and relief. 'Free,' he said. 'Our brother is chief now. He agreed with me that we had to find you, and I have. He wants you back home, Bridie. There's been another offer for you already.'

Too much. Too soon. She would go into all that later. But now, 'Where's Florian?' she said, looking over his shoulder. 'Are you allowed in here?'

'Massaging his master's beautiful body out there,' he said, tipping his head. 'I was told to take his place for the moment, assuming that I'm harmless.'

'But it's not just an assumption, Math, is it? It's true.' She took his hand to draw him further into the wagon, seating him on the chest. 'Come and tell me. Are you really as relieved as me about Father? He was a tyrant, wasn't he? No more beatings for you. We can go back home without his shadow hanging over us. Think of that.'

Math's reply came only after a thoughtful silence. 'It's like a weight lifted from my life,' he said. 'But you're right. They're not assuming, out there. They can tell. Florian and I could both tell as soon as we saw each other in the market. He was floundering about…' he laughed '…trying to explain what he wanted. I helped him out.'

'You followed us, then?'

'Yes, I guessed where you'd be. I waited, then followed on foot. Ran across country some of the way, with my pack on my back. It was not difficult to make contact with Florian. We seemed to connect. He usually sleeps near the Tribune, so he's glad to have me with him because he hates sleeping alone. I think he gets pestered. Now he has me to protect him. He's such a girl, Bridie.'

'He's been very kind to me.'

'Yes, but one thing I've discovered about being with this crowd is that they have a place for men like Florian and me. I've not been scorned or persecuted the way I am at home. Nobody cares about it. I'm allowed to be me. And you,' he said, looking her up and down. 'Whose idea was this? Not yours, I suppose? Is this what caused the trouble last night? Or was it your famous temper?'

There was no time to tell him all that had happened—it was more important for him to know what had *not* happened. Math's explanation of the phenomenon was short and to the point. 'A knee injury,' he said, 'when he was commanding a cavalry regiment. A horse fell on him during a skirmish, and he was kicked and speared too. It still pains him, Florian says.'

'Is that why he's so short-tempered?'

Math's hand reached out to caress her cheek. 'Our father *did* guard you close, didn't he, love? There's nothing quite like a constant nagging pain and no sex to keep a man on the boil, you know. And with you in his arms all night, I should think he's about to explode.'

Math's smile made her blush. 'But I thought that was because I begged him not to, and because he intends to sell me, eventually. The slave merchants offer high prices for—'

'And you think a tribune of equine rank bothers about things like that? He's wealthy, Bridie. The slave merchants have nothing to do with it. Now if you were to apply some of your healing to his knee, you'd make him a very happy man. I should think he'd be glad of something to ease the pain, now and then.'

'I don't particularly want to make him a happy man, Math. I'm more inclined to injure his other knee.'

'Forgive me if I don't swallow that rubbish,' he

said. 'I think we're both becoming more Romanised than our late unlamented father would have liked. And I'd lay any wager that your nights in the Tribune's bed are not as uncomfortable as all that. So how do you feel about trying to get home? Shall we? Or shall we wait?'

The offer of an alternative suggested to Brighid that Math had his own reasons for wanting to stay on course, as she did. 'Before I knew you were here,' she said, 'I decided to go all the way, if the Tribune would allow it. It's Helm's country down there, you know. Do you have news of him?'

'Only that he's headed for home. You're expecting he'll still be interested, are you? I'd have thought you could do better than that. I'm still sure you can.'

'I know you never liked him much, but they're a wealthy tribe, Math.'

'And more Romanised than us. You'd fit in well and he knows that. But you now have more choice, Bridie. With Father gone and our brother in charge, things will be more bearable at home. On the other hand, you could try to find young Helm and take your chances there, but he'll be getting you for nothing, won't he? I doubt he liked the sound of Father's bride-price for you. Perhaps that's why he left so soon.'

'Then what are we to do, Brother? The Tribune may not try too hard to find me if I were to disappear. He's promised to get rid of me, sooner or later.'

'You want to leave? It's quite a risk. And you couldn't foot it across the countryside looking like that. Where are your clothes?'

'In the chest underneath you. It's always locked. Always guarded, too.'

Math stood up. 'I'd better go. They're starting to move. We'll talk later.'

'Be careful, love. Florian is utterly loyal to the Tribune, remember.'

But when Math had disappeared, Quintus arrived to take her outside. 'You'll ride behind Tullus for a while,' he said. 'But let me give you a word of warning, Princess.' He hooked an arm around her waist and drew her into his hard chest as if he wanted her to feel every hidden contour under his tunic. 'Don't be making any plans to flee with that new lad. You'll go when I'm ready, and not before.'

'I have made *no* plans,' she said, fiercely.

'Then what was that long talk about just now? You hardly know him.'

'I asked if he had any news of the Brigantes, that's all.'

'And did he?'

'He's a gentle young man, like Florian, and lonely. We talked about how comfortable he feels in company with your people. I like him.'

His arm tightened. 'Yes, and they're all chosen for their loyalty to me. He'd better not be an exception.'

'Like me, you mean?'

'You will always be an exception, woman. But don't start plotting. I have not finished with you yet. Understand?'

It would not have mattered what reply she intended, for his kiss bent her in his arms, robbing her of both words and resistance, and when she clung to him, she was oblivious to the way one of her hands crept up to touch his soft falling hair. Not until the kiss ended did she realise where it had been.

She drew back out of his arms, placing a hand to her burning lips, but he took her wrist and held it away, studying her downcast eyes without comment. 'They're waiting,' he said, gruffly. 'Come.'

They pretended that nothing had happened, but both knew that it had. For in that tender gesture lay more than she had intended, and far more of herself than she'd wanted to reveal.

Chapter Five

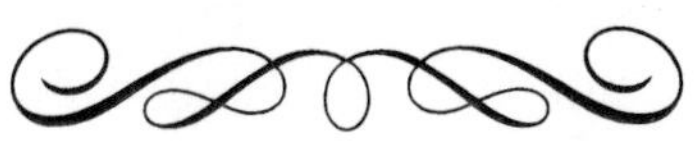

The news of her father's death and its implications gave Brighid so much to think about that Tullus soon stopped trying to make conversation for so little reward. Tribal fights were frequent and always fierce, but her father had seemed invincible. The Emperor, though, was a famous warrior renowned for his victories; this being the case, Brighid found it surprising, if not downright unlikely, that the information concerning the latest one would have been kept from the Tribune. She was sure he was keeping it from her, and now she would have to do the same or disclose the source of her information. Already he was suspecting her friendship with Math. Was he also suspecting Math himself? No, on reflection, perhaps not; her brother did not meet the image of a chieftain's son. She decided to limit their meetings after this.

One of her first decisions concerned her prayers

to Brigantia, whether to invoke mercy for her father's spirit or to give thanks for a deliverance she had never dared wish for. Her thoughts on the matter were as complex as the man himself, for in shielding her from the attentions of men, her father had apparently seen no paradox in exposing her to his own licentiousness both by day and night. His sons had disapproved of their father's insatiable appetite, and Brighid knew many mothers who would now be sighing with relief that their young daughters were safe from his favours. How sad it was that her little maid had caught his eye, had conceived before her childhood was over and then been denied any compensation, after all that. No, Brighid decided, she could not mourn the death of such a man, whoever caused it.

Accepting her lack of communication, Tullus was equally content when she asked him if there would be shops or market stalls at their next stop. 'I believe so, Princess,' he replied over his shoulder. 'Is there something you need?'

'If I could find a herb-seller, I could prepare something to ease the Tribune's pain,' she said. 'I assume that must be the reason for his short temper.'

Tullus's grey eyes twinkled. 'You may be right,' he said. 'But on the other hand, I would not be too surprised if he were to decline your offer. I believe the Tribune favours the professional healers at Aquae Sulis more than amateur medication.'

'Yes, come to think of it, I would probably distrust me, too, if I were him. But there's really no need, you know. Poultices are put *on* wounds, not swallowed, and, even if there was no improvement, he would not die from it. I've done it often enough to know what I'm doing.'

Lucan joined in. 'No harm in it. Perhaps we could put it to him,' he said. 'What kind of thing do you need, Princess? Mandrake root? Henbane?'

'No, not belladonna either. Or opium. In fact, I need only a few things I can't find out here on the wayside. See, there are nettles and marshmallow over there by that marshy ground, and elders, too, and willow. We've just passed a holly tree for its leaves and roots, and we already have a store of other ingredients: oatmeal, eggs, beeswax and wine, honey, lard and bread. Nothing poisonous there, sir.'

If Tullus and Lucan were surprised that the captive wished to alleviate her captor's pain, they were remarkably discreet about it, putting the proposition to their superior with an assurance that collecting herbs from the wayside would neither delay them nor constitute an escape risk. They would both undertake to guard her.

So they entered the settlement at the end of a thirty-mile journey with a sackful of leaves, roots and bark, while Math was sent to purchase the powdered roots of willow and mallow, and a pot of sheep's grease. It looked, he thought, as if his sister had decided not to injure the Tribune's other knee after all. Brighid herself had plenty of time to decide that it was in her best interests if she could somehow make herself as indispensable to the Tribune as Florian was. Known as Margidunum, the settlement was, apart from the usual cluster of houses and shops, a staging post on the main road with a large government hostel where Imperial officials and messengers could stay overnight. Private rooms opened on to balconies and columned arcades, in the centre of which was a paved courtyard with low-growing rosemary, lavender and houseleek, a stone statue of Mercury, the messenger-god, and white-robed men deep in conversation. Here was no venomous black-wigged hostess, but a friendly manager with a swarm of slaves at his heels to show the Tribune and his party to rooms on the ground floor while explaining to him the amenities, the baths, triclinium and exercise hall. And nocturnal company if he should require it, he added obsequiously.

By this time, Brighid was growing more accustomed to the undisguised curiosity of others, for although she wore a plain gown and shawl for travelling, even that was more flattering to her figure than her tribal dress. She had not learnt yet to keep her eyes lowered, but nor did she return the stares as she had done before. People found her green eyes disconcertingly remote, her expression far from servile, and when it was whispered that she was a tribal princess, no one was sceptical. To them, she lacked the proper demeanour of a slave, yet she had been obliged to leave behind the woman she'd been at home, accustomed to commanding her own household and being attended to. There, she would never have needed to persuade anyone to let her treat their wounds; they would have been honoured to be tended by the chieftain's own daughter. Amateur, indeed.

Not so Quintus Tiberius Martial, even though he was clearly in great discomfort after the day's ride in which his wound had chafed against the edge of his saddle. Throwing himself on to the couch as soon as the door closed, he beckoned a slave to remove his shoes.

'Remove those breeches, too,' Brighid told the lad. 'I need to look at the leg.'

'My leg is none of your business,' Quintus snapped.

'It *is* my business. If you die from blood poisoning, I shall be suspected, shan't I? Stands to reason. Therefore, I shall treat it.'

'Oh…do as she says,' he growled. 'But if you hurt it…'

'It *will* hurt. You'll have to bear it. Put it up on here.'

With her reluctant patient laid out and his naked leg cushioned for her inspection, Brighid sat beside the ankles to take a long hard look at the inflamed wound, the edges of which oozed nastily. It was swollen, too, and had clearly not received the treatment it ought. 'How long has it been like this?' she said.

'Since the Tribune received it some months ago, *domina*,' Florian said. 'It's never properly healed.'

Brighid touched the swelling. 'There's something in there,' she said.

'Can't be,' said Quintus. His eyes were closed and he was frowning. 'It was a metal spear and a horse's hoof, and the surgeon cleaned it up there and then.'

'Even so,' said Brighid, 'if it was clean, it would

heal and it isn't doing. Florian, will you and Max help me prepare a poultice for the Tribune? I need to open it up and clean it, and remove whatever is causing this mess.'

Math was familiar with his sister's healing processes and knew what she needed; while she made an infusion of marshmallow leaves and powdered willow bark to ease the Tribune's pain, the two lads pounded boiled nettle roots, lard and honey to make a plaster. Borrowing a bowl and pan from the kitchen, they boiled water over the charcoal brazier, tore linen into strips and tried not to wince as Brighid cleaned the surface of the wound with mint-infused water while bossily encouraging the patient to finish the dregs of his drink. 'That's the willow bark. Drink it up.'

'Urgh!'

'What *children* men are.'

As if on cue, Tullus and Lucan entered, clearly fascinated by the predicted scene on which they'd just been placing bets.

'Just in time,' Brighid said. 'You can hold him while I put this plaster on. He's bound to make a fuss.'

'I don't *need* holding down,' Quintus roared. 'Just get on with it. Any more poking about and I shall walk out.'

Ignoring the threat, Brighid nodded them into position, laying the cool linen on his wound with the pale greenish pulp next to it. The half-expected yelp did not come, but his two hands gripped the leg as if it might fall off.

'Let go of your leg, if you please, or your hands will get bandaged in too. This will soothe it and, by morning, will have opened it up enough for me to get inside. Now don't start being difficult again, *please*. You'll have to give the baths a miss this time. The boys will wash you down.' Soothingly, like a mother to a child, Brighid talked as she bound the wound and tied it, clearing away the bowls and linen with instructions to prepare a different poultice for the morrow.

'I shall not need it,' Quintus protested. 'It won't do any good.'

'*Do* it,' said Brighid as the two young men hesitated. 'The Tribune will take a short nap before his dinner.'

'The Tribune will do no such thing,' he argued. Nevertheless, within minutes he was asleep and Brighid was in whispered discussion with Tullus and Lucan about having their meal brought to the room on trays. This was a side of their captive the men had not seen until now, and a side of Quintus that neither of them had expected to see. Well, not quite so soon, anyway.

It was the delicious aroma of food that woke him to the sight of tables arranged with dishes of fish and stuffed poultry, vegetables and sauces, breads, cheeses and fruits, nuts, dates and ewers of wine. And as if by mutual consent, Brighid became the hostess, demonstrating her social skills down to the last Roman detail, thereby offering a comparison to her behaviour of the previous evening when she had been upset by the guests' hostility.

Heavy clouds brought an early darkness, and good wine brought a mellow conversation that eventually turned to Brighid's family. What kind of a man was her father? Being careful to speak as if he still lived, she told them how one of his hopes was to marry her into the wealthier southern tribes for political purposes, his use of the assumed title 'Princess' for his daughter being a part of this inflated ambition. Although not a king, he thought of himself as a king's equal in most things except birth. His sons were not named princes, however, for his intent was not to endow his offspring with more power than him but with marketability, and his sons could market themselves without his aid.

But when Tullus quietly asked her about the little maid and her death, she saw no harm in telling them of the reasons for her tragic wish not to live any longer and of her own intention to find a shrine at Aquae Sulis at which to make an offering. 'If I should get that far,' she added. 'It's for the Tribune to decide.'

'Your father has several wives?' said Lucan, breaking an uncomfortable silence.

'Concubines, not wives. His tastes in women are very...'

They waited politely for her to find the word, then Tullus purposely suggested the opposite. 'Particular?' he said. But by that time, Brighid had sensed that her revelations had begun to border on disloyalty and, instead of disagreeing, she reached for the silver ewer.

'More wine?' she said, smiling. 'I'm more used to mead, but I find this loosens the tongue just as easily.' To the three men, her silence on the subject of her father's morals said more about her than any further details could have done.

Outside, in the confines of the courtyard garden where Quintus strolled slowly between Tullus and Lucan, it soon became apparent to a trio of well-dressed slaves, employed by the hostel manager as escorts to lone guests, that here was some good company for the night. Like soft-footed decoys, they allowed themselves to be overtaken, then drawn into conversation with every hope of success, though none of them could have anticipated the watchful eye of Brighid. From the doorway of the room where the remains of the meal were being removed, she saw what was about to happen as the Tribune's arm became linked with that of one particularly voluptuous siren.

She quickly padded across the plot to his side. 'Time for your medication, Tribune,' she said, briskly. With a flash of green, her haughty glance caught the eye of the woman, causing her to blink with astonishment.

The hopeful escort bristled and moved closer to her prize. 'It's the first time I've ever heard a slave give orders to her master,' she pouted, clinging to his arm.

But Brighid's eyes hardened to the green of malachite and she was ready with her reply, snapping like a turtle before Quintus could get a word in between them. 'I am not the Tribune's slave, I am his *woman*. Now take your arm out of his and allow him to decide for himself what he will do.'

Without a murmur the woman did as she was told just as Quintus moved away from her side, touching Lucan on the shoulder in recognition of something between them that was causing the expression of pained amusement. Tullus seemed about to explode with suppressed laughter, but Quintus and Brighid moved away together without a word of excuse, regret or goodnight.

As the door of the room closed behind them, Quintus detained her with a hold on her arm. 'So,' he said, 'what was all that about, lass? Eh? You're concerned that I might have had *her* in my bed, are you?'

Brighid pulled her arm out of his grasp. 'Not in the least, Tribune. Have them all three in your bed, if you wish, but wait until your knee has mended first. I'm not spending my precious time and effort trying to mend it if you're going to undo it all again. And what would you have *me* do while you're busy entertaining that whore? Wait outside, or sit and watch?'

For a man with a bandaged knee, he moved surprisingly fast, catching her again before she could put any distance between them. 'Oh, no!' he said brusquely. 'Come back here, fierce woman! We'll answer that question when we get to it. Meanwhile, you're going to have to make more effort to keep a civil tongue in your head, or you might be waiting in a more uncomfortable place than this with a price tag round your neck. And let that be the last time you tell anyone you're not my slave.'

'You said I was to be—'

'You'll be whatever I decide at the time,' he snapped. 'Which ought to suit you well enough since *you* change your tune several times a day. I never know what you'll be next, starving captive or raving woman, unwilling, then willing...'

'Stop, sir! I have *never* been willing.'

Quintus smiled, admitting that his taunts were unfair. His arm tightened and the smile faded as he caught the full angry beam of her sea-green stare. 'No, lass, maybe not. But I've lit your fires, haven't I? Why else would you care who I take to my bed? And before you protest again that it's my knee you're concerned for, save your breath, for you must know full well that there are ways of getting round *that* problem. That lass out there would know half a dozen of them, I should think.'

'Let me go,' she said, pushing against him. 'This is lewd talk.'

'Is it? Right, so come over here and tell me more about these healing skills of yours. How did you learn them? Whose teachings do you follow?' Taking her by the arm, he walked her towards the couch, sitting beside her and enclosing her in the circle of his arms. It was warm and comfortable with the gusting draught blazing the charcoal brazier and flickering the oil lamps, the heavy patter of rain hitting the paving outside, the slamming of doors as guests fled, a man's shout and a woman's excited squeal. 'Well?' he said into her hair. 'I accept what you said earlier about not being able to help anyone unless they want to be helped, but how useful would your remedies have been in your maid's case? Do you have cures for everything? Even the mind?'

It was, she thought, as good a place as any to begin. So she told him how, since she was able to talk, she had shown an aptitude for recognising plants and their uses, and not only herbs, but the properties of things like spiders' webs and dung, soot and white of egg, beeswax and the sap of trees, butter and even urine. Everything in nature, she told him, had its use, and not only medication, but the planets, too, especially the moon's influence. The interpretation of dreams, portents like clouds and the weather, the behaviour of bees and birds—all had their own rules and charms. No, not magic, she told him, but the rules of nature, whether kept or broken, the meaning and messages offered up by the earth for inspection to those who learned to interpret them. She had never found it less than fascinating and, as she became more adept and successful at treating her villagers and the wounds of her father's warriors, respect for her had grown along with her reputation. She had been an important asset to them, though she didn't mention to him that a woman's bride-price was set according to her skills and that hers had apparently been beyond the Dobunni suitor's means. Either that, or he'd gone back home to consult with his father on the matter.

'Then I have acquired more than I realised,' he said softly into her ear. 'You ought to fetch a high price, Princess.'

'Sell me and you will have no one to treat your wounds, will you?'

'Hmm! As a Provincial Procurator, I hardly expect to receive any. Now, let's take a look at my knee, shall we? I'm curious to see how good you are.'

'The plaster has not been on long enough, Tribune. It needs all night.'

'Take it off. I want to see.'

'If you insist. But I warn you, I may have to probe it again.'

'Then it's better done without an audience.' Already his fingers were undoing the bandage. 'I would rather howl in private.'

She knew he would do no such thing. The Tribune was not a man to show weakness, in spite of that petulant show earlier, least of all before a woman. Slowly, carefully, she peeled back the slimy plaster, fully expecting to see little change, for this was merely to open the wound, not mend it, and only after a night-time, not half an evening. But to her utter amazement, the wound had begun to open cleanly enough for her to see, after only the smallest probe with her new tweezers, the head of a splinter sticking deep into the flesh. 'Hold your leg tightly,' she warned, 'and grit your teeth. There's a splinter here and I have to pull it out.'

The minor operation was over and done with by a count of twenty, the inch-long sliver of wood emerging smoothly as if waiting for release. She laid it upon the bandage for him to examine. 'So much for your army doctors,' she said. 'These things can cause a nuisance if they're left. Now stay there while I warm up the healing poultice that the boys made.'

'What is it?' he asked, suspiciously.

'Mostly boiled holly leaves, mallow, elder bark bound with sheep's grease and wine. It helps healing and takes the pain away. I think you should travel in the wagon tomorrow, to give this a rest.'

'I have a sheepskin. That'll protect it,' he said, automatically dismissing her suggestion as evidence of weakness. 'Is this what you used on your own people?'

'It would depend on the wound, the time of year and what was available. There are many other ingredients I could use. Is this why you're travelling down to the healing spa, Tribune? If so, it could be almost healed by the time we get there, if you'll suffer my treatment of it.'

With a hand covering his eyes, he flopped back as she applied the hot poultice, and she heard the hiss of his breath soften into its normal rhythm as the bandage was replaced. She knew how it must be throbbing.

The re-appearance of Florian with the two slaves was timely; Brighid was relieved to see that they bore her no grudge for taking on some of the duties that would otherwise have been theirs. Together, they made up more of the willow-bark potion to help with the pain, clearing up the room and preparing it for the night, fetching jugs of wine and tit-bits for when he woke, folding clothes and setting out fresh ones, and finally massaging the masterful shoulders and neck.

'Shall you sleep in here tonight?' she whispered to Florian as he finished.

Quintus opened an eye, answering for him. 'You will stay, Princess. Let him go to the lad.'

Florian could not hide his smile. 'It's best, *domina*,' he whispered. 'I'll return at dawn to help with the knee. I may have to sit on his chest.'

'Don't think I can't get up off this couch to box your impertinent ears, rascal,' Quintus muttered. 'I need no one to sit on my chest. Where's that potion?'

'Here,' said Brighid. 'Drink the dregs, too.'

'Getting your own back, are you, Princess?' he said, pulling a face.

'Oh, I could do much better than that, sir, if I wished,' she replied, taking the beaker from him. The door closed behind Florian and the boys as the Tribune's hand caught at Brighid's wrist, drawing her to his side where she stood uncertainly, her heart racing at the touch of his fingers. His eyes were closed, ready for sleep, yet he sought the soft warm smoothness of her arm, descending by way of her linen shift and the under-curve of her breast, then waist and hip.

'Then I am in your hands,' he whispered, smoothing his hand over her buttocks.

She trembled, able to move away, yet transfixed. *And I am in yours, my lord, am I not?*

The hand grew limp as sleep claimed him,

making no resistance as Brighid laid it gently upon his own body instead of hers, the rise and fall of his great chest under the sheet holding her attention as she played back the day's events and the dilemma that still held her in its merciless grip. She had had no private discourse with her brother since yesterday which might, she assumed, be due to his discretion or to the unfamiliar contentment of being in Florian's company by day and night. Whatever the reason, he had not offered any plan or suggestion for her release, either now or in the future and, without some discussion, she was obliged to reach the conclusion that Math intended to accompany her as far as possible and to help her to find Helm, the only man in the south of the country who could offer her his protection.

The problem remained, nevertheless, that each mile southwards made it more difficult for her to abscond, especially now that her outward appearance would do nothing for any attempt to blend invisibly into the background. It had been a clever move on the Tribune's part, one which could only be bettered by finding her original clothes. And even if they had not been locked away, the heavy gates of the hostel had clanged shut at sunset, a double guard keeping watch over the guests' safety.

More personal was the other problem, the one that had already begun to override her duty, her loyalty, her pride and her common sense, of which she had plenty. Not so infatuated was she that, given the chance, she would not turn her back on this man and make a run for it, wounds and all; not so in thrall to his lovemaking, or so newly awakened that she could not put him from her mind. Eventually. Yet her body told her something different, aching to learn more at his hands, to pulse with the elusive and unnamed weakness that churned her innards whenever he came close. Like a dowsing-rod over underground water she reacted to his presence, uncontrolled and wayward, shamelessly unable to resist as she ought.

Her mind had offered excuses, reasons. He would quickly discard her if she became too much of a hindrance. She would then become an abused slave instead of one who was cared for, that in itself being enough to keep her with him. His regular threats encouraged her to try harder to make herself necessary to him. Her healing had been a useful ally. He was impressed. At the same time, this would be a danger to her in another way, for she realised now that it had not been the *position* of the wound that had kept him chaste, but the pain of it. Curt and commanding he might be, as an ex-cavalry officer, but there was nothing like a constant pain to shorten a man's temper, as her brother had reminded her. How much longer would she be safe from him? Would his wound heal before they reached Aquae Sulis? Would her seeking of Helm be in vain, after all? Did she secretly want it to be?

Watching the undulations of his ribcage, she was reminded of the young Dobunni man, the chieftain's son who had singularly failed to impress her brothers, entertained by her late father as a good catch, if the price was right. Comparisons were futile, for although the young man appeared well put together and healthy, he was not of the Tribune's model, nor did he have the same presence and authority, though perhaps he thought he had. His look had not made her quiver inside, as she did with the Tribune, and although the touch of a Roman upon a Brigantian woman was a disgrace, there was no accounting for the body's preferences beneath the cloak of night.

No. She deceived herself. There had been lamplight.

No excuse there, then.

The shrine to Brigantia received an unusual amount of attention while Quintus was asleep, after which Brighid was content to leave her fate in the goddess's capable hands. Accordingly, she slept alone on the second couch in recognition of the choice being hers instead of his, a token gesture that gave her enough satisfaction to sleep soundly until dawn.

The almost ritual unveiling of the wound, carried out under the curious stares of quite a crowd, raised Brighid's standing in their eyes as nothing else had done so far, with the possible exception of her fierce behaviour of the last two nights. The inflammation had been replaced by the beginnings of new tissue, the swelling was reduced, and the pain now no more than a soreness. The uninterrupted sleep had made the patient marginally better tempered, even when the suggestion arose, yet again, that he should rest in the wagon for the next part of the journey. 'Forget it,' he said, tersely. 'Where can we purchase another horse?'

'Isn't your grey up to it?' Tullus said, observing the preparation of a new poultice over in the corner.

'It's for the Princess,' said Quintus. 'She can't keep on riding pillion. She needs her own mount.'

'Can she ride?' Tullus wanted to know. He spoke without thinking.

His two friends stared at him, open-mouthed.

'She's a *Brigantian*, Tullus,' Lucan reminded him. 'She can probably *fly*, let alone ride. Have you never seen those chariots?'

So that was how Brighid travelled, in some style, from the government hostel at Margidunum to the private villa at Corieltauvorum, an event she suspected had less to do with the overloaded hindquarters of Tullus and Lucan's mounts than on the dramatic appearance of the Tribune's woman on her own showy mare, the brilliant coat of which matched her hair exactly. It must, they all knew, have cost the Tribune at least three thousand *denarii* and was no doubt a reward for the Princess's competence. It was a reward Brighid was happy to accept for whatever reason, even if it puzzled her that the Tribune had provided her with an extra means of escape. Was he so sure of her? And was this to be Brigantia's solution to one of her problems, perchance?

Also lighter of heart and pocket, Lucan and Tullus quipped and quibbled in the sparkling sunshine, hemming Brighid closely with their mounts while keeping an eye on her horsemanship and soon reaching the conclusion that flying was not as ludicrous as it had sounded before they'd seen the instant rapport of rider and mare, the easy grace of Brighid in the saddle, the obedience of the animal to her signals.

'Bit of a risk,' Tullus said in an aside to Quintus. 'Isn't it?'

'Calculated,' Quintus replied. 'Looks good, though.'

'Better and better,' Tullus agreed, 'but stay on your guard, my friend. The lady may look good, but if she doesn't have a plan tucked up her sleeve, then she's not the woman I think she is.'

'Thank you for the advice, Tullus, but I don't need it. I have good reasons for making her more comfortable with her new appearance. Selfish ones, perhaps, but valid.' With that, he pulled his grey stallion ahead to speak with the leaders, leaving Tullus to raise an eyebrow in speculation at the selfish reasons for his superior's generosity. He did not think they were hard to fathom.

This latest mark of the Tribune's esteem, however, lifted Brighid's spirits higher than they had been for some considerable time, for although Roman women were more usually conveyed in litters carried by slaves or horses, only a few chose to ride their own mounts, even with polished harness, sheepskin saddle-cloth, and bells and tassels everywhere. Used to riding rough ponies bareback and receiving no help to mount, she decorously allowed the Tribune to lift her up on to the gleaming back loftier than even her father's stallion, arranging a soft blanket to cover her legs on each side. Sitting sideways was not for her. If this was how he wished her to be seen by their next hosts at the end of the day, then she would not disappoint him, or them. And this time, she would guard her tongue.

She had gathered houseleeks from the hostel courtyard that morning, with just enough time to bruise the fleshy leaves for the juice, to mix it with a fine oatmeal, mutton suet and milk to make a smooth paste, and to have enough left over from the plaster to carry with them during the day. Once again, her brother's help was a godsend, and while she told him—just for effect—how to do things he already knew, it also gave her a chance to ask him, in undertones, whether he had thought of any way out of the situation. It was as she had suspected. Math had given it little or no thought at all. 'Not yet,' he whispered. 'Be patient, sister. Give me time.'

Angrily, she turned away, wondering how much help he was going to be in the light of his new friendship.

* * *

'Well, Princess? Is this freedom suiting you better than the wagon?'

The Tribune's voice redirected her attention from a distant heron standing like a sentinel on the river bank, his knee just touching hers as he drew alongside. She turned to look up at him, towering over her, unsmiling, but with a glint in his eye that might even have been the sun's doing. His hair lifted in the breeze, parting it like sheets of dark silk and whipping it across his eyes. The grey stallion snorted at the mare, dilating its nostrils.

'The wagon has its uses,' she said, glancing at his hands, 'but this would always be my chosen method. Tomorrow, I may be allowed to canter, and the day after that, to gallop. No, don't look so alarmed, sir. I'm not being serious.'

'I was not alarmed, Princess. I was wondering which day you intend to fly,'

'I'm not sure that flight would be in my best interests, Tribune,' she said, sensing the direction of his enquiry.

'You'd not get far,' he said, quietly. 'Even on the mare.'

'No.'

'Are you going to ask about my knee? Isn't that what healers do?'

'How is your knee, sir?'

'Very comfortable, I thank you. I should have known of your skills earlier.'

'That might have been counter-productive, Tribune. I would have found it more difficult to resist the temptation, earlier.'

'To what, poison me?'

She nodded, glancing up at his face to watch it darken. But it did not. 'Hah! And now?' he said. 'Changed your mind, have you? Why?'

She shrugged, a secretive smile just lifting the corners of her mouth. Her reply was leisurely, casual, almost friendly. 'Oh, I had scrolls with it all written on, but now they'll have been destroyed and I cannot remember any exactly. It's no use if you're not exact, you know, and I might have got it wrong. My reward for that would not be so handsome as a chestnut mare, I don't imagine.'

'Is that what you think?' he said. 'That the mare is a reward?'

'Isn't that what I'm supposed to think? Everyone else does.'

'Then everyone else is mistaken. As you are.'

He was not, it seemed, disposed to elaborate any further, and as Brighid was not inclined to probe his reasons, she kept her lips closed and her gaze fixed at a distant point between her mare's pretty ears as they rode in silence for mile after mile, side by side, thought matching thought.

Chapter Six

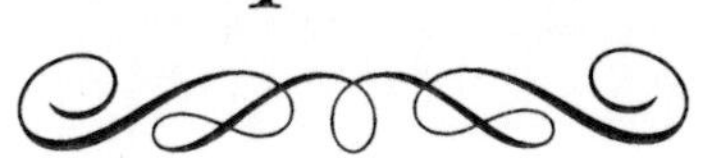

Despite the fact that Brighid had been taught, with her brothers, the language of the Romans and, inadvertently, to know something of their ways, her knowledge of their policies, laws and domestic habits reached her only at second- or third-hand along with her father's inevitable condemnation. Even when this information had sounded reasonable enough to her, he had denounced every aspect of their government and culture if for no other reason than that they had no business to be here in the first place, riding roughshod over those to whom the island rightly belonged. They had been over here for at least ten generations, and yet there were still men like Brighid's father who refused to adapt to the Roman presence, except for allowing his offspring to learn how to communicate with them. Their life-draining taxes he staunchly refused to pay.

So it was hardly surprising that Brighid had been raised on a diet of deep distrust and contempt for all things Roman, while secretly harbouring a curiosity to know more about how their shockingly indulgent standards of living differed from her own. It would have been strange indeed for her to show no interest at all, or even to agree entirely with her parent's bigotry when she had never been allowed to stray more than two miles from home. The town of Eboracum might as well have been Rome itself, for all she knew. Yet her father's loud-spoken dislike of the Roman system was too potent not to have left some impression on her. For one thing, she was a princess and therefore near the top of the tribal pecking order, and it was hardly possible in so short a time for her to shed the natural superiority acquired over her twenty-two years.

Some of the luxuries at the Lindum accommodation, however, had given Brighid a taste of what she'd been missing, the luxury of spotlessly clean floors and painted walls, delicate colours and decoration, the tiled bath with warmed flooring and water, feather beds and clean sheets, the drapes of linen she and everyone else wore for everyday use. Defensively, she reminded herself of the comforts she had left behind in the wide heather-covered hills of home, of the fabulous bronze weapons, the jewellery of gold and enamel, the cunningly wrought cups for beer and mead. There were priceless furs, weaving, dyeing and embroidery, the frequent visits of foreign merchants bearing exotic amber, pearls and coloured glass, hunting birds from the north, spices from the east. They had taken back hunting dogs, metal, corn and slaves and, but for her father's bullying severity, life might have been tolerable for her. Less so for Math.

The nearer they drew to the next overnight stop the deeper became the gulf between Brighid's conflicting memories of home and the inviting new world of gracious living where even the modest suburbs sprouted smooth-walled red-tiled houses amongst the older timber and thatch. Colourful robes marked out a predominance of wealthy citizens with slaves in attendance, and metal-clad Roman soldiers with brawny legs saluted the Tribune and his entourage as they passed, their anonymous eyes lingering upon Brighid and her high-stepping mare that must have cost a fortune.

On the furthest outskirts of the market town, a large villa spread out like a white crust upon a green-patterned cloth, trim round the edges and large enough to have housed a dozen families rather than the one wealthy farmer, his wife and daughter who came out to greet them. A messenger had been sent on ahead. They were expected. To Brighid, this was opulence on a scale that made her wonder, as they dismounted, whether her father had known of this kind of wealth and, if he did, whether his disapproval of Romans in general was based on envy or true patriotism. As it happened, the host and hostess, like their ancestors, were as British as him, the difference being their method of survival in a changing world.

It took only one glance for her to see that this villa was of quite a different order, both in scale and grandeur, from the retired commander's home at Lindum, for here the buildings were designed for comfort on three sides of a large garden with colonades, balconies and steps leading to other levels. Even more significant was the smiling welcome of their hosts who appeared to understand Brighid's status without any embarrassment, even when the Tribune introduced her as his personal healer. It was, Brighid thought, an ambiguous appellation if ever there was one, which the Lady Sylvana and her husband Cerealis took in their stride without batting an eyelid, the same of which could not be said of Tullus and Lucan, though they had enough discretion not to show their surprise.

The Lady Sylvana was glamorously middle-aged with a stunning pile of dark hair arranged in tiers of tight curls that had obviously taken an age to fix. Sparkling with gold, she waved red-tipped fingers and pointed red-tipped toes in flimsy studded sandals not made for mileage, whereupon Brighid hid her own red hands in the folds of her gown, hoping they'd not be noticed. The room she was to share with the Tribune, no questions asked, was more tastefully furnished than any she'd seen so far with the kind of reflective freshness quite new to her after the rough interior of a roundhouse. Yet she felt surprisingly at ease in this light clean environment as if this new phase in her life had been waiting only for the right moment to present itself. Caution and northern-bred common sense told her not to get used to it, for she must not imagine that her so-called position as the Tribune's 'personal healer' would guarantee her safety.

After the Tribune had bathed in the private bath-house and Florian had spent the usual time anointing the magnificent body, Brighid set about applying another dressing to the knee, whence arose an argument about whether Brighid would dine with him or not. If it had been her decision, she would rather have eaten alone.

'It's not your decision, but the Lady Sylvana's,' said Quintus, watching the bandage pass over and under his joint. 'She has asked for you to be there and I want you to be there, too.'

'There are good reasons why I cannot,' she said, crossly. 'For one thing, I am not used to your kind of dining. I don't eat lying down.'

'Is that all? It's not difficult. You'll be with me and I'll help you.'

'Another thing, I've not had chance to bathe. And I've nothing suitable to wear…and… Oh, never mind. You'd not understand.' Tying off the ends of the linen, she tucked them in and stood upright.

Before she could see it coming, he had lowered one leg to the floor and pulled her to him, clamping her hard to his chest and pushing her head on to his shoulder with his face only a breath away from hers. Any nearer, and her eyes would have closed. 'Like it or not, Princess,' he whispered, 'you must leave the barbarian behind and with each mile become used to a different way of life, everything except the title, which is a useful device, no more. Start now while there's still time, if you wish to convince me that you can be of some use.'

'So is the title of personal healer a promotion,

my lord Tribune? Or am I still to pretend to be your woman? You must keep me up to date, you know.'

'Sharp-tongued little viper. I think our hosts can work it out for themselves. And as for your not having anything to wear, women never do. It's a fact of life.'

She turned her face into his chest. 'There's more to it than that,' she said.

'I know that, too. You've caught sight of the glamour, haven't you? And you're making unnecessary comparisons. There's no need. Allow Florian to dress your hair, find the blue-green tunic, and you'll not need red-painted nails. She would kill for eyes like yours.'

Of all the things he might have said to reassure her, all the trite compliments men sometimes produce when they're trying too hard, nothing could have given her more confidence than to know she had something another woman would kill for. Especially a woman like the Lady Sylvana.

She peeped up at him to find the sincerity of his words, but his lips found her first, sending to oblivion the confused emotions, the jumble of losses and gains, hopes and fears that had dogged her, hour upon hour. She warned herself that she must not allow his lovemaking to become the answer to her problems, that she must seek her own salvation, somehow. But when his hand sought her breast, touching the scantily clad peak in passing, covering the round full softness while his mouth played upon hers, she knew in her heart that her plans were shifting like treacherous sands and that her intended use of him came a distant second to his use of her. In her attempts to convince him of her value, she had begun to convince herself of the need for change. Yes, she would have to do as the Romans do and be thankful her father would never get to hear of it.

In another way, she was later to give thanks that he would never see the villa's décor where pattern covered every surface, even ceilings and floors. Underfoot, bizarre mosaics of questionable artistry depicted nude actresses and mermaids, men fighting bulls and spotted leopards in chains, the gladiatorial theme rather at odds with their genteel hosts. But it was the couple's daughter, a girl of about seventeen summers, who reminded Brighid how often families breed children who refuse to fit the prescribed mould, and if Math could be a disappointment to his father, then so could young Flavia be to her mother.

While Brighid had taken an extra hour to reach her hostess's sartorial standards, the daughter's efforts resulted in a kind of austerity that was meant to be read as non-conformist and sexless. For such a lovely girl, it could not have been easy, but somehow she managed it. Nevertheless, she found much to interest her in her parents' guests, particularly Brighid with her fascinating combination of Britishness and Roman accentuated by the priceless ornaments. It was a look the girl's mother could never have achieved.

Flavia was spoilt and brash, leaving none of the guests in any doubt about the direction of her life, being intent on a career as a gladiatrix which, although frowned upon by the Emperor Severus, was still undertaken with dedication by a few high-born women who preferred danger and adulation to a life of martyred motherhood. The short-haired gangly-framed young woman astonished them with the revelation that it was her boyfriend, a Londinium-based gladiator, who had first taken her, unknown to her parents, to the local stadium to see the show. Naturally, they had done their utmost to persuade her from her course, but she was their only child and, using that as an excuse, had been unable to deny her what she had no intention of denying herself. Astonishingly, her father—shamefacedly admitting it was so—had built a covered arena in which she could practise with paid teachers in the belief that, since she was determined to take her life into her own hands, she had better do it in style. Her father, Flavia told them proudly, said she was good. Her boyfriend had said the same.

Reclining next to Quintus, Brighid saw him remove a date-stone carefully from between his lips and place it on the edge of his plate while his stockinged foot touched hers and drew away again.

Flavia's interest in Brighid extended further than her appearance and multiple skills to that of practice opponent. She was convinced the Brigantian Princess would have some fighting skills, whether with sword or spear. Didn't she?

Politely, her parents protested and begged the guests to excuse her enthusiasm. But Brighid had the means to extricate herself without giving offence, and it was only later in the privacy of their room that she and Quintus were able to share their thoughts about being used as target practice for a would-be gladiatrix. Not only had the young lady suggested it in all seriousness to Brighid, but to Quintus, Tullus and Lucan, too.

'As your personal healer,' said Brighid, 'I had to forbid it.'

Quintus yawned, noisily. 'Oh dear. I was quite

looking forward to it. But perhaps it's as well. I should not have known which bit to shorten first, her tongue or her silly ambition. Her father should take a strap to her.'

'And that would fix everything, would it?' said Brighid, saucily. 'How much did you learn about children, my lord, on your way up?'

'Enough to know that, if a lass chooses to act out a lad's games, she should be treated like a lad,' he said, unreasonably.

'It seems to me, sir, that that's exactly what they are doing, as far as they can. In all other respects, she appears to be a perfectly normal woman.'

'What…fighting? Where does that come in, for a woman?'

'It comes in at about thirteen summers,' Brighid said, letting her hair fall over her shoulders, 'and lasts for a few more. I remember it well. Rebellion. A wish to steer my own course. Antipathy to rules. Physical urges. Conflicting images of what I was. Wanting the kind of respect and recognition that doesn't come from merely being born female. If it's a passing phase, she'll grow out of it. If it's permanent, she'll at least have lived a shorter life by her own choosing, won't she? That has to be worth something.'

'Not to her parents, it doesn't.'

'She's a woman, Tribune. Her parents are trying to guide, not to dominate, and she has strong opinions. Is it such a bad thing that she'll find her way *with* them, rather than without them? I agree that what she's planning is outside society, and dangerous, but in the future she won't be able to look back and say her parents pushed her into something against her wishes. Tyranny is one name for that kind of over-protection, and that young lady…' she panted, waving an arm at the door '…will be better prepared for life than I was at seventeen. She envied me for what she *thought* she saw, my lord, but if she'd only known the truth, she'd…she…' Her voice faltered and choked as emotions became tangled with the words.

'She'd what?' His arms enclosed her, his lips against the loose hair on her temple. 'Think differently? I doubt it, lass. There's not a lot of thinking goes on in that head except what *she* wants, and life is not about what one wants at the expense of others. You know that. She has not given a single thought to her parents' wishes. You're angry because she has a kind of freedom you'd have liked, but there's a middle way, you know, between keeping a precious daughter safe and letting her off the rein too soon. They've allowed her to bolt straight into the most dangerous place on earth.'

His lips moved down her face, breathing in her warm scent while she struggled against the tiredness and fear of the unknown, the result, she told herself, of being plunged without preparation into a new and frightening kind of relationship 'Is this,' he whispered, 'your father's tyranny we're talking about?'

She nodded, knuckling a tear away. 'I suppose it is.'

'Well then, now you're free of it for a while, aren't you?'

'Out of the frying pan and into the fire, my lord.'

Instead of a direct denial, he swung her up into his arms and carried her across the lamplit room where shadows chased and bent across the soft blankets, the white-covered mattress and downy pillows. 'That remains to be seen,' he said, lying over her. 'I am not a tyrannical master, Princess, but I have to admit that your safety has become a priority with me too. Who in his right mind would not wish to keep hold of such a rare possession? Wise as well as beautiful. Fierce, clever, cultured, desirable. You reveal more of yourself each day. And you were brilliant this evening, as if you'd dined like that all your life. I was proud to have you beside me, though little did I expect I'd need your protection from a sword-wielding virago.'

'And my reward, Tribune? Another day not being sold to a slave dealer?'

'Is that what you wish, Princess? To stay with me?'

'As far as Aquae Sulis. Then I think you should free me to find my own future.'

'I'll take you there, but I shall not free you, lass.'

Indispensable? Brigantia, beloved goddess, did I not say? Indispensable as far as Aquae Sulis, no further than that. 'Why not? You have no—'

'Shh! Because I'm growing used to you in my bed and by my side in the daytime. My wound is healing, and last night we slept apart, so now we have some catching up to do.' Tenderly, he pushed a lock of hair from her face, letting his hand travel down over her body with all the authority of an owner examining his property.

She caught it as it slid between her thighs beneath the soft stuff of her gown, turning her head to avoid his questing mouth. 'Yes, no doubt, Tribune. But I am still a maid, if you recall, and I would rather be allowed to choose when and where to relinquish that state, and to whom. If you are not a tyrannical master, I think you should prove it by letting me give freely what is mine to give.'

'Ah, here we are again treading this fine line

between who owns what. If I were to argue the point, I'd say that, as things stand at the moment, what is yours *is* mine. Still,' he said, nudging her face back to his with his knuckles, 'I think I might be allowed a little tyranny before we sleep, eh? If I'm careful not to overstep the line?'

'May I not first prepare your medication, Tribune? It will help the wound to heal while you sleep.'

'Can I trust you, Princess?' he whispered against her skin.

'Come and watch. I do nothing in secret.' Taking his hand, she rolled away and drew him with her to the table where the pots and packets lay as Florian had left them, confident that whatever she added to the Tribune's drink would not be recognised by him for its properties. So when she laced the usual draught with a pinch of this and a speck of that, to improve the taste, he drank it down without question and returned to the couch, yawning again, to watch her finish undressing. Intentionally, she took her time, encouraged by the example of young Flavia, whose experience in getting her own way was streets ahead of hers, and while the Tribune's breathing settled into the regular rhythm of sleep, his eyes had closed long before she had finished combing her hair.

Several times during the night he turned to gather her close to him as if to continue some dream-like lovemaking. But the deep breathing resumed and the intended tyranny remained like a half-smile upon his face until dawn, by which time Brighid was making use of the women's time in the bath-house.

Stroking his stallion's velvet-pink muzzle, Quintus used the arched grey neck as a screen behind which to speak in subdued tones to his two friends before they mounted. 'Just keep an eye on the new lad, Florian's friend,' he said. 'I don't think his presence is as accidental as he wants us to believe.'

'Uh-uh!' Tullus grunted. 'Anything in particular?'

'Well, for one thing, he understood the Princess's instructions in her own tongue. It was a brief exchange, but there was no doubting it. And for another thing, he appears to know rather more about how Brigantes live than you'd expect from an ordinary York man. He claims to be a Roman citizen, his father a scriptor with a nice line in signwriting, but there's something odd about his knowing so much about how the chieftain was killed. I cannot help wondering if he's passed that on to the Princess. She seems to be thinking rather a lot about her father's influence at the moment.'

'Isn't that natural?' Lucan said, watching Brighid say farewell to their hostess.

'Maybe, but I would not be surprised if this lad Max is of the same tribe.'

'Could he be the young suitor from the Dobunni, do you think?'

'No! Not the right calibre for that, is he? Nor would he be speaking the Briganti dialect, nor has he travelled this way before.'

'How d'ye know all this?' said Tullus.

'Florian tells me everything.'

'But I thought…?'

'Yes, even so. But he knows which side his bread is buttered.'

'Don't tell me you've eaten *butter*, like the barbarians,' said Lucan, wrinkling his nose. 'Disgusting stuff.'

Quintus flicked an eyebrow. 'If you'd been in the army, my friend, you'd be glad to eat nothing worse than butter on your bread.' Sliding his hand down the horse's neck, he bounded up into the saddle with an ease that would have been impossible only two days ago, thereby missing the eloquent exchange of eyebrow-raising between his two handsome friends.

To himself, Quintus had already admitted, on waking, that he'd taken a risk last night in allowing the Princess some control of the situation, knowing why she was anxious to keep a tight hold on her virginity. But he did not believe she would harm him after treating his injury so efficiently and when she needed him to take her to where she could find the Dobunni tribe. Whatever young Max was to her, it looked as if he had the same aim in mind unless, of course, the lad was playing a different game.

Trotting away from the villa, Tullus and Lucan shared their amusement about the close encounter with a gladiatrix of such determination, though Brighid seemed too preoccupied to join in. She had passed several gifts to Florian to stow away in the wagon, beautiful alabaster jars of creams for face and hands, phials of perfumes and stoppered glass pots of sweet oils and unguents, pressed upon her by the Lady Sylvana as momentos of her visit. That morning, for the first time ever, Brighid had received a massage at the skilful hands of a girl whose precise routine had been more closely studied than she realised. It would be one more skill to add to Brighid's growing list.

It would have been difficult for Brighid to say exactly in what respect the spoilt young Flavia had made an impression on her, though she had soon recognised some of her own aspirations there. Her empathy had not met with the Tribune's understanding, nor would it have found a foothold in her father's attitude towards a daughter's role, for neither of them had suffered the kind of exalted confinement she'd had to put up with all her life. At seventeen, Flavia had a lover and the experience to go with it. A gladiator. Fêted and idolised, such men could afford to be choosy. Her parents had accepted that, too, though it must have cost them a few conventionally minded friends along the way. Brighid had heard of such men, lapping up the details of their deeds and misdeeds with a mix of disgust and arousal that had confused her adolescent mind. And now, here she was, mingling with those close to them and, to all intents and purposes, apeing their customs with pots and creams and cosmetics in her possession and a sneaking feeling that they would not be wasted. Would she resort easily to tribal life when she found Helm? In less than a week, was her resolve beginning to weaken? And where was Math when she needed his help most?

She managed to snatch a few words with him, but he had little to offer. 'We can't do anything,' he whispered, 'until we get there.' They had stopped for a rest in a flat sky-filled landscape that accentuated their sense of isolation with no distant feature to tell them where they were, as there would have been in their native hill-country.

'When?' Brighid demanded, as if he should have known the answer. 'Where on earth are we? How long will this take?' She had retired into the wagon to tear up some linen strips her hostess had given her when Brighid had apologised for the pink stain on the towel after her massage. The Romans, it seemed, even had a better way of coping with that, too, more comfortable by half than having to make use of basketfuls of moss. She sat on the wooden chest with her hands wrapped around a beaker of milk, frowning at her brother's vagueness.

'Another day or so and we'll be moving into their territory,' he said. 'You'll have to be patient, Bridie.'

'You *must* keep me informed, Math.'

'Yes, I will. I'll keep my eyes and ears open. Must go.'

'Wait! Ask about the Dobunni...where their chieftain lives. We don't want to pass it and have to retrace our steps.'

Math's hand was upon the canvas flap. 'And how d'ye think you're going to get free, exactly?'

Brighid's patience was running thin. 'I'm expecting *you* to plan it, brother. Or what good is it you being here?' Exasperated, she handed him the empty beaker and watched him disappear, only then seeing just below the tail-board of the wagon Florian's dark curly head looking up to smile at his friend as if he'd just arrived.

'She called him "brother",' Florian said to his master a few minutes later. 'I know the word. I heard it often enough in Eboracum and in Londinium, so it's not dialect. And the *domina* pronounces his name Math, not Max, sir.'

'Well done. Anything else?'

'Nothing I could understand, sir. But…'

'But what?'

'Please, don't hurt him, will you?'

'I've no intention of hurting him, lad. Just keep listening and watching.'

Florian continued with his massaging. 'Yes, sir,' he whispered. 'The *domina* has done well for your wound. It's healing nicely.'

Silence.

'I imagine the *domina* will soon be doing this for you too, sir.'

Quintus smiled into his towel at the hint of jealousy. 'You have nothing to fear,' he said. 'As a twelve-year-old, you were an expensive acquisition, Florian. You'll be earning your price for some years yet.'

'Really, sir?' Florian grinned.

Whether it was her sensitive condition or her growing anxiety about the nearness to their goal, Brighid's usual caution slipped when, at that night's hospitality, she rashly asked their elderly hostess if she knew anything of the Dobunni people. If the lady had kept the question to herself instead of repeating it at dinner, all would have been well, but it was thrown into the conversation as a perfectly normal topic with the added interest of why the Princess wished to know.

'Why? Because my family is of the Brigantes,' she said, thinking that she ought to be whipped for her stupidity, 'and I know that the Dobunni are powerful in these parts. But I don't know where one territory ends and another begins, not even ours.'

The host, a white-haired retired builder, provided her with all the information she had expected of Math that morning, that the people she had heard of were a little further south and that if they were to reach Corinium Dobunnorum by the next day, they would indeed find plenty of them strolling around the streets. Yes, he responded to

Brighid's look of surprise, they even minted their own coins and had their own tax-collecting depot. A wealthy tribe they were, some of whom actually co-operated with the government on various levels while some were more solitary and independent. Like most others, he added politely.

Brighid did not think her host knew much about the northern Brigantes, or he could not have held that opinion. But if she expected the Tribune to challenge her interest in a tribe of people so distant and different from her own, she was a little surprised to find that he thought nothing of it. Respecting her wish for some privacy, Quintus made no attempt to get close to her and made no objection when she wished to sleep on the spare couch in the room they'd been given. In fact, she would not have protested too strongly if he'd offered her the comfort of his arms at the end of the day, but he did not, and it was as if his only need of her was as the woman who tended his wound and who travelled beside him for the sake of appearances.

She had done both with spectacular results, so that when they rode through the huge four-arched gate into the large Roman city of Corinium, the attention given to the exceptionally fine woman with the blazing red hair sitting proudly on an expensive-looking chestnut mare was enough to part the crowds that thronged the busy streets. Carelessly, the thought flitted through her mind that if she had intended to lose herself in the dense throng of market-goers, she would need to make herself far less conspicuous. But just as she turned to catch the eye of her brother, who rode some way behind them, the Tribune leaned forwards to slip a length of rope through her mare's bit-ring, without explanation, keeping her close to his side and leaving it for her to decide whether it was for her safety, or restraint.

Although their stay of a single night at Corinium strengthened Brighid's impression that the citizens here were an affluent lot compared to any others she had seen, her need to know about her suitor's possible whereabouts remained unsatisfied, for she did not dare to risk broaching the subject again so soon.

It had been as they were preparing to leave the luxurious villa at Corinium next morning that she had been quite taken aback by her brother's hurried whisperings that he had some news for her.

Heartened by Math's sudden spurt into action, she had managed to hide her excitement until they stopped to eat at mid-day. 'I found out,' he muttered, escorting her to the wagon, 'that the chieftain's son spends some time at a place called Watercombe. He's friendly with the owner. Very Romanised is your Dobunni suitor, it seems.'

'Where is this place? Did you find out?'

'Somewhere near Aquae Sulis, I believe. A healing centre. That's all I know. Here you are. Let me hand you up. I have to look as if I'm making myself useful, Princess.'

'Not before time,' she said. 'See if you can find out how to get to this place.'

'Certainly, Princess,' he said for the benefit of the two guards. 'I'll bring your drink immediately.'

It was not Math who brought it, however, but Quintus who came to sit with her while she drank, sharing a platter of assorted shellfish fresh from the market, new bread, dried apricots and raisins. 'Do you wish to ride in the wagon?' he said, pulling the shell off a prawn and offering it to her.

'No, thank you,' she replied, taking it. 'I'm not uncomfortable on Clytie.'

'Who?'

'Clytie. Clytemnestra. You know. Agamemnon's wife.'

'Yes, I know that. I'm just surprised that *you* know.'

She stopped munching and turned to look at him, sharing his astonishment. They had spoken very little that day, and now his sharing of her food, too, in private, was like a warm caress over her heart that had begun to chill with cooling doubts. After his unexpected compliments two nights ago, she had assumed he was regretting it, regretting, too, the familiarity he had imposed upon her, taking advantage of her fears that he might soon discard her. But the expression in both their eyes was like a silent conversation that spoke of a comfort in each other neither had expected to find, affecting them with a certain kind of guilt. It had not been part of their plans.

He had not thanked her for healing his wound, nor had she thanked him for the handsome mare, for to do so would have moved their captor-captive relationship on to a different level, which neither was willing to acknowledge. But this long unaccompanied duet of perception where, in the dimness of the wagon, the two veils were lifted for a fleeting moment, said all that needed to be said—indeed, all that *could* be said—about their exact position in each other's lives, so that when her conscience reminded her of his refusal to set her free, she knew he had meant that he would not let her go. Which was not the same thing at all.

The strategy Quintus had planned was for his captive to ride beside him into Aquae Sulis in enough splendour to turn heads and for questions to be asked by visitors to the spa in the hope that her arrival would reach the ears of the Dobunni chieftain's son. Now, plunging headlong into those deep green eyes that darkened as he surfaced, his strategy lost some of its attraction, for while he had a duty to the Emperor, his heart had begun to play a cheating game with his loyalties.

'Are you sure?' he said.

Her reply was not prompt, her gaze straying to the open triangle of the canvas. She nodded. 'Yes, I'll ride beside you, if I may, Tribune, and you can slip a rope through my bridle.'

He smiled at that. 'To ruffle your feathers again?'

'No, sir,' she said, softly.

He felt her turn to look up at him again and heard, in the silence, what she had not spoken out loud, and his well-controlled desire for her tore at his innards. 'Then come,' he said, huskily. 'We'd better be away. We have some miles to cover.'

Chapter Seven

The town of Aquae Sulis sat snugly in a basin of land surrounded by wooded hills where a natural source of hot water had been bubbling up from the ground for longer than anyone's memory. Quintus's party might have made better headway if the road had not been packed with other travellers intent on the same destination through a countryside verdant with blossom, green hills and white sheep. So it was late when they arrived, tired and hungry. As usual, a messenger had been sent on ahead to reserve an apartment in one of the lodgings designated for visitors to the hot spring. Aquae Sulis thrived on the business of healing.

The town heaved with people flocking to the temple, the forum, the baths, the sellers of offerings, amulets and charms, yet Quintus's hope that Brighid's striking appearance would cause heads to turn proved to be too optimistic when everyone seemed much too preoccupied to notice who came and went. Nevertheless, she made by far the brightest splash of colour in the otherwise monochrome entourage and, if her appearance did not provoke quite the diversion Quintus had expected, his own eyes were diverted far too often, for Brighid's intention to be seen was for the same reason as his, and she had spared no effort to that end.

Swathed in ells of soft lichen-dyed linen of grey-blue and apricot, she had arranged the fabric to allow glimpses of her tribal adornments and to not quite conceal the thick braids of red hair piled cleverly on top of her head, held with dagger-like pins. With the horse's braids, bells and tassels to complement the picture, she looked every inch the Princess and, though the mare was tired, the dainty hooves pranced and danced amongst the crowds as if they'd come out only to greet her and her graceful rider.

The quip about the rope through her bridle, however, turned out to be more than mere words and, as Brighid was helped to dismount, the two armour-plated guards with Tullus, Lucan, Quintus and Flavian made a wall around her that left her in no doubt that she was still in every sense a captive. In view of her co-operation, she had hoped for some relaxation in the security, but apparently it was not to be, and the conspicuous guard outside the door of the room she was to share with her captor was obviously as much for her as for the chest placed at the end of the sleeping-couch. These precautions did little for her temper at being so confined, and she had decided to take no part in their conversation at dinner, to make clear her annoyance. But when the Tribune broached the topic of his business with the tax officials, she found it impossible to conceal her interest. This was the first time he had discussed it.

'We'll visit the tax office tomorrow,' he said to Lucan and Tullus, swinging his legs up on to the dining-couch.

Tullus cast an approving eye over the dining table laden with food from the local market stalls: hot pigeon pies, oysters and warm loaves, fishy sauces, cheese and sausages, olives, tuna with eggs, smoked ham, beans and stuffed vine leaves. 'Well, they'll know we're here by now,' he said. 'I only hope they haven't done a cover up before we get there.'

'It's not quite like that,' Quintus said, holding his hand out to Brighid to seat her beside him. 'The message I received is not that it's an inside job. They could have sorted that out for themselves. The problem is that some incoming taxes are appearing in the form of recently minted coinage, which suggests that someone is producing his own supply.'

'He'd have to get his hands on rather a lot of gold to do that, wouldn't he?' said Lucan, 'And have the men to do it? Are we talking about large sums?'

'Big enough to have been noticed over two years. I don't understand why they don't check it more thoroughly while the tax payer is there. Will you try some of this, Princess? Do you eat sausage?'

'There is nothing quite like hunger to broaden the palatte,' she said, taking hold of a hot sausage by its end as if it might bite her. She had by now accepted that Quintus expected her to dine with him, to be his woman in all outward appearances, if not in private. It served no useful purpose to protest that a captive slave would never do such a thing.

'Perhaps they're too short of staff to inspect it there and then. If the sacks are the correct weight, some well-known tax payers could be off and away before anything is noticed,' Lucan said.

'Nah!' said Tullus, dismissively. 'You've got it

wrong, my friend. They're supposed to count it out on the spot, but forgeries don't always show up until somebody takes a closer look. The mistake this forger is probably making is to send it in *always* looking too new. That's the biggest giveaway. Even money-changers' coins have that used look.'

'I thought,' Brighid said, 'that people were allowed to pay their taxes in kind instead of in money.'

Quintus explained, 'If they have consistent surpluses of something valuable, like corn, for instance, they may be allowed to pay in that currency at the discretion of the local tax office, who send it on to feed the army. But the Emperor prefers to pay his armies in gold, so if the tax payer has only base-metal coins, he must go to the money-changer to buy gold ones.'

'Which will no doubt cost him dear,' she said, pertly. 'Even I can see that. So if I were to mint my own gold coin, it would cost me less than having to buy it and then give it away again in taxes. No wonder my father refuses to pay.'

'And what would you use for gold, Princess? It doesn't grow on trees.'

'I would do what we do at home, Tribune, when we need gold. Our smiths render down the gold we take from those we conquer. They all have hoards of it. Or we barter with merchants. Or we know of rivers that yield it.'

'Mmm,' said Lucan. 'So what we're looking for is a man who employs his own smiths, who regularly conquers wealthy opponents, and who has a workshop where the noise of his forge doesn't disturb the neighbours. Or,' he added, reaching for another pie, 'he has his own private river or gold mine hidden away somewhere. Have I missed anything?'

'Leaving out the conquering bit,' said Tullus, 'where is the nearest gold mine in this delightful country?'

'Huh! Nowhere any of *us* would choose to go,' Quintus replied, waving an arm. 'The only gold mine that's still working is…' His eyes followed the direction of his hand, lighting up at the sudden realisation.

Three pairs of eyes fixed on the Tribune as his arm slowly lowered.

'Is?' prompted Tullus.

Brighid looked up at him over her shoulder. 'Is, as a matter of fact,' he said slowly, 'over there in the hill-country to the west. Cambria, it's called. A very wild crowd they are, too, and not easy to reach, but one of our fortresses happens to be where the miners bring up gold. Now isn't that interesting?' he said, softly.

'But if this mine is guarded by your men,' said Brighid, 'how likely is it, do you think, that they'd allow the gold to fall into the hands of anyone else? Surely the Roman army could keep it safe, couldn't they?'

'Certainly,' he said, 'but this is something we shall have to investigate. As I understand it, the mine is worked by local men, some slaves and convicts, and partly by concessionaires who are allowed to keep half of the gold they get out.'

'You mean the concessionaires have to go down…?'

'No, not personally. They provide a workforce.'

'Then they must be very unpopular,' Brighid said, biting into a rolled-up vine leaf. 'And wealthy. And unscrupulous. What *toads*!'

'And *they* probably speak with their mouths full of food, too,' said Quintus.

'Even worse,' she replied sharply. 'I'd like another sausage, please.'

'So we have to find out,' said Lucan, passing the dish of sausages, 'the names of these private concessionaires who own a stake in this mine. Would it include anyone from round here?'

'I don't see why not. As the crow flies, it's not

all that far, but the journey is not an easy one, although our men have built good roads there. Perhaps we ought to go and take a look.'

'Er…no, not me,' said Brighid. 'You might prefer to leave me here.'

'Yes, Princess. So I could,' said Quintus. 'And pigs might fly.'

'That would be a very serious omen.'

'Indeed it would. *Very* serious. More wine?'

An hour later, the three men sat with their wine in cushioned, creaking basket-chairs that sprouted loose tendrils, their conversation competing with the din wafting through an open window from the street. 'Close the window,' Tullus said to a slave, frowning.

The lad wrestled with the catch. 'It won't fasten, sir,' he said.

'I think,' said Quintus, waving the lad away, 'we may have to look for a better place than this. It won't do for more than a night or two.'

The roomy apartment was no more than adequate, well used by pilgrims and conveniently close to the baths for the infirm, but too close for peace. In Aquae Sulis, even-tide was as busy as noon-tide. The rooms had lost their freshness, cushions were frayed and grubby, walls were scuffed, furniture faded, the ornately decorated ceiling blackened by soot from the lamps. The stale odour of meat and spices leaked through every aperture. The two friends nodded in agreement. 'What has the lad been up to?' Quintus said. 'Anything to report?'

'Heard nothing, seen nothing,' said Lucan. 'If he is indeed the Princess's brother, they seem to be keeping well clear of each other. Is she…?' He glanced at the door.

'Guarded. She doesn't like it, but I never thought she would. Once we reached this place, the hunt for the suitor was bound to intensify, which is why one of us must attend her at all times. It's an extra burden we could well have done without, but…'

'You'd not consider letting her go, then?' said Tullus, quietly.

'No, not yet.'

Being experienced, his two friends did not ask him to explain, both of them having noticed how, in an unguarded moment, the eyes of their superior and his captive reflected deeper feelings than their bickering would suggest. 'Then I shall offer to escort the Princess tomorrow,' said Tullus, 'while you and my young friend here go about your business at the tax office. She'll wish to go to the temple, I dare say, and probably to the baths.

While she's in there, I might make enquiries about a more salubrious apartment for us.'

'Yes, thank you. I'll give you some money for her to spend. That should keep her occupied until we return.'

'And will you be making enquiries about your friend Alexius while you're there?' said Tullus. 'Surely someone must have some information about his disappearance? How long is it now?'

Quintus got to his feet, giving Tullus the impression that it was a matter too private to discuss. But he went to the window, speaking with his back to them. 'A year,' he said. 'He was sent down here to investigate the same kind of forgery problem, but I don't know whether the two are related. The last anyone saw of him was at the baths. All his belongings gone. And his two slaves. No one's heard of him since. He was my best friend, a superb soldier and horseman, but he ought not to have been allowed to investigate this kind of thing without the proper training. And he ought not to have tackled it alone, either. I'm going to find out where he's got to. He cannot simply have disappeared without trace.'

'No,' said Lucan. 'One of your countrymen, was he?'

'From Cadiz. We shared the same tutor. We were like brothers.'

'Then we'll find him,' said Tullus.

'I was not going to ask you to become involved,' Quintus said, turning back into the room. 'It might become dangerous.'

'All the more reason to divide it by three,' Lucan replied.

'You'll need us,' Tullus agreed. 'You have your hands full already.'

Tullus had not meant it literally, although it was a fair description of how Quintus spent the second half of the night, the first part being spent on the longer of the two couches while Brighid was already asleep on the smaller harder one when he entered. He awoke in the middle of the night, aware that all was not as it should be, to find her standing by the window where the moon, large and bright, filled the room with its soft beam, lighting her upturned face. He thought she might be praying, but after a moment or two he swung his feet to the floor and, making no attempt at stealth, folded her into his arms. 'What is it, Princess?' he said. 'Can't sleep?'

She hooked her fingers over his bare arms. 'Something's wrong,' she whispered.

'Where? Out there? Show me.'

'No, not out there,' she said with a trace of irritation. It was clear he'd misunderstood. 'It has happened before. A feeling…a terrible…' she shook her head as if searching for the word '…a terrible omen of danger…something bad…very bad…black…threatening.'

'It has happened before? When? When you were captured?'

'No, it's not like the second sight. Nothing as clear as that. It was when my father took my maid. I felt her heart break and I knew she would die from it. And now it's here again, telling me…'

'Telling you what? Something here, in this house?'

'I don't know. I really don't know. I can't see *what*, only that it lies ahead. Perhaps it *is* this place. Yet I think danger is one step ahead of us, waiting, no matter how we try to evade it. I don't think we *can* evade it.'

'Princess,' he said, turning her round to face him, 'listen. You are well guarded from danger. I am an experienced soldier and Tullus and Lucan are strong and intelligent enough to be aware of hazards in a place like this. You are not used to towns. Tomorrow, we shall move to a better place, somewhere quiet and more comfortable. And you will not go out alone. I shall not let any harm befall you. Now come into my bed and sleep with me.'

'I cannot sleep. And I should not be…'

'Forget that. I want you close to me, so we shall ignore convention.'

'I thought you…'

'Don't. Not until you know me better.'

That was not likely to happen, she thought as they lay closely entwined, unless she were to ask him about himself before they must part for ever. Surely it would not be long before Math brought her some positive news to add to his latest unhelpful offering. So she coaxed Quintus to tell her about his youth in Cadiz, his ambition to become a cavalry officer in the Roman army, his successful career and quick rise to become a tribune. The Emperor Severus had kept him by his side in more recent years, sending him and his friend Alexius here to the island of Britain ahead of his own arrival. The governor at Eboracum, Gordianus, was a fool, Quintus mumbled into her hair. She did not ask him for details of his wound, for she knew that some men were not so proud of being disabled, even temporarily, and he was the type who would pretend it was better long before it was. She had dressed it before dinner and had been quietly satisfied by the rapid healing, but would not agree to leave it unprotected, as he had wanted.

She was asleep before Quintus had finished his rambling *curriculum vitae*, so she did not know that he kept sleep at bay on purpose to intercept the first sign of danger, the omens of which had woken her too soon. It was not by any means the first time he'd lost a night's sleep, but it was the first time he'd watched over a woman whose fears were so convincing. Not for a moment did he doubt the truth of what she felt.

Like all night fears that take on a more rational guise in the light of day, Brighid's deep inexplicable concerns had now been shared and, if not exactly halved, at least alleviated by the Tribune's assurance that he would not allow any harm to befall her, which seemed to rule out the slave-merchant threat for the time being. Yet strangely enough, it was not any harm to herself that menaced her, but to him. There was no more to it than that. As before, the fear seemed to concern someone close to her and, like it or not, no one was closer to her than the Tribune. Was it to do with the business he had to investigate? Taxes were a sensitive issue. Provincial Procurators had powers, and had never been the tax-payers' favourites.

'Go and make some enquiries,' she whispered to Math as he dropped a handful of leaves into a pan of boiling water. She had been escorted to the kitchen by one of the guards while Florian massaged his master's back, making any useful conversation impossible.

Above the bubbling, the clattering, the raking of red-hot charcoal, Math managed to mumble a reply of sorts that to Brighid was frustrating in the extreme. 'I can't. Not yet, Bridie.'

'Why not?'

'Florian and I have to attend you and Tullus while the Tribune's at—' He stopped as the guard moved closer to look.

'Give it a count of thirty, then strain it. Do you think you can manage *that*?' she snapped in Latin, missing the look of astonishment that passed between her brother and the guard.

She intended to visit the temple that morning and perhaps to talk to people and to find out the location of the place known as Watercombe where Helm might be found. The escort of Tullus, Florian and Math would not make things any easier. Busy market places, temple precincts and hoards of people going in all directions were, however, still new to her, and even Math did not behave in the way one would have expected of an Eboracum man where that city was several times the size of this. So when Tullus tipped his head at Florian, his sign-language was read as, 'Keep your eye on him.'

Accordingly, Flavian took hold of his friend's tunic sleeve, moving him forwards. 'You're supposed to be watching out for the *domina*'s comfort,' he said, 'not standing gawping at the buildings. Keep up, man.'

The buildings were impressive, even to a town-dweller, the pale stone carved into elegant pillars, steps and sculptures. There were white-plastered walls, open arcades and the massive barrel roofs of the bath complex, red-tiled and shining in the sun. Everywhere there were colonnades with wide open spaces beyond which people clustered around open shrines, watching unwilling goats being dragged towards red-robed priests. Visitors strolled, gossiped and squatted, many of them infirm, carried in litters and in arms, on crutches, or wrapped closely against inquisitive stares. Yet there was no hubbub, only the sound of double-pipes, the cry of a fretful child, the high intonation of a priest's voice from the open door of the temple, and the hushed exchange of visitors.

Brighid's visit to the temple precinct that morning was all the more significant when she discovered the connection between Sulis, the local goddess of the healing spring, Minerva, her Roman counterpart, and Brigantia, yet another manifestation of both goddesses. To find that her own deity was here, albeit under an assumed name, was an indication, surely, that this visit had been planned by Brigantia herself. She would be there at the sacred well, waiting for Brighid's personal communication. Waiting to make things happen.

'Up there, see?' said Tullus, pointing to the triangular pediment high above the temple columns. 'The Gorgon's Head. Symbol of the goddess Minerva.' Surrounded by garlands, winged victories and sea-monsters, the huge stone carving looked down upon the crowds. 'Do you wish to visit the sacred spring, Princess?' he said.

'Yes,' said Brighid. 'But please allow me to go in alone. I cannot abscond, Tullus. Look, if you stand here, you'll be able to see me.' The entrance through the portico was, in fact, wreathed in steam from the hot spring, for it was from this source that the water bubbled up from the ground and was piped to other rooms.

'Shall I go in with the *domina*?' Math volunteered.

'No, you stay here, lad.'

Brighid did not argue. She did not want Math to be with her either.

Half-expecting a small gushing well similar to the ice-cold springs at home, she was amazed by the way this hot spring had been tamed by previous centuries of Romans to surge upwards into a pool completely enclosed by a high-barrelled vault of stone glistening with green slime. Ferns sprouted like tufts of hair from every join, lit by daylight that streamed through an arched opening where steam rolled against the cooler air. The surface of the pool, an irregular oval, steamed and swirled like molten green glass across which Brighid could just make out the outline of two stone water-nymphs and, in the wall behind them, three openings through which people leaned to look down into the waters. The glint of metal flew through the air, followed by a greedy plop as the water swallowed the offerings.

On her own side, three stone columns stood on the water's edge with lintels across the top and two more nymphs between, their green feet lapped by the water, their frozen gestures imitating the live arms in the openings on the opposite wall. Beside her stood a family gazing down into the depths where, when the steam parted, small objects could just be seen scattered across the bottom, shining gold, copper and pewter, nothing identifiable. One woman stood at the other side of her in silent contemplation, though her expensively clothed shoulders shook with sorrow. As one hand reached up to pull her pale green linen further over her head, Brighid saw a wrist adorned with gold and gemstones, hands long and smooth, lashes wet with tears. Outwardly, she appeared to have everything to be thankful for, yet her distress was unmistakable.

Without thinking how it might be interpreted, Brighid reached out to place a gentle hand on the woman's arm, closing her fingers tenderly over the fine green stuff to feel the firm arm beneath, although she was not prepared for the slight flinch, as if she had touched an injury.

'I'm so sorry,' Brighid whispered. 'I didn't mean to…'

The woman turned, stiffly, with an attempt at a smile through lips swollen with weeping. 'It's all right,' she said. 'It's nothing.'

In those conditions, it was difficult for Brighid to get more than an impression of the woman's demeanour, although her bearing was that of a woman older by some ten years than Brighid herself and whose eyes, even reddened by tears, were large and dark. Natural compassion prompted Brighid to find out more, to offer sympathy, but presumably the lady had come here to solve her problems by other means, and it was not the place of a stranger to interfere with that. Even if there had been time.

Reminded of her own reasons for the visit, Brighid chose not to impose further upon the woman's misery. Sliding a gold band down her arm and over her knuckles, she tossed it into the middle of the pool. *Help me, beloved goddess, to find safety and happiness before I grow too old to enjoy life. Protect me and those I love.* There had been no time to have the bracelet inscribed with a message, but Brigantia would know which offering was hers. She stood for a while before turning to go, only then realising that the lady had disappeared.

Outside, the dark silhouette of burly Tullus was bending over a crumpled heap on the ground when Brighid joined him and immediately recognised the pale green gown of the lady whose arm she had touched. 'She's fainted,' said Tullus, squatting beside her. 'I suppose it happens all the time. Can you do anything for her, Princess?'

'Carry her over here,' Brighid said. 'Lay her on the steps. Now, let me loosen her scarf. She needs some air. Florian, go and find some cold water... over there under the colonnade. Max, don't stand and stare. Go outside the courtyard and see if the lady's litter is waiting. I don't *know* what name, lad. Go and ask.'

'She looks very off colour,' said Tullus, diplomatically understating, as usual.

'She was standing next to me in there,' said Brighid. 'Poor lady.'

The dark eyes flickered open, blinking away tears of shame. 'Sorry,' she whispered. 'I don't know what came over me. The heat...?'

'Hush, lady,' said Tullus. 'It's the change of temperature. You won't be the only one today. Take a sip of this water, if you will.'

She sipped, gratefully, while they studied her face, no longer covered by the green linen or in shadow. It was a sad, lovely, gracious countenance with shades of unhappiness below her eyes, her pale skin beginning to show lines around the full mouth. Clearly she was still a very lovely woman, the thick dark brown hair delicately silvered.

Math came trotting back to them. 'Yes,' he called, 'there's the lady's litter waiting just outside the gateway. *Domina* Helena Coronis is the name.'

'Did it occur to you not to shout it across the precinct?' said Tullus, glaring at him. 'Could you tell me, *quietly*, where the lady lives?'

'Watercombe, sir,' said Math, trying not to catch his sister's eye. 'Perhaps it would be best if I were to follow on behind, just to make sure she gets there safely.'

'There's no need,' said the lady. 'It's not far. Only a mile or so. I'm quite recovered, I thank you. Really, yes, I'm perfectly well now.'

Brighid stared at Math, then at the pale green lady who had suddenly become all important to her. She could not let her go without making some more permanent contact. This was exactly what she'd been waiting for. A woman from this place called Watercombe who was bound to know Helm. Her prayers answered so soon.

But Tullus, a stickler for the courtesies, took the lady at her word and, as deaf to Brighid's attempts as to her brother's offers, simply picked her up in his arms and, with a command to the other three not to move a foot, carried her out to the waiting litter, returning with an air of one whose good turn for the day was complete. It took all Brighid's control, during Tullus's very brief absence, not to round on her brother with a torrent of questions in their own tongue that would elicit some real information for a change. To make and then lose such a contact was almost unbearable, but with Flavian standing by, there was nothing to be done except to fume in impotent silence and to hope for another chance, perhaps tomorrow.

Her thoughts remained in utter confusion throughout the day, not the best of conditions in which to explore the convoluted bath complex and the facilities of which she could not take advantage during her courses. Fate seemed determined to thwart her. Having worked up an appetite, they sat on a stone bench in one of the squares and snacked on roast chestnuts, chicken wings and warm cheese-bread bought from one of the many vendors, and Brighid did her best to be amicable, knowing that Tullus would rather have been elsewhere.

As it happened, Tullus had more than a passing interest in the extremely complicated system of water-pools and channels that diverted the water beneath the floors. Rome, he thought, must have employed some very fine water-engineers to have built such a place as this over what had once been a muddy hole in the ground.

Brighid had been more interested to see how

many sellers lined the precincts, peddling everything a visitor could need in the form of jewellery, charms and amulets for offering to the sacred spring, coins and tablets of lead inscribed on the spot with an appropriate message, curses written backwards. There were shallow pewter and silver dishes for libations at the altars, small bronze figurines of gods and goddesses, gemstones of every hue. Most fascinating was the man who sold a range of metal votive offerings designed to the buyer's own specifications, tiny legs and feet, an ear or a finger, a breast, a head in silver or pewter according to one's injury and pocket. The perfume-seller's stall was like a hive of bees, buzzing with excitement, reeking of scent and twinkling with coloured glass, and Brighid would have spent some more of the Tribune's money if her thoughts had not been elsewhere.

They came to the market where, for a short time, she tried to forget the appendage of three hovering males amongst the colourful fabrics, leathers and wools. She bought several more robe-lengths of fine linen with embroidered borders, skeins of threads for sewing, nets for her hair, two more pairs of leather sandals, a length of wool for a cloak and a leather bag large enough to take her belongings. She would be prepared, when the time came for her to go, and she would be dressed to impress.

Tullus had not achieved anything like her success, having intended while she was in the baths to enquire about a change of apartment, not thinking that she would be giving that pleasure a miss. It looked as if they would have to suffer another noisy night. But Brighid's mind was still overwhelmed by what she had seen and by the names Helena Coronis and Watercombe. If only she had been able to talk with the lady in private.

Back in their rooms, to which Quintus had not yet returned, her immediate need was for the newly acquired luxuries of soap, hot water and clean linen clothing next to her skin. Instructing the guards to allow no one to enter, she washed herself from top to toe and was pleased to discover that her courses had all but ceased. If escape really was as imminent as she hoped, then her personal timetable was in her favour.

Dried, and still glowing from her ablutions, she took her lengths of linen to the window, flinging them over herself to judge the effect of the new bright colours against her skin, gathering them to see how they draped and finding that one piece had a pulled thread, which must be eased back into place. Her head was bent upon the niggling task when the door opened. 'No!' she cried. 'I told you…!' Too late.

'Yes,' said Quintus, 'so I heard. May I come in, Princess?' He was already closing the door behind him, taking in the scene of her naked back with a long trail of linen held in her arms. The light fell upon her tumbled hair as it had done at their first encounter, and this was how he would like to have seen her then, angry still, but naked. The graceful swell of her hips, her long smooth thighs, the soft peach of her skin against the gold ornaments and swathes of coloured linen lent her the image of a pagan goddess, wild and fiery, indignant at being interrupted, but fearful for the vulnerability of her position.

'No,' she said, hitching the bundle further up. 'Can you not wait, sir?'

His face reflected his thoughts like a mirror as he strolled towards her. His day had been long and irritating, and this was not the greeting he would have liked, though he might have expected it. 'I think I've been remarkably patient to wait as long as this, woman. Don't you? By now, most slave owners would have found out more about what they'd bought.'

'You did *not* buy me. No…keep away! You may not…'

'All right, you were a gift, but no less mine. What have you been doing all day? What did you purchase? Is this some of it?' He took the bundle from her and held it up, removing the shield she'd tried to hide behind. 'Mmm, a good choice of colour.'

Teasingly, he left her no way to evade him, and now there was only the cool outdoor scent of him between them and the slightest touch of his white linen toga upon her breasts.

'You may not see me like this, Tribune,' she scolded, placing her hands over herself, feeling the responses of her body betray the words as soon as they were said. He had already seen her like this, but that did not give him permission to do so again.

But he took her wrists and eased them away, upwards, until they were pressed against the wall above her head and held there as his lips found hers, drinking deeply like a man parched with thirst. Their breath mingled sweetly as an ache of emptiness filled her lungs. In her excitement at the longed-for fruition of her plans, she had tried to push her newest physical experiences to the back of her mind as a distraction she could not afford. Yet her body would not co-operate, flaring like dry tinder under his first touch, trembling for more, all thoughts of escaping converting instantly to shameless surrender. And when his free hand slid over her hip and thigh and on like a shadow to the space between her legs, she waited too long to savour the breathtaking flare of excitement before gasping a protest against his kisses.

'No…oh, no, my lord…not….not there! No, *please*!'

'Your courses have finished,' he whispered, keeping his hand in place.

'I have not bathed. Tomorrow, perhaps. Give me more time.'

'I'm not sure that I have more time to give, woman,' he said, taking his hand away and releasing her with a groan. 'Is that water still warm?'

'Yes, my lord,' she said, angered by her own weakness.

'Then wash me down before we dine. If I have no time to go and bathe, and I may not take my pleasure another way, then at least I can be ministered to. And if you intend to visit the baths tomorrow, then do it early. You'll be coming with me to see a water engineer. Tullus will be interested and I'm not leaving you behind.' He unwound himself as he talked, pulling his tunic over his head with a ripple of muscle and sinew, revealing himself to her with a casual indifference that seemed to imply how little he cared whether she was aroused or not, only that he had been prevented from enjoying himself.

Brighid hurriedly donned her shift and set about washing him, fully aware that he could have done the job more efficiently himself and that this was just another way of making use of her while putting an end to her innocent diversion with her purchases. Not only that, but she felt he had it in mind to embarrass her with those parts of his body that had not yet recovered from their moment of lovemaking. Although the phenomenon was no surprise, she was more insulted than embarrassed, for he could not have forgotten that she was still a maid and that, until she had had the experience, the apparatus he was so proudly displaying was more like a threat than a delight.

The longer she performed her task with very little contribution from him, the more angry she became at his sudden ungentlemanly change from caring bedmate to peeved slave owner. Politely inviting him to bend so that she could reach his neck, she felt behind her for the bucket of cold water left by the boy and, swinging it up above him, emptied the lot over his head and shoulders. 'There, my lord,' she growled, 'that should cool things down a bit, I think.'

His leap into the air would have done credit to an Olympic athlete as, with a bellow of shock, he turned his dripping body to face her in disbelief. 'You...you little...*barbarian*!' he gasped. 'What was that for?'

Like lightning, she had dropped the bucket and retreated, half-soaked, to the far side of the room, facing him like a tigress. 'It was for *you*, you great surly brute!' she yelled. 'You've been asking for that for days. And if you have the gall to ask me to tend your blasted wound, you'd better beware, for I intend to cauterise it with a hot iron.'

'Pass me a towel, you bad-tempered little minx.'

He could not have known how accurately a Brigantian Princess, when angered, could throw. The bundled towel landed on his ear with a hard thwack, even before the words were out. *'Please!'* she reminded him.

'Mop this lot up, or it'll leak through the ceiling,' he commanded.

'Mop it up yourself. It's your bath, not mine.'

He stared at her. 'Little *vixen*! Do as I say.'

'Go to Hades!'

Padding wetly to the door, he yanked it open,

roaring like a wounded bull for the two boys to come up immediately. They almost tumbled into the room, goggle-eyed at the spreading pool of water in which their master stood, the *domina* in her wet shift, the scattering of empty bowls. They were fourteen-year-old lads, not unintelligent and not without a normal sense of the ridiculous and, as they began the task of mopping up, their almost hysterical giggles grew out of control until tears began to fall down their rosy cheeks, accompanied by little moans. Such a thing had never happened to their master before. Yet as they mopped and squelched, snuffling and squeaking, their glances at the Tribune's usually severe expression revealed that, every now and then as he rubbed his head with a towel, his shoulders heaved as the towel muffled a roar. Several times.

The *domina* was folding up her pile of dress lengths and packing them into a large leather bag, punching them angrily, her damp shift clinging seductively to her knees. Quintus closed the door behind the two boys. 'What's that for?' he asked, still laughing.

Brighid did not look up. 'For the market. I'm sending them back. I'll get your money refunded. I can do without anything of yours, even your miserable gifts. I can get finer from my own people, and I can get more respect as a bath attendant, thank you.'

'Don't go, barbarian,' he said, teasingly. 'Who would put me in my place? Who would tend my wounds? Warm my bed? Grace my dining couch and ride—?'

'Wash your feet and suffer your—'

'Hush, lass. It's over. Let it go,' he said, scooping her up before she could dodge away. 'I did not mean it to—'

'Yes, you did! You know you did. I am a Princess, Roman, and I will not be treated like a whore for your pleasure after a day's work. Find yourself a girl at the brothel down the street.'

'Not while I have you,' he whispered, rocking her in his arms. 'I ought not to have tormented you. Now calm down, fierce woman, and wear one of your new purchases. I want to show you off tomorrow when we make our visit. Come now, lass. Forget your anger, will you?'

'I don't want to go visiting. I'm not interested in water engineering.'

'He has a big garden with fountains, and his wife runs a healing centre. I thought you'd like to see that.'

'I've travelled enough.' *A healing centre?*

'It's not far, only a mile or so. A place they call Watercombe because of all the springs there.'

She held her breath. There it was again. Watercombe, where she might at last find the man who could rescue her. They knew of him there. It was a miracle. And the woman Helena Coronis would be there too. *Thank you, Brigantia.* 'I'll come,' she whispered, 'because I do not want to stay in this place alone.'

Gently, he kissed her forehead. 'Good. Now put something decent on and let's go down to dinner. I'm starving and I can smell something good.'

But why, she thought, if the lady from Watercombe runs a healing centre, did she need to seek help from the sacred spring of Sulis-Minerva?

Chapter Eight

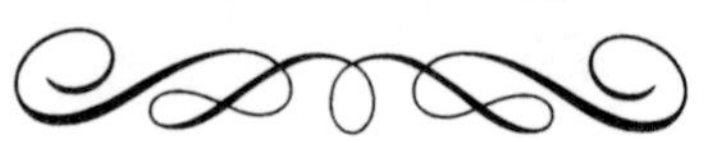

After heavy rain during the night, the countryside was awash with tumbling streams, bright sparkling greenery and blinding sun bouncing off limewashed walls. This was Aprilus in its very best garb, dressed to celebrate their short journey to Watercombe, a villa built on a wooded hillside over natural springs.

The dark sense of dread had visited Brighid again that night, completely at odds with her exhilaration at finding Watercombe so easily with no effort on her part. She had actually managed to feign reluctance, though she had taken great care with her dress and hair, which she knew the Tribune would believe was for him instead of for a certain one of Watercombe's many guests. If Helm was not there, she would have to make an excuse for another visit.

She had gone to the baths early that morning,

taking advantage of all the facilities on offer, a full massage, a hair wash, scented oils and skin toners, pedicure and manicure and another visit to the shrine to see if there was a sign of the Lady Helena. She had even asked if anyone knew of her but, until she mentioned the name to the man who sold the limb-shaped offerings, no one could help. He, however, had looked up and smiled. 'These are made at Watercombe,' he told her, 'at the Lady Helena's healing centre. I make them myself.' There had been no more time to explain, for Tullus approached at that moment and she had no wish for him to know of her particular interest in the place.

Now, approaching Watercombe from the valley below, the size of the villa was revealed as being much greater than any of them supposed, a sprawling complex of white-walled buildings nestling into the hillside, its red-tiled rooftops shining pink in the sun, its gardens terraced into the slope where white-robed guests strolled and sat beside shimmering pools of blue water. On the approach, other visitors rode or toiled on foot up the hill, splashing through limey puddles and labouring under the weight of disease and old age. The Tribune's party, on the other hand, had no such problem for yesterday Quintus had only to mention his reasons for visiting Aquae Sulis in the same breath as their less-than-comfortable lodgings to be told by the men at the tax office that he could easily solve both issues at Watercombe. Why not go and pay a visit? When they had mentioned that the owner was also the brilliant hydraulics engineer who serviced the water systems at the baths in town, as well as designing others in the area, Quintus knew that Tullus would certainly wish to see the villa as soon as possible. If the Princess had not taken so long making herself ready, Tullus would have set off an hour earlier, having also heard that the villa was a show place for garden-lovers as well as a cult centre for pilgrims.

The track led them round to one side of the villa past a series of bath-houses attached to a two-storey block set across the end of the atrium. Here they were welcomed. Either, Brighid thought, the steward welcomed everyone with the same warmth or, more likely, that their arrival had been seen from a distance. They were, after all, a well-presented bunch with four slaves in attendance, if one counted Math as one, the horses alone advertising a certain affluence. The steward's quick eyes took them in at one glance, his deferential bow just the right depth to avoid servility.

'Welcome, my lords,' he said, having noted Quintus's purple bands. 'Welcome to Watercombe. And to my lady also. Is this your first visit?' His eyes shifted back uncertainly to Quintus as if he was not quite sure of the lady's status.

'Quintus Tiberius Martial,' said he. 'Tribune. Yes, this is our first visit to Watercombe.' *As if you didn't already know that*, he thought.

'My lord,' said the steward again, adding an extra head bow for good measure, 'we are honoured.' Without looking, he snapped his fingers into the air to summon a slave. 'Ask the Lady Helena if she will be pleased to come to the atrium. We have some distinguished guests she will wish to greet personally. Hurry, lad!' He turned back to Quintus. 'If you would come this way sir, we can speak in more comfort. Your horses will be taken to the stables. You need have no fears for their welfare. A handsome mare you have, my lady.'

'She is indeed,' said Brighid, enjoying the special treatment alloted to knights and their ladies. It had been the same at home, although here the grandeur was of a different order, shining with tiles and limewash, mosaic floors and coloured walls, grass in tidy squares with trees like enlarged pine cones. In the atrium was a square pond with a central fountain, more powerful by far than the others she had seen, disappearing into the blue sky with a flash of sparkling light. Her father would have been amazed.

Satisfied that the Tribune's lady understood the language, the steward probed a little further. 'You have come to seek the healing, or is this a social call? If it's the former, I can send for our chief physician to attend you immediately.'

The Lady Helena could not have been far away, her appearance making it unnecessary for Quintus to commit himself to anything more specific before he'd taken a look at what was on offer. The price would be academic, for nothing here would be cheap—even those pedestrian pilgrims would have saved up for years to get here. Their hostess's face gave no sign of the previous day's malaise, nor did she betray the slightest indication that she had already met four of the group in the temple. Apparently then, it looked as if she did not want the steward to know of her visit. As introductions were made, none of them gave her away by asking if she was recovered, for they could tell by her appearance that whatever had upset her had passed, her eyes clear and brown but with persistent dark shadows. Her smile was almost radiant, showing white even teeth rare in women of her years. 'My lords,' she said, 'you are very welcome. Have you come far?'

Slaves bearing trays had followed her into the atrium with silver flagons and delicate beakers of glass in pierced pewter holders. Wine and water were mixed and handed round, biscuits and dates to be nibbled, bowls of water placed with a pile of napkins for sticky fingers. Healing, apparently, began with food hygiene. They sat in basket-chairs to talk while Florian, Math and the two young lads stood aside, awaiting instructions, and Brighid noticed how the lady's eyes avoided hers for most of the time while she spoke almost exclusively to the men. Avoided, that is, until Quintus told her that the Princess was his personal healer, at which her sudden recognition made Brighid want to laugh as the mental mistake was remedied in a gush of polite astonishment. It had been dark in the shrine and she had been weeping.

'A healer. Really?' said Helena Coronis, taking a longer and keener look at her beautifully groomed guest. 'You are not from these parts then, Princess?' Something in the way she spoke, the guarded look in her eyes and a certain stiffness—which might, of course, have been no more than a rheum in her neck joints—made Brighid wary of how much she herself gave away at this stage, remembering her unaccountable fears.

'I am from the north, my lady, yet I discovered yesterday that my own deity is represented at the shrine of Sulis-Minerva, so I am well protected, you see.'

What exactly Helena Coronis made of that was anyone's guess, but she smiled graciously as if she was impressed by Brighid's tact. 'We must compare notes,' she said, shifting her attention to Quintus. 'Are you here to solve a specific problem, my lord, or for insurance against one?'

Silently, he shared the joke with Brighid before he replied. 'I have an old wound,' he said, 'which is now responding to treatment, but—'

'But which would benefit from some water therapy,' Brighid interrupted, severely, knowing how he would dismiss it as nothing, given the chance. She did not want him to dismiss it. Having got this far, she could use the Tribune's wound as a reason to stay, giving her time to plan while providing them all with a change of lodgings. Two birds with one stone. 'I was saying to you only this morning how much daily swimming would help, my lord.'

Quintus swivelled his eyes towards her before his face caught up, and the slight pause before he agreed told her that he had understood her message. She wished to stay here. 'Yes, I know. I had intended to swim daily in the public baths, but we are not satisfied with our apartment so close to the centre of things.'

'You need peaceful surroundings, Tribune,' said the Lady Helena. 'I know what these apartments are like. Well used and basic, and not the best environment for a healing process. Why not take a look round Watercombe? We have rooms still available this early in the season, and you need not commit yourself until you've seen what facilities we supply. Everyone is welcome, even if it's only for the rest.' Her glance fell for a moment upon Tullus, and Brighid had no doubt at all that she was remembering how his strong arms had carried her like a child to her litter only a day ago. Almost at once her glance slid away to Brighid, her arm gracefully waving towards the green-painted wall behind them where a series of alcoves housed figurines of gods and goddesses with lamps burning before each. 'You see, our own *lares* over there represent most deities. We try to cater for everyone's needs here, whatever they are. Diets *and* deities.'

'How long have you lived here?' said Tullus.

Brighid thought the lady blushed a little before

she replied, non-committally. 'Oh, for some years. I started it with my first husband, but it's my present husband who made it what it is now. He's a water engineer, you know. He's built Watercombe up from very humble beginnings. Now, shall we take a stroll round? I'll show you the healing rooms first, since they're nearest. Just through here.'

Brighid had already begun to reap the benefits of her transformation from tribal princess to supposed Roman citizen, but now she saw yet another side to her newest status as the Tribune's personal healer. Following one pace behind, it was impressed upon her yet again that if she had not been so determined to find her erstwhile suitor, she could easily get used to being the woman of Quintus Tiberius Martial. Last night she had lain in his arms again, perhaps for the last time, and although he had not ventured further than before, after her prickly reaction earlier, his kisses might easily have persuaded her to find out exactly what it was she'd been holding on to for the sake of a man she hardly knew. After guarding herself so closely, she could only hope that Helm would appreciate the danger she'd been in. More than that, she hoped he'd be worth the wait.

Keeping one eye on the tall soldierly figure of

the Tribune, she wondered if her recent night fears were a warning that, when they parted, her life would revert to a system even more constrained than the one she'd left behind. Was she doing the right thing? Was there a better alternative? Would the Tribune keep her for as long as it suited him before finding a woman of his own class? A woman of good family, with connections, wealth and culture? Was she beginning to love him already? Was it her imagination, or had he suddenly begun to walk with a slight limp again?

She was saved from dwelling on these matters by the appearance of the Lady Helena's young daughter, a sweet-faced child of four summers with her mother's dark good looks, who took an instant fancy to Brighid and the exotic appeal of her gold ornaments and elaborately braided hair; young Carina felt that to hold the Princess's hand might endow her with the same sense of theatre conveyed by her mother's guest. A little later, Carina was delighted to tell her, away from the others, that the stunning mosaic floors were specially made in local workshops, but that Mama thought the dancing ladies ought to be wearing clothes.

In the healing room and the temple, their brief visit was conducted in whispers, patients occupying the small cubicles for private consultation with white-robed ladies and an ancient white-haired man. A crowd waited patiently outside. None of the Tribune's party had known what to expect from a privately run concern like Watercombe, but none of them could fail to be impressed by the businesslike approach to people's suffering where every kind of problem was dealt with by dream interpretation, water therapy, medicine and meditation, divination, physiotherapy and sound advice. They must, Brighid remarked, employ many specialists. 'Yes, we also have a priest here,' Helena Coronis told her, pointing out the shrine-building, 'and an expert in dreams. It's an important part of our treatment that most of our guests undergo to discover the cause of their problem. Over there are the sleeping cubicles where they stay for a night under supervised conditions. In the bath-houses we have a massage room, aromatherapy and the facial and physical rooms, the exercise hall, the surgery and birthing-room—'

'And the perfumery, Mama. That's the room I like best,' said Carina, bending down to study her reflection in a pool of green water.

They walked along gravel paths and up white stone steps to higher levels where more pools shimmered with orange-gold fish darting and diving beneath water lilies. Every fountain was of a different design, waterfalls gushed out of fern-covered retaining walls, and it was Carina who happily pointed out the various springs that fed the pools and cascaded down past the house through channels into the bath complex. 'Papa did it,' she said, proudly. 'He's clever. He knows all about water.'

Lucan pointed to red-tiled rooftops appearing through the trees. 'I can hear hammering,' he said. 'What's over there? New buildings going up?'

'The workshops,' said Lady Helena, 'for maintenance, you know. There's a water-powered mill for grinding our flour, too, granary and storerooms, a large garden where we grow our own produce, a kiln and drying ovens for the grain. My husband has done wonders in the last few years.' Absently, one hand came to rest softly over her forearm, the arm that Brighid had touched the day before; it seemed to Brighid that, as the lady quickly averted her face, the praise of her husband's efforts was like an incantation she had learnt to recite when asked, her tone rather lacking the conviction of a genuinely proud and appreciative wife.

In view of the distress of the previous day, Brighid thought the lady was putting on a good show of contentment with her beautiful home and thriving business. That it brought in substantial wealth could not be doubted when everything pointed to the family's affluence. Lady Helena's blue sheer-silk *stola* was embroidered with gold threads around its hem, with more gold and lapis lazuli hanging from her ears. She was certainly blessed with wealth and material comforts of every sort and, if she was ill, then surely she was in no better place to find relief.

The large two-storey block they had passed on the way in turned out to be the guest apartments leading to the bath-house and exercise hall, but the difference between these beautifully appointed rooms and the ones in which they'd spent the last two nights was enough to persuade Quintus that the extra expense would be justified. The rest of his retinue, he said, could stay where they were in Aquae Sulis. He had already caught Brighid's admiration of the garden scenes on the walls, the green-and-white décor, the tasteful furnishings. There was a carved wooden couch with a white tasselled blanket and huge green cushions, a tigerskin on the floor, a bronze candelabrum and a stove on tall legs to warm chilly nights. On the low table was a silver jug, silver beakers and a bowl filled with early roses. In an alcove stood a bronze figurine of the goddess Venus with buttocks shining like an apple—placed there, Brighid guessed, to aid couples who were having problems conceiving.

Leaving Tullus and Lucan to visit the exercise hall, Helena Coronis took them back to the atrium to arrange for their things to be brought from town. The appearance of two young ladies walking arm in arm attracted Brighid's attention, and she thought they might have stopped to talk had not Helena Coronis been with guests. From across the pool they waved to each other with a smile. 'My elder daughter,' she said, 'and one of our long-stay guests.'

'Your daughter?' Brighid said, watching young Carina skip over to them and take their hands. 'I thought…'

'By my first marriage. Clodia is seventeen now. The other young woman is Dora, short for Theodora, staying here until her babe is born. Lovely girl. Her husband is a friend of ours.'

'And your two daughters get on well together, I see.'

'Thank the gods, they do. They're the loves of my life.' It was a bold statement that she did not try to amend to include her husband, as though it mattered little what construction was placed upon it.

'You are fortunate,' Brighid replied, as Quintus strolled away to meet Florian.

'I suppose I am…' the lady sighed '…compared to some unhappy wretches who come here. But I wanted to thank you for…well…'

Brighid shook her head. 'We are both healers,' she said. 'Perhaps we can talk some time?'

'That's why I'd like you to stay here a while, if your master will allow it. Your…er…the Tribune needs medication still, does he?'

'Remedial exercise mostly. Florian over there is his masseur, but the Tribune needs rest, too. Watercombe will be better for him than the public baths.' Looking at the subject of their conversation, neither of the women thought there was much wrong with him that some strenuous exercise could not remedy. But Quintus stood in conversation with Florian and Math where it looked as if there might be trouble brewing, Quintus standing with hands on hips, looking down his nose at the two lads before him. Florian was almost in tears.

At once it occurred to Brighid that Quintus was sending her brother away, as he had said he would when they reached Aquae Sulis. She ought not to interfere, yet she needed Math's help now more than ever. She went to stand beside him. 'Please, my lord,' Florian was pleading, his eyes brimming with tears. 'Not even for a few more days? He's been such a help to me. *Please?*'

Quintus half-turned to Brighid, almost expecting her to intercede. 'He has been a great help,' she said, trying to sound impartial, 'and Florian will need a partner in a strange town. Perhaps Max could be my personal helpmate? Just to complete the image?'

'Oh, yes, sir,' Math said, 'I could serve the Princess well, I assure you. I'd be happy to protect her wherever she goes, if you'll allow it. More than happy.'

'Hah!' said Quintus, cynically. 'You'd have to keep your wits about you, then. I fear the shoe might be on the other foot.'

'Give him a chance,' Brighid whispered. 'Just while we're here?'

'Stop howling, man,' Quintus said to Florian. 'You can keep your mate and the Princess can have a new helpmate, and *you*,' he said, glaring at Math, 'had better earn your keep, or you'll be off! Now go to the lodgings and bring our things back here.' He placed an arm across Brighid's shoulders in an unusual display of public affection frowned upon in Roman society, even amongst married couples. 'And you, my beautiful slave,' he said in a low voice, 'had better earn your keep, too, if you want to stay at this expensive place. Don't go wandering off with that useless young lout unless Florian goes along, too. He's all promises, but I know perfectly well why he wants to stay.'

'You do?' Brighid said, feeling a tightness in her chest.

'Well, of course I do. Ah, Lady Helena, it's all arranged. Our belongings will be here in a few hours.'

It was only a few moments later, when they were joined by Lucan and Tullus, that they met the husband of Helena Coronis strolling along the gravel path with his stepdaughter and her friend on each side of him. They were laughing at some private joke and so did not see the group surrounding his wife until they were only a few yards away, giving Brighid time to take a long look at the man of whom his family were so proud. The man to whom Helm was a friend.

They made an interesting trio, the pretty Clodia, long-haired, slender and gangly; her friend Dora, heavily pregnant and almost certainly an ex-slave, if her very short cropped hair was anything to go by. Here was something of a mystery, Brighid thought, for pregnant slaves were not usually afforded any special treatment unless….unless? She had expected the Lady Helena's husband to be about the same age as her, so it came as something of a surprise to see a man of younger years, well built and looking as if a regular five-mile run before breakfast kept him in trim. He was not quite as tall as Quintus, perhaps because his head was shaved almost to the scalp, though the severe style suited his healthy glow. Looking up, his blue eyes quickly assessed the group ahead of him, lingering over Brighid before stepping ahead of his two companions to make a short respectful bow to Quintus, whose rank he clearly recognised.

'Allow me, my lord,' said the Lady Helena, 'to present my husband, Publius Cato Valens. The Tribune Quintus Tiberius Martial.'

'My lord.'

'And his two friends, Lucan and Tullus.'

'Sirs.'

'And the Princess Brighid, the Tribune's healer.'

'Princess.' He was far too diplomatic to address anything directly to her at this early stage, so his remark was made to Quintus instead. 'Our guests do occasionally bring their physicians along, too, my lord. Comparisons are always healthy, I say.'

'The comparison between Watercombe and our

lodgings in the town is both healthy and rewarding,' he replied. 'It's a beautiful place you have here, Valens.'

'Ah, so you're staying in Aquae Sulis. On business, or for recreation?'

'Your good lady has been kind enough to offer us rooms here. Which pleases my friend Tullus particularly. He's very interested in your use of the local water.'

The blue eyes dodged across to his wife's face before resuming their expression of polite regard, but Brighid felt his wife stiffen very slightly as if that look held more than approval. Or less. 'Excellent,' he said, agreeably. 'So you're to stay with us. I'm sure she will make you comfortable. She excels in the art of good hospitality and I shall personally show you round the water systems, at your convenience. Perhaps you would do us the honour of dining with us this evening, before your treatment begins? After that, they may decide you need starving. Who knows?'

Quintus smiled. 'Last chance, then. Thank you.'

'Have you met my stepdaughter, my lord? Clodia, come forwards.'

Shy, but willing to please her handsome stepfather, Clodia allowed herself to be presented to the new guests before going to stand beside her mother, as if to make way for Dora to endure the same formality. But it was her mother who reached out to draw that young lady to her side as if to shield her bulge from exposure. 'And Theodora,' she said, kindly, 'stays with us until she can join her husband. Is it tomorrow he comes, my dear?'

'Yes, my lady,' Dora whispered. 'I believe so.'

'Is he far away?' Quintus asked.

As if to pre-empt any gaffe on her part, Valens replied rather quickly. 'Oh, Helm has his own rules,' he said. 'He goes about on family business. You'll meet him.'

Helm? The name struck Brighid with a sickening thud, reverberating around her head in a void while people mouthed words she did not hear. The cold chill returned to freeze her limbs, her face, her tongue, even her thoughts. Helm. Dora's husband. His wife. His *wife*?

'Princess?' Quintus's voice reached her from the far end of a tunnel, like a distant whisper. 'What's the matter?'

The group had begun to move away along the path, chattering, leaving her with numbed legs and unfocused eyes. She began to feel nauseous and faint, but knew she must fight it. No one must know.

'What is it, lass? Tell me.' His arm and body steered her in the opposite direction, and she walked with him in a dream, willing one foot to move in front of the other like an invalid. A hard ball formed at the back of her throat, making her pant for breath like a stranded fish. 'Tell me?' he insisted.

'I can't. No…I can't. Don't ask me.'

'I *am* asking you.' When she could only shake her head, he took her arm and walked her along the pathway to the guesthouse where their room on the ground floor had its entrance under a covered walkway.

It was peaceful enough for her to hear the heavy thump of her heart, to hear the creaking shift of her world, her plans, her future. What a fool she had been to think she could mark out her own destiny when men always held the upper hand. Keeping herself pure for him. Travelling hundreds of miles to seek him out. Forfeiting her dignity, her identity, her pride. This, of course, must have been the meaning of those warnings. Not for the Tribune, but for herself. Treachery. Betrayal. Her first time away from her father's protection, and she'd been taken for a ride. Literally.

So much for her prayers.

One thing was certain, she must get away from here as soon as possible.

He closed the door and stood by it, as if he knew. Waiting.

Brighid stood in the middle of the room, not wanting to touch any part of it. 'We have to go… no…*I* have to go. You must free me. I cannot stay. I'm sorry. I really *cannot* stay here. Those warnings were right.' Spreading her hands, she looked around her at the tasteful prosperity, the high point of her material education. It had been for Helm she had transformed herself and he had married a shaven-headed slave, after all that. How he would laugh when he saw her.

Unconsciously, her hands cupped her face, her eyes searching for a grain of sense. 'What have you seen?' he said. 'Tell me what it is. Unless you tell me, I shall not be able to help. Is it him… Valens? Is it the girl….the slave? Being pregnant? Is it the husband? The one who comes and goes?'

Her cry was muffled by her hands and she shook uncontrollably. 'Just let me go,' she whispered. 'Please.'

'Is this how Brigantian Princesses go on, then? They flee, do they, when the going gets rough? Would your father have been proud of that?'

Her head jerked out of her hands at his question.

'Would?' she whispered. '*Would?* Then you know. You've known all along, yet you said nothing to me about it. You cared nothing about my loss. How could you *do* that? How could *any* man be so unfeeling?' Her body tensed like a tightly coiled spring, her fists clenched.

'Feelings don't come into it. I'm being paid to find things out. It's what I do. It didn't suit my purpose to tell you, that's all.'

'That's *all*,' she spat at him, her green eyes flashing in anger. 'How much more important does news have to be before you can forget how much you're being paid, my lord? Do you have a heart somewhere in that fine chest of yours, or did you lose it along with your humanity?' With a sob, she flung an arm into the air, stabbing with one finger. 'Don't tell me. Let me guess. You knew about Math, too, didn't you? You almost said as much when you agreed to let him stay here with us. Tell me, my lord, what *don't* you know?'

By now, Quintus had arranged himself sideways on the couch to watch her ride out the storm, knowing that anything he could say in his defence, or by way of explanation, would be twisted out of all recognition. She had a point, but he was not inclined to concede it, suspecting how little love there had been between her and her father, and that her distress was more about his silence than about the losses she had suffered. 'Of course I knew,' he said. 'What do you take me for? A green lad with cloth between his ears?'

'Then you must have brought me all this way for a purpose, not for the reasons you gave me and not to warm your bed either. You've not had your money's worth there, have you?' she shouted.

'Keep your voice down,' he said with a glance at the door.

That was like a red rag to a bull, for the weight of her words lay in the volume as well as the content. 'Nor *will* you!' she roared at him, ignoring his command. 'You want something for nothing…no! Get away…no…no! You were using me, weren't you…to lead you to something…and like a fool…' Snatching at a soft woollen coverlet, she hurled it, hoping to divert him, but he caught it and flung it aside as his other hand grabbed her wrist, twisting it behind her before she had time to evade him.

Clamped hard against his chest, she was hoisted high into the air and dumped like a sack on to the wide couch and, without being allowed a moment to recover, she found herself pinned down by the weight of his body and the tight grasp of his hands. His grim expression warned her that she could expect no mercy and that, once he knew about Helm's role in her life, her main reason for remaining chaste had gone. The requirements of potential slave-merchants had ceased to be a threat, for she knew his desire for her was on a tight leash, and this attempt to chasten her was only a short step away from her complete surrender. Held down with such force, there was nothing she could do but toss her head wildly from side to side and to kick like a furious mule. To no avail.

'Now, barbarian, *you* can answer *my* questions,' he growled, glaring into her eyes, his brows lowered like thunderclouds. 'For a start, you can tell me about the man called Helm. The father-to-be. He's the one you're most upset about, isn't he? The one who's not so high in rank that he can marry a slave woman. Tell me about him.'

To his astonishment, the lovely green eyes welled with tears as the helplessness of her situation overwhelmed her. The realisation that none of her schemes had worked was more than she could bear. Betrayal and disappointment flooded into her, along with the knowledge that she had lost control of her plans, her body and her heart, too. Yes, she would have gone with Helm if he'd been free, choosing security over an uncertain future. But now her heart was no longer hers to give. Sobs racked her and gobbled up her attempt at words, her face contorted by the pain of failure.

The merciless grip on her wrists slackened and, though she could not see, the steely eyes piercing hers softened with concern. Taking a fistful of her linen gown, he wiped her eyes and pushed damp strands of her hair aside, shocked by the vehemence of her distress. Here was something he'd not anticipated. Had she given her heart to this man? Was that it?

'I have to go,' she sobbed. 'You *must* let me go now.'

'Shh! You're going nowhere,' he replied, harshly. 'You hoped to find him here, didn't you?'

She nodded, too confused to deny it.

'He's the one who came to seek your hand, then disappeared again.'

Another nod.

'So who told you he'd be here at Watercombe?'

'Math.'

'Ah, Max. The brother with divided loyalties. Well, he's not been as much use to you as you'd hoped, has he? I suppose this Helm would recognise him?'

'Yes. How did you know…about him…seeking my hand?'

'I'm asking the questions. But you may as well

know that I was using you to lead me to him. He's high on the Emperor's "wanted" list. Now we only have to wait for him to appear, ostensibly to visit his wife. Did you and he form an attachment while he was visiting your father? Did you spend time together? Alone?'

If there was a hint of envy in his tone, she did not recognise it. 'We exchanged no words. I saw him, that's all. And he saw me. My father did not keep me informed.' Angrily recalling those events, she pushed a tear from her cheek. 'And you need not think we became lovers. He can marry as many women as he likes, but no honourable man takes a princess as his *second* wife after a slave girl, for anyone can see that's what she was. And if my father had known, he'd have thrown him halfway across the moor for his impertinence. We have our pride, Roman.'

'So I've discovered. Well, Helm won't be too pleased when he discovers that you're now *my* woman, will he? He's in for a shock there.'

'I'm *not* your woman!' she snarled, though the edge was taken off its effectiveness by a sob catching at her breath.

'Then I shall be putting that right in the very near future,' he said. 'For which I have the contemptible Helm to thank.'

'He was not the keeper of my virginity, sir!' she retorted, hotly.

'No? Just coincidence, was it? You're not too good at deception, are you, lass? And your anger is all about being used when you thought *you* were pulling the strings. I doubt you've shed one tear for your father since you discovered his fate, not the way you grieved for your maid. Eh?'

'My losses have been great, my lord.'

'Then stop thinking about them and put your mind to how best we can make use of the situation,' he countered, callously.

Stung by his lack of sympathy, she turned her head aside. 'No woman of status likes to be *told* that she's being used,' she whispered, 'even when she's being given in marriage. Why do you pursue Helm? Has he commited some crime?'

'He's an ambitious chieftain's son,' he said, sliding to one side of her, 'with high ideals about putting a British king on the throne. That's why he contacted your father, hoping for an alliance that would provide men and funds. It has to be nipped in the bud, or we shall have yet another revolution on our hands.'

'I see,' she said, attempting to roll away to the other side of the couch. But Quintus bridged his arm across her, scooping her back to him and settling her under him once again.

'So,' he said, grimly, 'if you're thinking of warning him…'

'Why would I do *that*?' she retorted, trying again to push herself away. 'I owe him no allegiance.'

'You kept your virginity for him though, despite what you say.'

She lay still, looking up into his eyes, hard as marble, and troubled. 'You harp on that string at great length, Roman. Why not put your mind to how best you can make use of the situation?' Mimicking him, she realised as soon as the words were out that he would place a different construction on the advice.

His hand moved softly over her breast, cupping the perfect fullness and sending a shudder of excitement into her thighs. 'Excellent advice,' he whispered.

After her struggles, her gown had slipped off one shoulder, almost exposing the breast beneath, the proud nipple just below the surface inviting his touch. Her attempt to hold him off stood no chance against the power of his great shoulders and, as her body arched, she felt his teeth pull down the fabric, taking her into his mouth like a greedy infant, and all she saw was the side of his handsome head and feel the tender assault that sent hot waves of yearning into her deepest parts. She cried out, helpless against his strength and the sensation, against her longing for him and his love, emotions that engulfed her in surge after surge, holding her weightless and whimpering. She touched his hair, sinking her fingers deep into the silky mass as he moved to her other breast to begin suckling again while his hand slipped between her thighs into that place she had denied him only yesterday. This time, they parted for him without persuasion, all sensations merging into one, all signs of danger suspended.

Tenderly, his fingers explored, touching and fondling, and this time there was no reasoning in her to stop him, only the breathtaking revelation that, after this, life could never be the same without him. But it was Quintus himself who could tell how close she was to capitulation when she whispered typical words of contradiction that meant, he believed, that he must relieve her of all responsibility. 'No…no, my lord!'

'Shh!' he said, softly. 'Time has run out on you, my beauty. I know why you've been keeping yourself chaste and I have aided you although it went against all my needs. But he doesn't deserve you and I do; before you meet him tomorrow, you'll belong to me in every way. I shall risk no misunderstandings about that. Now, we have to go and eat with the rest of them. We have some plans to make.'

His hand withdrew like a warm shadow, leaving her aching, wanting him, trembling with emptiness. His kiss was hard, demanding her obedience, and she put up no argument against his determination to solve the problems in his own way. Which, she thought, cynically, must have been what he intended all along. Not for one moment did she believe that his heart had softened towards her, or he would hardly talk of deserving her, would he?

Chapter Nine

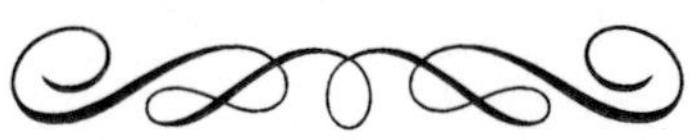

Having stepped out of one set of problems straight into another, Brighid turned her immediate attention to the new suite of rooms in which their belongings were being unpacked and arranged. There was nothing for it now, she realised, but to accept the circumstances with a good grace and not to do anything that would make the difficult situation any worse. Perhaps, after all, she had underestimated the Tribune's ability to be in command of every detail, just as she had misjudged the loyalty of the love-struck Florian. She should have heeded his warning.

But without labouring the point, Quintus was not unaware that her assessment of him was at this moment being revised and that a new respect, and perhaps trust, would help to oil the wheels of their ambiguous relationship. Certainly he needed no one's permission to do as he wished with his own property, but the Princess was no ordinary woman and theirs was no ordinary alliance, nor was he the kind of man to take what he wanted from a woman without due consideration, even though some kind of drastic action was called for to prevent Helm believing she was still a good prize, worth a sudden abduction. It was a callous and calculated reason for taking a woman's virginity, to prevent someone else from doing the same, but Quintus was a soldier with a soldier's methods. If it would divert her mind from whatever Helm had to offer and bind her to him instead, it would have gone some way to solving that particular problem. He could then dispose of the lad according to his Emperor's orders and get on with his other investigations. The pregnant slave Dora could hardly be counted as either a help or a hindrance, Quintus thought, when there were all kinds of reasons why Helm had not declared his previous marriage to Brighid's father. Perhaps it was not a true marriage at all. Who knows what these chieftain's sons got up to away from home?

They took a mid-day meal al fresco on their private terrace during which Quintus handed out instructions on what not to say or do, this being an unknown set of circumstances calling for some caution. To young Math, his command was that he should stay out of sight of both Valens and, when he arrived, Helm, too. The revelation that his identity had been known to the Tribune for some time was a source of embarrassment to him. 'Yes, sir, if you say so,' he said. 'But I was to have been my sister's personal companion.'

'Yes, I know. Things have changed. I know more now than I did then. You will stay behind the scenes or return to Aquae Sulis. I don't want you being identified. It can only complicate matters. The Princess will be escorted at all times either by me personally, or by Tullus and Lucan, or by you two guards.'

The two burly guards nodded agreeably, their faces now revealed as rugged, deeply lined and as concerned as two favourite uncles. Devoid of their armour plating, scrubbed and dressed in brown tunics, they were no longer threatening.

'You don't trust Valens, then?' said Lucan.

Quintus's eyes were half-closed against the sun as he watched distant figures wander along the terraces, and his frown was no more than a shadow across his brow. 'A man of his standing is unlikely to take a local tribesman as his personal friend unless there's something in it for him, and

I want to know what it is. I doubt he's going to offer us an explanation.'

'Won't Helm wish to speak to the Princess in private, once he recognises her?' said Tullus. 'If you don't allow that, we're losing a chance to discover what *he's* doing here, aren't we?'

'I admit that he'll want to know what the Princess is up to, but I doubt he'll explain his presence here, except to visit his wife. There has to be more than a simple friendship between him and Valens,' Quintus said, wiping a hand across his jaw, 'some business or other. One way to find out is through the woman who's expecting his child. I wonder if you,' he said, looking at Brighid, 'might try to get to know her better.'

'Do you indeed, my lord?' she said, fixing him with a murderous glare. 'You'd like me to offer her my friendship, would you? You astonish me.'

Quintus countered the look, then his slow blink swept over Florian, Math, Lucan and Tullus before coming to rest on the two genial guards, whose participation had begun to take on a new interest. 'You two, come with me,' he said, rising. 'A word in your ears.'

'No need to go,' said Brighid. 'I've heard enough. You stay here while I go in to make a *scalding* hot plaster for your leg.'

'Right,' said Quintus, resuming his seat. 'You do that.'

Math watched his sister's dignified departure. 'With respect, I think you may have said the wrong thing sir,' he said.

'Did she ever kill anyone with that look, young man?'

'That's usually the intention, sir. She's still perfecting it.'

'Uh-huh! I don't suppose I have long, then.'

Brighid would have liked to hear what was being said to the two guards, guessing that it was sure to concern the fate of the man to whom she had unwittingly led them. Well, she thought, crossly shaking out one of the new linen lengths, it would serve the double-dealing louse right, whatever they decided, quite forgetting in her quest for vengeance that he would leave behind a wife and unborn child. Now, where could she find something to remove all these creases?

Her search led her to a corridor along which guests could reach the gymnasia, the baths and, for slaves, the laundry and kitchens. Without a maid, Brighid's appearance raised a few eyebrows, but she soon found a space where she could damp the linen and lay it under a screw-press, which is where she was joined, most unexpectedly, by Helena Coronis. 'You should let your maid do that, Princess,' said the lady through a hiss of steam. Brown-clad slaves moved like ghosts behind wicker cages draped with white togas and sheets, and the clatter of water hitting bowls softened her words. She took hold of one end, ready to draw it through the press as Brighid released the screws.

'Yes, I lost her just before we left Eboracum. I'm having to fend for myself,' she replied. 'I miss her sorely.' Brighid stopped feeding the linen into the plates and looked up. 'There, that's one length. Now for the green.'

Helena Coronis held laughter in her eyes at last. 'That's how it's done. Were you sorry to leave Eboracum?'

'Not at all,' Brighid admitted. 'The prospect of visiting the shrine at Aquae Sulis where my own deity resides was too good to miss.'

'Brigantia?'

'Yes,' Brighid said, twisting the screw again. 'She's also known as Minerva down here, I believe.' She looked across the table, but her hostess was still gently smoothing the linen into a neat pile, her dark pleated hair now uncovered, glistening with droplets of steam. Her hands were long and deft, her sleeves showing bare wrists where the fabric had been pushed up and, just below the cuff, soft smudges of grey-blue and crimson bruised the delicate skin. No wonder, Brighid thought, she had winced when her arm was touched. It was no accident, however, that when their eyes met, Helena Coronis made no attempt to cover her injuries, as if she wanted them to be noted, their origin to be deduced. Only then, when she knew Brighid had seen, did she adjust the fabric over her wrists and continue to smooth the linen.

'I wanted to thank you,' the lady whispered, 'not only for what you did yesterday but for saying nothing of our meeting. My litter-bearers will say I was visiting friends. They are very loyal.'

'You need have no concerns, my lady. Tullus is the soul of discretion.'

'Please thank him for me.'

'I will.'

'And tell him that—' her eyes darted sideways '—my husband has friends at the tax office.'

Brighid stared at her, her hands once again idle. 'Friends?'

'Yes, officials. There we are. I think that's it. If you need some help with the sewing, I can send you some girls. I would let you have Dora, but she's getting near her time.'

'Is that why her husband is to visit?'

'Oh, yes, to be sure.' Such a casually spoken reply was bound to be some way from the truth.

Carrying the pile of linen across her arms, Brighid was about to turn away when she was levered back into the door recess by the lady's arm, the hand covering her mouth. Obediently, she flattened herself, clutching the linen to her chest as several men crossed the end of the corridor led by Valens, the lady's husband. 'He's showing them to baths and boiler rooms,' Helena Coronia whispered.

'And you don't want him to see you talking to me,' Brighid said.

The lady's eyes closed with a sigh. 'I don't wish to face an inquisition about what I said, what you said, and why. That's all.'

'But I'm the Tribune's healer,' she said, looking down at her layers of folded linen. 'I've been treating his wound.'

'Oh, I have no doubt of that at all. That's probably why he forgets to limp sometimes, especially up and down the steps.'

Their laughter was almost inaudible. 'It was me who wanted to stay here,' Brighid said. 'We had to have a reason to stay in such a lovely place, even though the knee is almost mended.'

'At this time of the year, business is only just starting to pick up. I wonder if you would pass on a piece of information to the Tribune, though I would not want him to acknowledge that it comes from me. Tell him, when he is asked who recommended Watercombe to him, to say that it was Nonius.'

'But he said it was a man at the tax office who—'

'Yes, dear. Nonius is the head of the tax office. My husband's friend.'

'Then I shall certainly remind him of that, my lady. It was Nonius.'

'Until this evening then, Princess.'

'Thank you for your help.'

'I'm sorry to hear about your maid. Let me know if…'

'Yes. Thank you.'

Brighid's return to the suite was greeted by Math and Florian who had no time to wipe the frantic expressions off their faces before the door closed. One of the guards stood outside on the wooden-railed balcony, arms folded across his chest. 'Where in the name of Zeus have you been, *domina*?' said Florian, with a hand clapped dramatically to his forehead. 'We were told to find you. Fast.'

'I don't mind you claiming success,' said Brighid, laying her linen down carefully. 'You found me in the laundry doing this, and I came back like a lamb, you see, and now you can help me to cut it up. My shears are in that workbox, Math. Where are the men?'

'Invited to tour the water systems,' he said, eyeing her with suspicion. 'And next time you go off somewhere, you'd better say where you're going or we shall get it in the neck.'

'I am most unlikely to say any such thing,' Brighid responded, rummaging for her tools. 'What on earth would you two find to do if you didn't have me to look for? Florian, don't just stand there. Help me.'

As if Brighid's imperious manner was somehow Math's fault, Florian sent his friend a look of resentment that changed to a grin as he saw the grotesque face being aimed at her back. 'Certainly, *domina*,' he said.

The time it took for Quintus and his friends to be conducted round the site was all the time Brighid needed to sew the straight seams and hems of the violet gold-embroidered linen she intended to wear that night. It also gave her the chance to think back over her meeting with Helena Coronis and the various messages she had slipped into their conversation that seemed to explain her sorrow at the shrine. If her younger husband was ill treating her, that would also explain why he was so firmly excluded from being one of the loves of her life, and why she showed signs of unease when he looked at her. Another hint was the head of the tax office who, for some reason, the lady wished to take responsibility for recommending their stay here. Did it matter who recommended it? And was it significant that Valens had friends there?

Certainly the lady's assistance was more an example of helping a guest to deceive her husband than of wifely support. Yet the two daughters had shown no reserve in his presence. One had walked and laughed with him, the other had run to hold his hand. The affections of a four-year-old were quite transparent. There could be no problem there, then.

The tour of Watercombe's hydraulics system kept the men in conversation long after Valens had left them, for although the workshops had been excluded, their interest in the water power, the heating systems and the utilisation of every drop of water, both waste and pure, was both genuine and well informed, all three being familiar with the engineering of other countries. Impressed by the owner's capabilities, it was some time before they all went off to the baths, leaving Brighid with the distinct impression that this might be the sole topic of conversation all through dinner and well into the night. There had been a time in ancient Greece, she understood, when dinner was a men-only affair. Not so the Romans—more was the pity, she said to Math. What had the Tribune decided to do with Helm?

'Come on!' she cried. 'He must have known you'd tell me.' She thought he looked different, more relaxed, happier, his eyes softer. Very handsome. No wonder Florian was attracted to him.

'The Tribune wants to know what he's doing here,' he said, reluctantly. 'They have to watch his movements. He doesn't believe he visits just to see his wife. He's sure he needs money for this enterprise of his, whatever it is.'

'Don't you know?'

'No. Father never discussed anything with me, did he?'

'It's a plot by Helm and his tribe to raise an army against the Emperor, Math. Getting powerful men behind them. Like Father. That's why he wanted a connection with the Brigantii. That's why he offered for me.'

'He *thought* Father would fall over himself to have a Dobunni man as a son-in-law, that he'd even *pay* him to make it happen. He didn't know our father very well, did he? Father expected payment from *him*. A large one. Too large for Helm. He's a nasty piece of work, Bridie love. You're well rid of him. Whatever your feelings are for your slave master, I believe you'll fare better with him than with Helm. Whatever you do, don't agree to go off with him. Once they've found out what they want to know, they'll kill him.'

'They?'

Eloquently, Math tipped his head towards the guard who stood outside the door with his back to them.

'And what of his wife and unborn child?'

He shrugged, shaking his head. 'She's not part of the equation,' he said.

'Typical!' she whispered, savagely. 'So what makes you think *I* shall be better off with the Tribune, I wonder, when a woman and child have no part in the equation?'

'You're not…?'

'Of *course* I'm not, idiot! But it's only a matter of time, isn't it?'

'Is it?'

'Yes,' she whispered, turning away. 'I'm going to bathe. Come with me.'

Later, she had a chance to pass on the message to Quintus.

'I have something to tell you, Tribune. From Helena Coronis.'

'Oh? Then tell me.'

'She wants you to say it was a man called Nonius at the tax office who recommended Watercombe to you.'

His eyes widened fractionally, his slight frown jerking his head down before he spoke. 'You're sure it was Nonius? He's the head—'

'Yes, of the tax office. A friend of Valens.'

The deep brown of his eyes appeared to absorb the information while he searched over her shoulder for a place to store it. 'Well, well,' he said, quietly.

'You must not say that she told you this.'

'Of course not. But this suggests…'

'That she's telling you something about her husband. And there's something else, too. I saw her arms covered in bruises. She knows I saw them. She gave no reasons for them being there, but I think she was telling me that *that* was the reason she was at the shrine yesterday, when we first met.'

'When she fainted?'

'Yes. She asked me to thank Tullus and to say thank you for not letting on that she was there. Obviously, she's anxious for her husband not to know.'

'But he has every right to know, as her husband.'

'That's not quite how it came across. Not to me.'

'How did it come across? To you.'

'As if she was afraid of him.'

'Too big,' he whispered.

'What?'

'Too big. Your eyes. Your mouth. I could eat you.' His face had moved closer as she talked, his eyes half-closed with desire, his mind already veering away from Helena Coronis and her husband.

'I would spoil your appetite for dinner,' she whispered back.

'There is that danger,' he said, placing his hands on her waist, searching her voluptuous body with his eyes while pulling her gently towards him. 'So I shall wait until afterwards.'

'You'll still be talking waterworks at dawn,' she teased.

'Is that what you think, Princess? Let's see, shall we?' His silky wayward hair brushed her forehead as he bent her to him, taking her mouth in a tenderly tormenting kiss meant to remind her of his intentions, and of the way he hungered for her.

But as they walked across to the triclinium through lamplit arcades, the enigma of making the man called Nonius responsible for their being here was held at the back of Quintus's mind like a knot that wouldn't stay tied. If the Lady Helena was setting her husband up, which was not impossible, then she was perhaps hinting that Nonius would be the very last person to want a Provincial Procurator snooping around Watercombe and that, if Valens believed it, his friend Nonius would have some explaining to do. Added to that was the flimsy excuse Valens had offered when Lucan had asked to see the workshops. There had, in fact, been plenty of time, but no inclination. He was brought sharply back to the present when Brighid observed that he was again forgetting to limp. Behind them, Tullus and Lucan exchanged looks of concern. The Tribune had spent several hours that afternoon clambering over rough ground, half-built hypercausts and steps without the slightest discomfort.

It was the first thing Publius Cato Valens asked about, noting the convincing wince of pain as Quintus arranged himself on the couch of honour at the head of the three-sided arrangement. Tenderly ministering, Brighid arranged the toga over his legs before joining him. 'Quite painful after all that scrambling,' said Quintus, 'but it was worth it. One can't allow an old wound to get in the way of learning. What a blessing it turned out to be when I mentioned it to Nonius. He was determined I ought to visit Watercombe to seek a cure.'

'Nonius...at the tax office? *That* Nonius?' Valens's attempt at nonchalance was sadly overdone.

'The very same. Do you know him? Bald. Well made. An excellent man. One of the best.'

'Hmmm!' said Valens, scratching his nose. 'I wouldn't know.' His blue eyes were hard like stones, softening as they rested upon his lissome stepdaughter. She was arranged on the couch near her mother, who preferred to sit in a wicker chair with padded arms rather than with her husband. Intercepting a smile between Valens and Clodia, Brighid was intrigued to see how the girl blushed and looked down, and how his eyes caressed her before catching Brighid's inquisitive glance.

Immediately, the eyes changed, challenging her with a look of frightening directness. 'Princess,' he said from the other side of Quintus, 'tell me something about your ornaments, if you will.' She thought he must mean their symbolism, but apparently not. 'Are they solid gold, or hollow?' he wanted to know.

She smiled, as if he had made a joke. 'I doubt if I'd be able to walk in here with them on if they were solid,' she replied. 'No, they're made of sheets of beaten gold, and the smaller pieces are twisted and coiled gold wire. Not too heavy.'

'But valuable, eh?'

'Invaluable to me, sir.'

'Hmmm, yes, of course.' He stared hard at his fingernails before abruptly swinging the conversation round to the food arriving at the table, to the fine wine the slaves were pouring, and Brighid could see why Helena Coronis would have been attracted to his glowing robust health and restless energy, a certain rough directness that would have taken her widowhood by storm. Refusing to take no for an answer, blustering his way over her threshold, he would have been careful to keep his bullying under control, and she would have been reassured by his fondness for her daughter on the verge of puberty, a difficult age for a girl to accept a rival for her mother's attention. He wore a voluminous toga of cream linen with panels of brown-and-gold stripes that echoed the gold sheen of his shaved head, and his hands were strong, gold-ringed and well manicured. But as well as his physical attractiveness, Brighid wondered what direction Valens's fondness for Clodia took, having noticed how often his eyes wandered over the pale pink chiton bound beneath her young breasts and the curve of her hip as she reclined. When her chiton slipped off one shoulder, Helena Coronis eased it back into place, earning a frown of irritation from her daughter, who apparently wanted it to stay.

The meal was a tribute to their hostess. Simple healthy fare, Valens had told them, all locally grown produce; only the wines and snails had crossed the seas. They started with honeyed wine, stuffed kidneys in sauce and tiny cubes of roast venison, with the snails as a merry talking point. Before them, a verandah gave on to a garden lit by lamps and flickering lanterns. Behind them were panels of garden revelry, dancing girls and eager satyrs, swags of flowers, ribbons and masks leering from the top borders, more to the host's taste, Brighid felt, than their hostess's.

Inevitably, the conversation turned to Valens's alterations to Watercombe and of his contribution to other hydraulics schemes, consultancies and planning. His work had taken him the length of the country. He knew the family with whom they had stayed on their way down, whose daughter

Flavia was a budding gladiatrix. His face lit up at that for, he said, looking pointedly at Clodia, he was determined to have his stepdaughter try it, too.

Eyes turned to Clodia for her reaction. Perhaps her stepfather was teasing. Her eyes were downcast, but she was smiling, disregarding her mother's sharp glance that silently pleaded with her husband to say no more of that. Laughing at the discomfort he had caused, Valens tipped back his head to drop a morsel of food into his mouth, looking round at the silent faces as he chewed.

'You approve of that, do you?' said Quintus.

The reply was predictably unfeeling. 'Yes. It shows what a woman is made of.'

'Well,' said Quintus, keeping his voice level, 'I can suggest a dozen or so better ways to find out what a woman is made of without resorting to violence, my friend. They might be somewhat slower in nature, but at least no one gets injured in the process. Does the Lady Helena share your urgency, Valens?'

'The Lady Helena,' said Valens, 'shares all my opinions. Don't you, my dear?'

Helena Coronis was pushing the food about on her plate, clearly struggling with an answer. But Tullus, who reclined on the other side of Clodia, took the situation into his own hands by asking her, in a tone that demanded her immediate attention, whether the eels were from the local river and if the mulberry sauce was homegrown, too. 'If so, my lady,' he said, smiling at her, 'I think you may have to write a recipe book one of these days. These are the best eels I've eaten in years. I think I might just injure myself, to prolong our stay.'

'Thank you, my lord Tullus,' she said, returning a grateful smile. 'Yes, all our fish is local and the fruit, too. Our cooks are trained to prepare for special needs. Some of our patients suffer from having eaten the wrong kind of food.'

The dangerous moment had passed, yet there was not one of the guests who had missed the tension between host, hostess and daughter, and not one guest who failed to sympathise with the Lady Helena's dilemma.

Brighid's fears that the talk would all be of waterworks were not borne out, for Quintus, Tullus and Lucan made a concerted effort to speak of their hostess's food management, her clients, her skilled practitioners working there, and her opinions of the large bath complex at Aquae Sulis. After his encounters with the knotty problem of Nonius, and the gladiatrix, Valens appeared to be relieved to make only brief contributions, although his frequent and prolonged observations of Brighid made her wish for the meal to end.

Not unaware of the scrutiny, Quintus made his ownership unambiguous by reaching a long arm over her to offer morsels from his plate, a poppy-seed fritter dipped in honey, a piece of roast hare—which she took, but did not eat—a lamb sweetbread to eat with her salad. Yet more than once, during that splendid feast, Brighid felt the warning danger and the inexplicable dread clouding her enjoyment of being seen as the Tribune's woman, and, because Valens was on the next couch to hers, it was virtually impossible for her to touch Quintus with her foot without it being noticed. The warmth of him at her back, however, reminded her that this was to be her last meal as a virgin, and for some time at least, the succulent dishes might as well have been hay.

As she had foreseen, the men stayed to talk, but the chance she had hoped for to speak again with her hostess did not materialise when Clodia was escorted away by her mother with what seemed like an exaggerated concern for her safety, and Brighid had only Florian for company as far as their suite of rooms. Rejecting his offer to act as lady's maid and, in the process, conveying something of her sense of dislocation, she had not the heart to refuse when he suggested that a back massage might be just what she needed after their eventful day. It might also, she thought, be what she needed to prepare her for the night ahead, provided the Tribune's wine consumption did not send him straight to sleep.

It was, however, the other way round, for Brighid soon fell asleep under Florian's gentle hands before he'd finished, so that when Quintus entered, he was greeted by the sight of her smooth undulating back gleaming like silk in the low lamplight, her loose hair blanketing her face, her gold ornaments piled to one side of the small table where Florian had lovingly arranged them. Florian himself was perched on the edge of the couch with his back to her, arms folded patiently. He pushed himself upright with a last look at the sleeping Brighid and a grin for his master. 'Over to you, sir,' he whispered on his way to the door.

Playfully, Quintus aimed a swipe at his slave's curly head. 'Imp,' he whispered. 'By the way, where's the lad?'

'Safe, sir. With me.'

Quintus nodded. 'Early start tomorrow. I'm to be treated.'

'Yes, sir.' Florian's dark eyes returned to the couch, sparkling with laughter. 'Indeed you are. Goodnight.'

He stood for some moments looking down at her, denuded of all ornament except the glorious mass of her hair, a few fine threads of it stirred gently by her breath, a frayed web of copper filaments lighter then the luxurious lashes that swept her cheeks. He had noticed the way Valens's eyes had gobbled her up and knew by the way he'd looked at his stepdaughter that a woman would not be safe from him for long, if he could find a way. Perhaps that was at the root of the problem with his beautiful but older wife.

The unusual perception of protectiveness that had been growing inside him over the last few days and nights, mostly ignored, now began to make its presence felt again as his senses feasted upon her, the warm scent of Florian's perfumed oil, the faint sound of her breath, the silken skin and soft shadows that delved into the cleft of her buttocks. She was magnificent. She was his to protect against harm, theft and whatever it was she had been warned of in her subconscious. Fate had worked her magic, turning the Princess away from the man she had hoped to find towards himself. He had felt it during the meal, her need to be seen as his woman, not for pretence, but for real. Their fingers had touched, and she had trembled, giving off waves of desire and disturbance like minor earth tremors. Warnings of his intentions had made her sharp and edgy, as if she was about to face a challenge, and he knew that conflicts still remained concerning his reason for taking her last precious gift. She had no choice but to recognise his rights as her owner, although this was not the way to take a Princess's most prized possession unless he was prepared to offer her something as valuable in return. His hand reached out to touch the soft bed of her hair, wondering if she would regard his protection as a fair exchange, yet suspecting that a woman of her calibre would demand more. Strangely, the idea did not fill him with alarm, as it might have done weeks ago.

'Roman,' she whispered, groping for his hand.

'Yes, barbarian. It's me. Are you asleep?'

'No. Do you want me to bandage your knee?'

'I shall do better if it's unbandaged, I think.'

Pushing her hair away, she smiled sleepily and rolled over to rest on one elbow, presenting him with a different view of her naked body while looking him up and down to remind herself of his extraordinary good looks. He wore a loose white linen tunic with rolled-up sleeves under a toga of deep forest green with a wide blue, purple and gold border in the Greek key pattern scrunched into the folds. She lifted an arm to him, reaching for his face, and he bent to her, hooking her arm about his neck as he scooped her up to nestle close like a child. Her hair fell over his arm, her body still half-clinging to sleep.

'I didn't want to wake you, Princess, but I fear I must.'

'Because of…of him?'

'That was the reason, originally. Now it's only half the story.'

'Oh? What's changed?'

'I think I have. I want you for myself. It's true that I don't want to risk him still being interested in you, but that's not the main reason any more. I can't spend another night with you in my arms without making you mine.'

'You've been too long without a woman? Is that it?'

'No, that's not it either. It's you, exotic creature. It's you.'

If Brighid felt that odd explanation to fall short of the satisfactory, she said no more on the tricky subject just then, because she was where she expected and wanted to be, relaxed and too sleepy to wrangle about motives. His profile was chiselled by the light from the oil lamp, his hair raked back and slipping into ridges over his ears, his beautiful wide mouth set and determined, unsmiling, as if a decision had been reached at last. She felt his ruthlessness and was excited by it, absolved from further dissent, all responsibility lifted by the strength of his arms.

She had seen him naked before, but soon he was warm and peach-coloured in the soft light, his great shoulders wide above her, his arms like buttresses gathering her into his embrace. His deeply modelled chest pushed her gently into the feather mattress, and against her breasts she felt his heart beating in answer to her own. She offered him her lips, holding his head between her hands with her fingers deep in his hair, quivering with delight at his overwhelming closeness after the interminable mealtime when his proximity had almost driven her crazy. She would give him what he desired, and she would accept the consequences, whatever they were, for this was an experience no right-minded woman would relinquish, even a princess as proud as she. Now, her father's fury would never reach her.

Making love to her as if for the first time, as if

that chastening episode at the bath had never happened, he explored her lovely body like a master with his pupil, awakening new responses in her that caused her to cry out with too much sensation and to writhe in ecstasy under his hands, tongue and lips. Vaguely, she recalled the fears of previous times when she'd had to call a halt to his loving, leaving him wanting more, and her wondering what more there was. But he knew her body better than she did, having already sampled the latent passion, the generosity of her giving, the deep well of her desire. He knew how slowly to stroke and tease, how much to ignore the grasp on his wrist, what words to subdue the fierceness that mingled with the ritual protests of a maiden, protests meant to test him, to be overcome with kisses that silenced and held her, ready for the next audacious caress.

No longer fearful, she saw no reason to make it too easy for him. With her pride still intact, she would make him employ every device before she would grant him access after so many days of wanting her, and she would leave him in no doubt that taking the maidenhead of a Brigantain princess was a rare privilege. That was the plan. But Quintus was experienced, overcoming her reservations and delaying tactics time after time with tender force, taking advantage of each weakness, gentling her with skilful fingers in places not even she had discovered, which now made her gasp and moan and pant his name in breathless whimpers.

He lifted his head from her breast, pulling at the proud nipple with his lips, transferring his attention to her mouth, whispering, 'Trust me, my beauty. This will be uncomfortable. A short pain. I'll try to be quick. Hold on. That's good... brave woman...there...shh...there...'

As he spoke, the venturesome hand broke through the sensitive barrier to cause a spasm of pain that he soothed with rhythmic strokes and soft words of encouragement and then with kisses upon her trembling mouth. 'Shall I go on?' he said.

'Yes,' she gasped. 'I'm all right. Go on, Quintus. It's nothing.'

With his thumb, he brushed a glistening drop of moisture from her eye. 'I'm sorry. I'll be careful. Lift your legs...wrap them round me, if you like.'

Obediently, she did as he suggested, delighting in the warm weight of him, the strange intrusion of his body that entered her where his fingers had been a moment before, pushing, waiting, pushing again, past the soreness, filling her completely.

She heard his stifled sigh, felt his rapturous shudder and knew that this was what he had wanted from her since their first stormy meeting when there had been only a grain of common ground between them.

She felt him wait for the emotion to pass, for his kiss to take her mind on to another plane, existing only through heightened sensations with no room for thoughts. She was not aware of exactly when he began to move inside her, nor did she mind the initial discomfort beneath the slow smooth strokes that had the power to rock her upon the mattress. All she knew was that these were sensations beyond her imaginings—and she *had* tried to imagine them—not only being entered in so tender a place, but being part of a man's body, the sole object of his attention, beloved, desired, seduced and mastered by the one man who mattered to her, the only one she had ever wanted to receive her most treasured gift. Yes, she had made it difficult for him, in her own pernickety, truculent way. It was a matter of principle to her that he should see her pride, though she would not know until some time later how much he had enjoyed her little show of vanity, her pretence of unwillingness.

But now she was in an undreamed-of place

where he had set the tempo, which he knew well how to do, and although his natural urge was to give in to a barely controlled energy, he knew that this first experience must meet her needs more than his. So he was surprised and elated when his careful preparation generated a passion he had not expected so soon, a wild abandon, a heat of very unmaidenly ardour that urged him towards a climax he had tried desperately to hold back for her sake. Moaning with desire, she dug her fingers into his waist, her head tossing in a whirl of her hair, green eyes heavy with blazing fire. 'Go on, Quintus. More…more…I want all of you… faster…don't slow down…don't spare me…I'm not a child.'

'Are you sure I'm not hurting?'

'Yes…no…it doesn't matter.' Her fingernails dug in again.

He needed no more persuading, for this gift was more than he could have hoped for. Unleashing his restraint, he plunged into the glorious coupling, feeling her body respond like a wild horse in a joining of wills heading for the same distant goal. Incredibly, he heard her wail as he quickened, spurring him on to let go of every reservation, of every thought but release, to finish with her in a mind-dizzying turmoil that shook them both to the core. Together.

They reeled in each other's embrace, half-laughing, half-crying in disbelief, in Brighid's case because it *was* unbelievable that her body should have gone off with him so wantonly, beyond her mind's influence.

For Quintus, there was something even more unusual for him to recognise, that made him hold her close in his arms after drying her down, gathering her hair and smoothing his hand where he had used her so ungently. Beyond words, when thoughts began to return, he found a place in his mind that had lain dormant until now where a flame had started to burn more brightly, a place he could not name, for it was more than comfort, or desire, or lust, more than plain satisfaction or pride in achievement. Or gratitude.

Lovingly, his lips touched her brow. 'Are you all right, beautiful woman?' he said.

But she was already asleep.

He, however, lay awake for some time, wondering what exactly was happening to him to cause this most unusual ache in his breast, the sweetest ache he had ever experienced.

Chapter Ten

There might have been time next morning for Quintus to discover more about Brighid's frame of mind if Florian had not come quite so early to prepare his master for the day ahead. Having just taken her into his arms to wheedle something complimentary out of her, Quintus was not best pleased when Florian's quick tap on the door was followed by a flurry of activity that clearly signalled some kind of crisis. Clothes baskets were dragged open and delved into, bowls were sloshed with water, windows noisily unlatched. Florian was obviously not himself.

'What in the name of Zeus is the matter with *you*?' Quintus roared, dropping his embracing arms. 'Have you lost your manners? Did I say come in?'

Petulantly, his bottom lip quivering with distress, Florian looked over his shoulder first at

Quintus and then, with resentment, at Brighid. 'He's gone!' he said. 'I *knew* he would, eventually. I should never have—'

Quintus slid off the bed. 'Stop!'' he commanded. 'That's enough snivelling. Simmer down, lad, and tell me what you're talking about. *Who's* gone?'

Florian brushed away a tear with the towel he was folding. 'Math,' he said. 'He's not been in all night...well...not with me, anyway. I expect it's that young—'

'No, Florian,' Brighid said. 'He would not. I know he wouldn't. He'll have gone back to Aquae Sulis for something.'

'Not without telling me, he wouldn't,' said Quintus, taking the towel. 'Go and get those two lads in here. They can start searching while I put some clothes on. Go on! Hurry up!' He went to the bowl and began to douse himself.

Brighid sat on the bed, her mood of retrospection replaced by sisterly concern. 'You think something has happened to him?' she said.

'No, of course not. Florian is being hysterical, that's all. This is the first relationship he's had, so he's still unsure. There'll be a perfectly simple explanation for it.' With water pouring over his head, the words that were meant to sound comforting lost something of their intended effect.

'He *might* have gone to Aquae Sulis,' she insisted.

'Mmm. We'll soon find out. Put some clothes on, lass,' he said, rubbing his hair, 'before those lads get here. He should have stayed indoors as I told him to.'

'He should have gone back home as *I* told him to,' she muttered, wishing she *had* said it. This was a disaster. Hardly the way to celebrate their new relationship, now as far from his mind as last year's summer, just another event for him, like any other. She had slept the whole night long without waking, without a word between them, sharing the same pillow and, for all she knew, the same dreams. She had been ready, just now, to tell him what she had discovered about herself, and about him too. Now, Math must come first.

Please, beloved Brigantia, keep Math safe. Please.

They could not be seen to be searching, Quintus told them, because officially her brother was not there. They would have to make up reasons to be wherever they were looking: baths, pools, the garden areas, the granary and malt ovens. Then someone must go to town to ask at the lodgings. He himself would have to keep to his schedule, or questions would be asked. Lucan and Tullus would have to search, too, without arousing suspicion. And when he was found, the lad would be thrashed and sent off, though this threat was not made in Florian's presence.

'And you, Princess,' he said, 'must go nowhere alone. Now, order some breakfast for us, if you will.' When she frowned, he took her face tenderly between his hands, touching her lips with his. 'Don't worry, lass. He'll not have gone far. We'll find him. But we have to eat, and we have to hide the fact that there's a problem.'

'Yes,' she said, taking his wrists. 'But I'm afraid for him.'

'No need. He's stronger than he looks.'

'Then you think…?'

'No, it's best to keep an open mind, sweetheart.' Still holding her face, he kissed the tip of her nose. 'And you were am-a-zing last night,' he drawled.

That made her smile. 'Was I? So now you're hungry?'

'Ravenous!' he whispered with half-closed eyes.

That breakfast, taken hurriedly while discussing where and how to conduct furtive searches for Math, was to be the last real meal for Quintus until the dawn of the next day. His first visit to the healing centre, which included a full medical examination, a series of tests to establish his fitness, a review of his diet, bodily functions and sleep patterns—all of which he felt were quite unnecessary—took most of the morning, at the end of which he was told he must fast in preparation for the dream interpretation in which he would participate that night.

His first reaction was to decline the invitation for, of all things, he had been looking forward to spending the night very much as he'd spent the last one, in Brighid's arms. The priest would not take no for an answer. It was essential, he said, for a complete physical overhaul, and why else would he have come to Watercombe if not to sample all the amenities? Dreams, said the elderly priest, were the window into the soul. Correctly interpreted, they could explain the mysteries of man's behaviour and put him on the road to a happier life of fulfilment and prosperity. The Tribune must not deny himself one of life's greatest experiences. Was he afraid?

Quintus was no coward, but nor did he believe there was anything to rival the great experience he'd had last night, nor did he particularly relish sharing with this old man and his colleagues the contents of his private life through any kind of window, especially one induced by drugs. Although their use had not been mentioned, he knew they were administered to induce sleep and to cause vivid dreams, and Quintus preferred to know the herbalist on a more personal level before he drank anything he had prepared. He was hard pressed to contain his scepticism.

Nevertheless, he agreed. As an investigator, he saw that it would give him the chance to find out exactly what *did* happen during these magical rites as opposed to what was *supposed* to happen. He would fast in preparation—that would be no great hardship. Nor was sleep deprivation.

Mindful of Quintus's instruction not to go out alone, a command that her brother had obviously ignored, Brighid went with Lucan to tour the extensive gardens, ostensibly to stroll and talk while taking note of every hidden pathway that might indicate Math's whereabouts. There were plenty of people with whom to mingle, to pass and greet, to give them an excuse to pause and to observe the landscape, the more distant grottoes and water shrines where springs bubbled from the earth or trickled down walls. Higher up, beyond the reach of disabled pilgrims, a narrow path led to upper terraces that wound between low conifers, with wooden benches where Brighid and Lucan sat to watch the guests below.

Brighid's keen eyes scanned the scene while Lucan's observations were closer at hand, beside and behind them, swivelling him round to see the bank of grass at their backs, stalks of which had been flattened under the new growth. 'Why would anyone clamber up there, I wonder?' he said. 'It's not a path, but it's certainly been trodden.'

'Let's take a look,' said Brighid. 'Stay behind the tree so we won't be seen. Wait, I shall have to hitch my gown up.'

With Lucan in the lead, hauling her up, they followed the faint pathway through bushes and then through a hazel wood to a small clearing where there was little to be seen except a row of small grassy mounds of varying heights, one of them dug so recently that only bare earth showed in stark contrast.

'Graves?' said Lucan. 'Could they be?'

'No flowers. No markers. It's unusual, but they could be. Perhaps they're infants who didn't survive their birth. It does happen.' She crouched, suddenly overcome by the appalling tragedy of it, remembering her maid and the manner in which she had lost her infant. Not even a grave or the decency of a burial, not a prayer or an offering for her safe passage. Lucan waited, saying nothing, only guessing at what thoughts passed through her mind. As if she was certain of the contents, she stroked the grass of the nearest mound like a mother smoothing the covers of her child's cot. 'Little thing,' she whispered.

Their return was slower and very subdued, both of them sure that they had stumbled across a cemetery, of sorts, and that here at Watercombe there must always be fatalities as well as cures. Brighid pulled her gown into shape and composed herself before continuing down, terrace by terrace, towards the longest pool where Tullus was waving to them. Beside him, deep in conversation, were two men dressed in short white tunics, one of whom they recognised as Valens.

Brighid stopped abruptly, turning to Lucan in consternation, the green of her wide eyes showing him what he'd already guessed, that the other man must be Helm, the Dobunni chieftain's son who had already met Brighid. 'I cannot!' she whispered. 'It's too soon…. I didn't think…I'm not prepared…what am I to say?'

'Princess,' Lucan said, gently, 'he is a complete stranger to you. You greet him as you would any other stranger, saying little. Just be your usual self, haughty and contained. He will not wish to recognise you, either.'

'No, of course he won't, will he?'

'And you need not answer his questions. He'll be the nervous one. Ready?'

'Yes, come on. I have to face the little toad some time.'

Lucan smiled and led her forwards. 'That's more like it,' he said.

The three men watched their approach, one approving, one highly suspicious, and one open-mouthed with astonishment at her transformation. The latter, a sandy-haired bearded man approaching thirty, had a frothy waterfall moustache and eyes of flint grey under equally generous eyebrows. His physique was worthy of his status, wide and muscular, but far from graceful, functional but coarsened like a native fell pony in its winter coat. His red mouth opened and closed as his bewildered expression turned first to Valens, then to his heavily sandalled feet.

Aware of Valens's intense scrutiny, Lucan called out to them, 'Been admiring the gardens while the Tribune takes his medicine. They're a credit to you.'

'Well met, Lucan,' said Valens, 'and to you, Princess. Allow me to present my friend Helm.

We go back a long way, he and I. Helm, meet the Tribune's other assistant, Lucan Decimus Galla, both of them here under false pretences, but we allow them to stay because we need the money.'

Brighid refused to smile, but watched from beneath heavy lids as Lucan and Helm sized each other up like two wrestlers. Helm's eyes, however, were avoiding hers, though she noted a flush of red suffusing his neck above the white tunic. It took no more than a glance.

'And the Princess,' said Valens, 'is the Tribune's healer. Now if I had such a healer, I would not bother coming all the way to Watercombe.'

They were all supposed to laugh at that, but Tullus made the point that they were already on the way there when the Tribune and his healer met. But Valens's attention remained fixed on Brighid, not only her face but all the way down and back up again, twice, and she knew exactly what was passing through his mind, as did both her friends. What was passing through Helm's mind behind his bushy brows was just as easy to speculate but, to his credit, he made a valiant effort to recover from his shock when it was clear that some word of welcome was expected from him. 'Welcome to Watercombe, Princess,' he said, gruffly. 'You are some way from your territory, I believe. Valens tells me you are of the Briganti.'

'Do you know our tribe, sir? Have you been so far from home?' She knew he was unlikely to admit to it without explaining his reasons, and she did not believe he was quick-witted enough to make up a convincing story without getting into a tangle.

'Er…no,' he said, glancing at Tullus. 'Never.' Had she known it, he was already in a tangle.

'I met your wife yesterday. Congratulations.'

'Congratulations?' Ambiguity was not something he found easy to deal with, either.

'On the expected addition to your family. Have you known your wife long?'

Helm was not enjoying the situation. Already he was floundering. 'About half a year,' he volunteered, too guilty for accuracy.

Brighid nodded, smiling at the forced error. The baby was due any day.

As usual, Tullus came to the rescue. 'Time goes fast down here in these valleys,' he said, 'and men never know how long they've known their wives, Princess. Ah, look, here he comes, fresh from the clinic.' Over the shoulders of the other men he saluted with one hand in the air. 'Come and meet the friend our host told us of last night. Helm of the Dobunni, I present Tribune Quintus Tiberius Martial.'

As if he knew how much Brighid craved his support at this critical moment, he went straight to her side and, with a noticeable disregard for convention, placed his arm around her waist and pulled her in to his side, not looking at her but at Helm, challenging, under the guise of an introduction, whatever thoughts he was harbouring. It was cleverly done, but to Brighid it was like a healing unguent over her heart, calming the soreness while transferring all responsibility to him.

She placed her hand on his, feeling the warmth of it spreading over her hip.

Unsmiling, Quintus nodded at Helm. 'Well met,' he said. 'Are you here on business, or pleasure?'

'Entirely for pleasure, sir. To make use of the bathing facilities and to see my wife. Perhaps to take her home with me.'

Brighid thought this rather strange when the reason for Dora's stay was to have her baby here in safety. But it was none of her business and Quintus appeared to find nothing to comment on. For the length of the garden, the men conversed amiably with Brighid clamped to her lover's side by his arm. Yet there was a tension she knew to be the result of this inevitable meeting for which nothing could have quite prepared her, and although she kept her eyes becomingly lowered, she knew without looking that Helm was puzzled and fascinated by the change in her, her refusal to acknowledge him, her sudden appearance here in his territory, and her relationship to the Tribune, whose presence had unsettled both him and Valens.

Their host talked loudly as if to prevent the conversation turning to other matters, and it was only when they merged with a throng of visitors near the atrium that, as she turned away, she caught a look from Helm that, as plain as spoken words, begged her for some moments in private. She blinked and looked away, responding to Quintus's hand on her waist. A private conversation would not be possible. Math had told her that they would kill him, but it seemed to her that both Helm and Valens were already aware that the guests in their midst were mixing *their* pleasures with some undisclosed business. Business that probably concerned them, too.

Her need for news about Math was her first priority. 'Has anyone seen anything?' she said as soon as they were alone.

Silently, they shook their heads.

'Oh, for pity's sake!' she cried. 'Why not? Has anyone been sent to town?'

'Florian and one of the guards went earlier,' Quintus said. 'They'll be back when they have something to report. The two lads are still looking. So is the other guard. Tullus has been looking, too, and you and Lucan have been searching, presumably with no success, and I have been pummelled black and blue by some heavy-handed imbecile who appears not to know the first thing about massage. It's the last time I shall let him anywhere near me. There, Princess. Does that answer your question?'

Brighid glared. 'Yes. Thank you. I'll send for some food.'

'I can't eat anything. I've been told to fast.'

In the brief silence, Tullus cleared his throat. 'Lucan and I will go to the guests' hall and eat there, if you'll excuse us.'

'Yes,' said Quintus, 'you go and enjoy some succulent ham served on a bed of—'

Lucan grasped his shoulder. 'Peace, man. It will be disgusting and we shall not enjoy one mouthful. We'll keep looking, Princess. Don't worry.'

'Don't worry,' she whispered as the door closed. 'Of *course* I'm worried.'

At home, if a man was missing, a search party

would have been dispatched immediately with orders not to return until he was found. Here, apparently, one must wait, be patient without worrying, pretend that nothing was amiss. Her brother was amiss—what could be more important than that?

The air between them vibrated with unspoken accusations of inefficiency and lack of motivation that she knew were unjust, for no one knew better than the Tribune how to handle problems of this kind, not with her father's rowdy methods but with caution. Yet her brother might, at this very moment, be suffering terribly, alone.

Quintus held out a hand. 'Come here, lass. Come and tell me what that Dobunni savage had to say when he saw you.'

She went into his arms with the merest show of reluctance, but no word was exchanged for some time, their mouths being otherwise engaged in satisfying their hunger for each other. But when he would have gone further, urgently pushing her gown off one shoulder, she protested, squirming away to avoid his hands. 'I cannot…cannot do this, my lord. Please stop.'

He stopped immediately with a sigh that understood the problem. 'Yes, I know, I'm an unfeeling brute. You've had a difficult morning, my Princess, and your mind is on other matters. I know. No need to explain.' Pulling her into his arms, he cradled her against him and pushed away a heavy screen of red hair to place a kiss on her forehead. 'Now, tell me about it. Have we baffled him, do you think?'

She told him what little there was to tell, about the graves that she and Tullus were sure were those of infants, though the evidence indicated as little for Watercombe's success in childbirth as for their standards of massage, which any Roman was well able to judge. Perhaps, they said, the quality of treatment at Watercombe did not deserve its high reputation, after all. When Quintus told her about his own experiences that morning and his agreement to spend that night at the temple, she was horrified at the danger. 'No,' she said firmly. 'You cannot. You *must* not, my lord.'

'Why? Because you'll miss me?'

'Because you'll be walking into a trap. Valens is already suspicious and so is Helm, and that kind of treatment is too open to abuse for them not to take advantage of it. The wrong drug, an overdose, a weak patient, and he can die. I know the kind of stuff they use, my lord: mandrake root, thorn apple, henbane and deadly nightshade, mugwort and opium. They mix them with wine to disguise the taste, and all it needs is an extra grain for a man to become insane. It's not just dreams they induce. The patient rambles and raves, and they have to hold him down. It can cause vomitting and…well, other things. You'll not know a thing about it until you wake up in a sweat. *If* you wake.' She was sitting ramrod straight, her face a picture of deep concern.

'You care. Don't you?' he said, stroking her arm.

'Of *course* I care! How can you doubt it?' she said, brushing off his hand.

'Rest easy. I have no intention of taking their concoctions. I shall pretend to, and I shall feign sleep, but I shall spend the night watching. I'd not take a draught from anyone but you.'

'Promise me. Don't let them dupe you. Or dope you, for that matter. Remember my portents. There's something wicked about this place, and now Math has disappeared. Who'll be next? Don't let it be you, my lord.' Taking hold of his sleeves, she shook him with an angry impatience, only half-believing that he could survive where others had failed.

'Hush, lass. It won't be. I'm flattered to know you're concerned for me.'

Then don't be. What would happen to me if I lost you, too?

'Oh, you great...*ox*!' she growled, struggling in his arms.

But the memory of their passionate night, of her initiation, and of the bliss that followed was still in both their thoughts, too recent to be quenched by the latest upsets, still simmering in spite of her protests. At the back of Brighid's mind was the blackest menace of the empty night ahead, a night she had thought would be theirs together, but which would now be spent alone in fear and longing. However confident he might be of surviving the night intact, she could not let him go like this, without the loving he so obviously craved.

Her struggles abated, and she bent herself into him, reaching up to link her arms around his neck, whispering sweet insults into his waiting mouth. 'Great...ox,' she murmured. 'Why should I be concerned for you? I helped to mend your leg only because I grew tired of your bad temper. And now you have me for one night, and then you leave me...'

'Oh, lass! Hush. I did not plan it that way,' he said, kissing her eyelids, her nose, her lips.

'How do *I* know that?' she whispered, teasing him with her green-jewel eyes.

He used actions rather than words to explain, understanding by the soft yielding of her body that her needs were as great as his, beneath her reticence. With his mouth still upon hers, he stooped to lift her higher into his arms and was delighted when her legs wrapped him, her body pushing against his aching member with only their tunics between. It was a blatant invitation he had not expected so soon in their relationship.

Blinded by the sudden torrent of passion that shook them to the soles of their feet, he supported her thighs and heard her moan with pleasure and anticipation, not knowing that his hands pressed upon the parts of her that can make a woman wild with eagerness. He felt her pulling frantically at the fabric separating them, felt the sudden heat of skin upon skin, her soft moistness opening for him, as ready as he was. He felt her lowering herself upon him without a trace of modesty, the rippling ecstasy of his entry and the delicious squirm as she settled, arching her torso in rapture, crying out for him to take her without delay.

Breathless with desire and almost savage in their intensity, they clung together, giving and taking equally in perfect unison, hearing only the ragged panting of cries and words, encouraging, approving, delighting. Then, as the oncoming rush of mindlessness overtook them too soon, he swung Brighid round to the wall to quicken the pace and to hold her hard against him until the blinding end, the explosive starburst that left them both shaking and trembling, laughing with exhilaration. It had taken no more than three minutes, but the fervour and spontaneity of those brief moments showed Quintus another side to the amazing woman in his arms that he had already suspected, the immense passion that extended into every part of her life. This woman would never become a passive victim of circumstance, not even though Fortune might be looking the other way. Still locked in their intimate embrace, he carried her to the couch, too breathless to speak, too overcome to do more than cling together and let roaming hands smooth brows and hair, their lips lapping up the laughter.

She wanted to plead with him not to go, to stay here with her. Her thumb brushed tenderly along his dark eyebrow. 'Be careful,' she whispered. 'Be on your guard. Those priests are professionals, remember.'

'So am I, sweetheart,' he murmured, taking her thumb and kissing it. 'Don't be concerned for me. With this to think on, I shall do nothing foolish, believe me. I'll be back in the morning.'

Florian and the guard returned from the town of Aquae Sulis later that afternoon with the disappointing news that Math had not visited the lodgings. His mysterious disappearance affected them all. Nor had there been any sighting of him at Watercombe, in spite of the searches of the seven others. If she had been allowed to follow her premonitions, Brighid would have packed her belongings and left immediately, but with Math still missing that was impossible. They would have to stay until he was found.

'Can't you demand to have the place searched?' Brighid said as the light began to fade. 'You have the authority. And what does it matter whether he's seen or not? Somebody's seen him, obviously.'

'Tomorrow,' Quintus said. 'If he doesn't appear by morning, I'll have the place turned inside out. This is getting ridiculous.'

Knowing he would keep his promise, Brighid had to be content.

Arranging to meet Brighid for dinner, Tullus and Lucan accompanied Quintus to the temple after their friendly bath, which sharpened their hunger, as usual, but served only as a source of irritation to the one who had agreed to fast. There was really no need, the men told him, if he did not intend to co-operate in the experience. But

Brighid knew better. They would smell food on his breath. There would be other signs, too, too delicate to explain. He had to be seen to be hungry and Quintus agreed with her.

In their apartment, Brighid collected her toilet kit and went with Florian to the women's baths where high-pitched laughter and squeals echoed round the vaulted ceilings, and the slap of sandals on wet tiles mingled with the clapping of palms upon clients' oily backs. The sight of a handsome young male slave in the women's bathhouse caused not the slightest concern, and Florian's natural discretion helped him to fade into the background until Brighid needed him, exactly like a maid.

There was a young female slave there, however, who was bold enough to ask him about the young man who had attended the Princess the night before, a dark-haired young man with the bent nose and soft eyes. He had indicated, she said, that he might be there again tonight.

Florian's aching heart shone through his eyes, and he was forced to swallow quite hard to keep his voice level. 'He's…er…gone missing,' he whispered, having neither the inclination nor the ability to hide his despair. 'Been missing since last night. You've not seen him?'

The girl, a pretty, short-haired, fair-skinned lass, turned even paler, chewing at her bottom lip. 'No,' she said, her blue-grey eyes clouding over with concern. 'Oh, *please*, beloved Sulis, don't let them…' Quickly, she placed the back of her hand to her mouth, but not before Florian had heard.

'Don't let them…what? Who are *they*? You know something.'

She shook her head. 'No, I don't. Not about your friend, anyway.'

'Who, then?'

'Young men disappear. That's all I know. Look,' she said, matching his pleading dark eyes with her blue ones, 'I shall get into trouble for talking, but I come here with my mistress every year and she warns us not to go anywhere alone, girls as well as boys.'

'Girls, too?'

'They don't disappear but, well…see for yourself.' She nodded towards a group of young women who had just entered the hot room swathed in white towels, one of whom he recognised. 'She was a slave here last year, and now look what's happened to her.'

'But that's Dora, the Lady Helena's friend.'

'The Lady Helena's *slave*, young man. They've

married her off because her mistress won't have her living here once she's had the baby.'

'Why not? Doesn't she like them?'

The girl rolled her eyes. *'Because,'* she whispered, 'it's her *husband's*.'

'Valens?'

'Shh! Yes, him,' she muttered, hardly moving her lips. 'So tell your mistress to watch her back. And her front.'

'I will. But are you telling me that Dora was *forced* to marry?'

Her frown was pitying. 'Where have *you* been all your life? Don't you have any women slaves in your house? Where'd you get the idea that a woman slave has any choice in the matter? You must know what happens when they have infants the owner doesn't want?'

'No. Tell me.'

'Up on the hill beyond the gardens there's a clearing in the trees, and row after row of tiny graves. Unmarked. They didn't all die naturally, but because they were not wanted by the father and his pals. All female slaves working here are used in the same way, like it or not. That one over there…' she indicated Dora with a tip of her head '…is one of the fortunate ones because she was a personal maid to her mistress. A husband was found for her. She'll be able to take her infant home.'

'Perhaps he fell for her. He must be a hero to take on another man's child.'

'Or perhaps he owes Valens a favour.'

'Yes, or the Lady Helena,' Florian said. 'I don't suppose you could find my friend, could you? I've looked everywhere I dare.'

'Is he your lover?' When Florian nodded, she continued, 'I thought so. It's all right, we only chatted to pass the time. He was not interested in me, only as someone to chat to. He's very nice.'

'Yes. Could you help? You might know other places to look.'

'Yes, I know lots of secret places.' She smiled, mischievously. 'I'll see what I can do. And don't ask me why they disappear. None of them have ever come back to say what happened, and, unless you come back to Watercombe year after year, you don't realise that it *is* happening. Slaves run off all the time and pilgrims collapse for all kinds of reasons.'

'In the temple? At night?'

'Oh, regularly. Why?'

'My master's there. Oh, it's all right, he's strong.'

'Your mistress is waving to you. Don't forget

your towel.' She held it to him as he stood, noticing his fine straight legs and muscular calves.

'Thank you. You're very pretty.'

She smiled, wondering what compliments he paid to his lover.

Florian's first impulse was to tell the Princess what he'd just learnt about the terrible fate of slaves' infants, wrenched from their mothers' arms like so much detritus left over from men's lust. The girl was right. He had lived a sheltered life as the Tribune's masseur and what he had heard sickened him to the stomach, wrinkling his nose in disgust at the way men treated vulnerable females, devoid of any feeling or responsibility. Dora was indeed fortunate to have been spared, for whatever reason. But the Princess was in a hurry, scarcely noticing Florian's silence as being in any way different from his earlier melancholy, so the chance to speak did not come and Florian had to resign himself to waiting until she would stand still and listen.

There was also his need to inform her about the strange disappearance of men like Max, but what was there to tell the Princess except that it was no new occurrence at Watercombe? How would that help? Max had not been in the temple, and not for one moment did he believe that his master was in danger of collapsing there overnight. No one had discussed with him, Florian, exactly what the temple experience involved, so there was no reason for him to be more alarmed for the Tribune than he was for his beloved Max.

The route from the bath-house to the rear of the guests' apartments was the one Brighid had taken to the laundry the day before, past a series of smaller rooms and curtained cubicles where perfumes mingled and wafted along the corridor and lamps flickered in the draught. As the two people most committed to finding Math, his sister and his lover, Brighid and Florian found it mutually excusable to ignore caution and to push aside a curtain here and there, just in case a figure reclining on a masseur's couch might be Math, drugged. Or worse.

One room, slightly larger than the others, had a single lamp burning on a ledge, an open wax tablet and stylus on a table, an open basket-work container beside it and another one beyond, closed with a leather strap. 'Keep guard while I take a look,' Brighid said, not needing to explain.

'Be quick, *domina*,' said Florian. 'Someone is still working here.'

The open basket was half-full of beeswax candles, rolls of gauze and linen bags of ingredients that Brighid easily identified by their perfume: frankincense, musk and spikenard. She was just about to unbuckle the strap of the other container when Florian ducked his head under the curtain. '*Domina!* Quick!' he whispered.

It was too late. No sooner had she stood up than the curtain was rattled to one side to reveal Valens holding Florian by the scruff of his neck, pulling him inside and steering him towards the wall. 'Stay there, whelp,' he said. 'Princess. How can I help you? Is it perfumes you require?'

For the first time, Brighid became aware of her appearance since leaving the bath-house, scantily dressed ready to prepare for dinner, her hair damp and tumbled, her skin glowing against the gold collar and earrings. Her expression of defiance was meant to hide her acute embarrassment. She had not expected anyone to see her like this, least of all Valens. 'Thank you, no. I have to admit that my curiosity gets the better of me sometimes. The curtains make these little places so easily accessible, don't they? Now, I hope you'll excuse me. I must dress for dinner.'

'Plenty of time, Princess. I also have an insatiable curiosity to find out what is concealed behind fabric coverings. In fact, my curiosity has plagued me ever since we met.'

'Perhaps another time, sir. If you wouldn't mind…?'

But Valens had no intention, now he had her alone, of releasing her so easily, and he stood squarely before her only an arm's length away while the backs of her legs pressed against the open basket, preventing her from moving. Over the man's wide shoulders she could see Florian's scared eyes staring at her before looking sideways to find an escape, if only she could hold the man's attention. 'I'm sorry you have been plagued, sir. I assure you, there's nothing more to me than meets the eye. Is that what you meant?' she said.

Slowly, with feline stealth, Florian moved towards a curtain on the side wall that appeared to connect this chamber to the next one. And, while she kept her eyes on those of Valens, plotting their insulting journey over every detail of her body they could find, she cursed herself for her stupidity for allowing this predator the chance he'd been waiting for to question her without interference. She steeled herself for his questions, determined to show no warmth, to reply courteously and to give him no opening for a move on her, if he should be so foolish. But he was a man who abused his wife, and who probably had as few morals as her late father. And he declined to answer her question. 'You were searching for something, Princess?'

'I am a healer, sir. The scents of sandalwood and frankincese drew me in. Is this the room used by the aromatherapist?'

'A healer, you say. And what more are you to the Tribune, I wonder? His slave, that's obvious. Captured, were you?'

'I am no slave, sir!' Foolishly, she swallowed his bait and saw the resulting smile in his cold eyes. 'No man owns me,' she added, hoping this might explain things.

The smile stayed, however. 'Ah, but that's always going to be a problem, isn't it? A woman like you should always *belong* to a man, preferably one who can offer her a permanent home with all the luxuries due to her rank. Does the Tribune offer that? Has he made you an offer yet? Can he protect you against danger while he's busy with his tax investigations? He *is* a Provincial Procurator, isn't he? When he's not taking the cure, that is.'

'Should you not be directing such questions to the Tribune himself, sir? We've hardly known each other long enough to talk about the future.'

'Then let's talk about the past, Princess. Did

you actually get to meet our friend Helm when he was up in the north?'

She felt the blood drain from her face, sending a cold shiver of fear across her scalp. He knew, but how much had Helm told him? 'I do not know your friend Helm,' she said. 'We have never spoken.' It was the truth. They had not spoken and she did not *know* him. His offer had been made to her father.

So, she thought, since he had made no reference to any offer of marriage made by Helm, he had not been told of it. Which meant that Helm had gone to speak to her father for reasons the Tribune had given, for contributions to an uprising of tribes against the Emperor. Helm had used his offer of marriage as a screen for a more important matter in which Valens was presumably concerned, since he knew about the visit.

She had seen how a man's eyes could darken with desire, but this man's undisguised lust was written in every line of his face, on the tip of his tongue that licked at the corner of his mouth, on his nostrils that flared like a stallion with a mare. Compared to the Tribune, this man resembled a primitive wild boar with no control over his savage instincts. No wonder Helena Coronis sought help from the sacred temple of Sulis, where he was not there to see. What had she ever seen in the man except some kind of security?

He had made no move towards her and she knew it was because he believed that Florian was still in the room with them, listening to every word, recording every movement. Once he discovered his absence, he would know his time to be limited.

'Which reminds me to ask you, sir,' she said, 'why your friend Helm was visiting my father and why he chose to deny it yesterday? You are obviously in his confidence.'

As if he resented the change of subject, his slight frown and the quick shake of his head came together. 'Contact with other heads of tribes, I suppose. He'd not want to admit it in front of a Roman Tribune and his sidekicks, would he, in case it was misconstrued as conspiracy. I expect your father was partial to a little conspiracy now and then, Princess? Chieftains usually are, aren't they?'

'If you mean against the state, sir, I think not. He had enough on his hands fighting local battles to bother his head with national conspiracies. He was never one for giving money away unless it would benefit him personally.'

'Is that so? Then you might like to share a few private words with my friend Helm, Princess. I can arrange it for you.'

'I think not. Your friend is a married man. It would not be seemly and the Tribune would not agree to it.'

'And do you do everything he asks?' When she hesitated, his eyes strayed again to the gold around her neck, then further down to her breasts as if they were bared to him. 'You hesitated, Princess. That's good. I trust you will keep this lad's mouth firmly shut on what he sees and hears.' He glanced over his shoulder to where Florian ought to have been. 'We don't want…' Swinging round, he uttered an oath before turning back to Brighid, his eyes narrowed dangerously. 'You knew!' he purred. 'Well done. Another time, perhaps. Eh?'

There was no need for a reply to his implied suggestion, for the clatter of sandals on tiles could be heard approaching, and the murmur of voices asking which one, and where. Turning on his heel, Valens threw aside the curtain just as the corridor filled with men, facing Tullus and Lucan with a hastily assumed smile of surprise that fooled no one. 'Ah, my friends, you've come to spoil our discussion. What a pity. We were arguing the properties of the hot spring that people insist on drinking when they'd be better off bathing in it. But it's time to eat, Princess, and I've kept you. Do forgive me. Enjoy your meal.' He bowed to

Brighid, inviting her to leave his room to suggest that it was she who had intruded on him, not the other way round.

Brushing past him, she felt his heat, wrinkling her nose at the odour of his lecherous sweat, and she wished there had been time for her to return to the bath-house to wash away the memory of his deeply intrusive eyes. There had never been a time, she told herself, when she had been more grateful for an interruption, or when she had longed for Quintus more. Asked if she was all right, she could only nod her head. But Tullus felt her shaking as her hand slipped through the crook of his arm, and Lucan could see by her pale green stare and white cheeks that words would come later, when wine would moisten her dry mouth.

Chapter Eleven

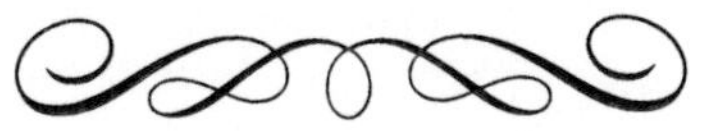

Lucan helped himself to another spoonful of succulent vegetables. 'Right,' he said, 'so now we know where we stand.'

'Where?' said Tullus, laying down his knife. He'd carried it with him since he was a lad: horn-handled and embellished with silver.

'Well,' said Lucan, 'our host now knows we're from the tax office, doesn't he?'

'He knew that before.'

'Now he's certain of it. I don't know what difference it makes, but it might. And for another thing, Helm has told him about his visit to the Princess's father. So why, I wonder, did Helm bother to deny it?'

'Because I refused to recognise him,' said Brighid.

'It also indicates,' said Lucan, choosing not to follow that line, 'that Valens is involved with

Helm's recruiting conspiracies in some way. What is it that Helm needs for his revolutionary schemes?'

'Money and men,' said Tullus. 'I expect.'

Florian had been invited to dine with them, to reward him for his help and to console him. He had been silent until now. 'I have something to tell you, my lords,' he said. He had lost his appetite, and he seemed lost without Quintus, too, and his talk with the girl at the baths had deeply upset him, as had Brighid's constant unavailability. So he told them what the girl had said and saw their knives being laid aside, one by one, their food left to grow cold while frowns reappeared and faces paled as the sordid facts emerged about Valens. The information about the disappearance of young men hit Florian and Brighid especially hard, filling their eyes with tears while Tullus and Lucan were stunned into silence.

'Why did we come here?' she whispered. 'I knew it was not good. I should have listened to myself. Those graves, Tullus, are where Dora's child would be destined if she'd not married Helm, so there must be some good in him.'

'Yes,' said Lucan with some cynicism, 'and one must ask what inducement he needed to marry a slave girl who's carrying his friend's child. But what interests me most is this disappearance theory. Who are these young men, exactly? Are they all pilgrims needing treatment, given dangerous potions to drink?'

'My lord is in the temple,' Florian said. 'Will they try to poison him?'

Brighid laid a hand over his arm. 'He won't be collapsing, Florian. He doesn't intend to drink anything they give him. Don't be concerned. He'll have the place searched tomorrow, if that girl can't tell us where to find him.'

She had found some comfort in sharing her recent alarming experience with her friends, which had reinforced the fact that her position as the Tribune's healer was indeed a precarious one, since it had never been discussed or defined. Her blithe brave comment about living in the present had been enough, since her capture, to keep her mind focused. But now her relationship with the Tribune had shifted and, whether it pleased him or not, plans would have to be made for her future. If marriage to her was not a possibility for a man of the Tribune's rank, then perhaps he would return her to her elder brother, the new chieftain.

That night, the bleak thoughts, and the disturbing ones, kept her awake for hours while her hand strayed into the cool space where he should have been, her mind tumbling and rioting through the lessons of love he had taught her that day.

In one of the narrow cubicles that encircled the Temple of Dreams, Quintus sat on the edge of his low bed to search with bare feet for his sandals. The horsehair mattress was obviously not intended for any sleep other than drug-induced, and though Quintus had spent the night in some very strange places as a soldier, he resented paying through the nose for the use of smelly pillows and two worn blankets. A small lamp burned on the table beside the bed, and an empty beaker, the contents of which had been poured down a wide crack between the wall and the tiled floor that a visiting rat would easily have negotiated. He had sent back the first drink of yellowish wine, complaining that there were stains on the rim. But after an hour of sacrificial rites and the mysterious ablutions of white-robed assistants, priests' intonements and plodding rituals, perhaps they thought that such details would not be noticed above the pangs of hunger.

Eventually he and the other ten inmates had retired to their cubicles, stifling yawns, later to be visited several times by the aides who remarked loudly that his sleep appeared to be tranquil and that perhaps he ought to have been given something stronger. Sounds reaching him from the next cubicle told him that his elderly neighbour was putting on a better performance, mumbling and yelping in the throes of some terrible nightmare. He was also visited by the two large white hounds that had played a picturesque part in the earlier ritual, sniffing at him but leaving the curtain with a space through which he could see the temple lamps burning on the altar. Constant movements prompted him to investigate and now, sitting on his bed, he watched a man being carried from a cubicle on the opposite side, the aides returning empty-handed moments later. The transfer was so silent and smooth that Quintus assumed he had simply been moved to another bed.

Still groping blindly for his sandals, he realised he would have to get down on his hands and knees to retrieve them from some dark corner. They were at the far end, bringing with them a thick roll of filth that he shook off in disgust and pushed back out of sight. Then, to satisfy a sudden curiosity, he took the lamp down to floor level to see further under the bed where black lumps, the detritus of years, lay hidden. Holding his breath, he reached under to grab the largest piece, hoping it was not a dead rat, but determined to use this as evidence of the squalid conditions, so different from the spotless apartment prepared by the Lady Helena's staff.

Clambering back up, he shone the lamp's light upon the filthy trophy and saw that he was holding a stiff leather boot of a style quite different from his own, but astonishingly familiar to him. And when he blew off the top layer of dust, it seemed to prove what he already knew, that this had belonged to no other than his missing colleague and childhood friend, Alexius Tito Gaditanus. Other than Alexius, who had his own way of doing things, no one he knew had ever worn army boots of this style with civilian dress, for they were too heavy to look elegant. The upper was completely enclosed and cut with ties that extended from the same piece of leather, threading through slits in the ankle flaps. One could never lose one's laces or suffer from cold feet, Alexius had said, ignoring all the teasing.

Quintus saw that his hand was shaking. *Alexius, my friend, where are you? By Jove's breeches, I shall tear this place apart till I find you. I swear it.*

At home, Brighid had been used to venturing out at night to observe the moon and stars or to wait for the dawn to break over the hills. Her father had never forbidden her that kind of communication, for he had understood its importance to her. But now, both guards stood at the doors and she was confined as surely as she'd been in the cell at Eboracum, with not even her maid for company. She could, of course, have had Florian to stay with her, but he had agreed to take his misery and weepy eyes to Tullus and Lucan's room for the night. He had been severely disturbed by what he'd been told at the bath-house that evening, and although together they had decorated their favourite shrines with flowers, for it was the Kalends of May, he would not be comforted.

At home, she mused, the first day of May was called Beltain, the night when all the young men and women would be dancing under the night sky, cavorting round the fires that would invoke fertility for crops and cattle, running off into the shadowy woods to make love, though nothing like as good as her recent experience she was sure. If only he could have been here now to do it all again.

A sound reached her from beyond the door to the terrace. Someone was whispering. Instantly alert, she sat up in bed, her ears straining to recognise the voice. Was it Valens demanding admittance? Like a hare in danger, she leapt out of bed and, without waiting to see who had opened the door just wide enough to slip through, she hurled herself at the tall figure whose head was hooded with the end of his toga. She heard the breath whoosh from his lungs and a sound like *hah!* that might have been a laugh, then felt the painful iron of his forearms blocking the rain of blows she hammered against him in the dark.

Wildly, frantically, sure of nothing except that this intruder ought not to be there, she writhed and kicked as his arms closed round her and lifted her as if she was weightless, and it was only then, when she felt the familiar tilt against him and breathed in the cold scent of the night air on his skin, that she knew she was mistaken. It was not Valens.

The dam of her relief, resentment, fear and frustration that had been deepening since yesterday burst upon him as if he were the one responsible for it and, instead of allowing his greeting, she scorched him with her indignation, calling him every insulting name in her own tongue, of which thankfully he could only guess at the meaning. Not only was he verbally assaulted but physically, too, for once he had tossed her on to the bed and tried to hold her there, her fists came back to pummel at his chest and shoulders, her teeth to nip, her heels to drum against his wrapped legs. Panting with anger at her own helplessness, at his ability to govern her newly discovered desires, his control of her nights and days, liberty and restraint, she did everything in her limited power to pay him back for every uncomfortable change he had made to her life since her so-called release from capture.

'Don't you think you can…' she railed at him '…walk in here any time…'

'Hush, lass. You can calm down now.'

'…of the day…or night…and just…'

'I can, barbarian.' Taking her thick plait of hair in one hand, he closed in on her, stopping her tirade with a kiss that left her weakened and too breathless to continue. 'Now,' he said, 'can I get a word in edgeways?'

'No,' she whispered. In the darkness, she felt his smile on her cheek.

'What, then?'

No reply.

'Is this how tribal women greet their lovers on the eve of Beltain?'

'Remind me,' she retorted, 'what am I at this moment? Tribal woman or Roman or Briganti? Slave, healer, mistress…?'

'Mine,' he growled, 'to do with as I please.'

'I see. So you came back to tell me so, did you?'

'Lass,' he whispered. 'Are you not glad to see me?'

With a sob, she threw her arms about his neck, burying her fingers deep into his tousled hair. 'Have I not just *shown* you, Roman? Do you think I greet all my lovers like this?' Steering his lips towards hers and slanting her face, she kissed him the way she'd done in those dreaming hours of restlessness when she'd had only memories to remind her, this time with the full length of his body over hers and his hands already searching over her skin.

At some stage, he paused to unwind the long toga that threatened to submerge them in its layers, coming back to her naked and warm, to make her whine with excitement at the masterful sweep of his hands that lingered, in tune with her cries, playing her like a harp. Once again, every part of her took on a new meaning, awakened to new sensations by his touch, by his lips and tongue. Her skin came alive even to the light brush of his hair that caressed her eyelids, the soft touch of his ears across her lips, the rough unshaven chin that met her breast. There were other ways of doing this, he had told her but, for her, the tender weight of his body over hers was the best and sweetest experience imaginable, the delicious waiting for him to move into her that provoked inexplicable contradictions of possession and permission, of being taken, and of wanting to be taken. Yet not once during their loving had he implied that she had no choice or that she was not being considered enough. Unlike that time in the bath-house when he had chased and caught her, there was no part of this episode that she did not welcome and want more of.

In spite of her earlier passion, she was greedy for the kisses she had missed. The loving that had been made brief by yesterday's urgency was now lengthened by her need of his comforts, taking her mind into a void of sensations and well away from the evening's dangers, of which he knew nothing. Then, when her body trembled with desire and her cries pleaded for release, he slid into her with a moan that revealed how much she had tested his discipline. 'Oh…woman!' he whispered. 'Forgive me. I cannot be gentle.'

'Yes,' she breathed into his ear, 'so be ungentle with your woman, my lord.'

'But you're still new.'

'No,' she teased. 'I'm vastly experienced. And

it's Beltain night. A night for wildness. For abandonment, not gentleness.'

In her innocence, she had not realised that light-hearted banter could be a part of something so intensely serious, nor was this unfamiliar side of him anything less than endearing and exciting, when his usual demeanour was authoritative, and more laconic than chatty. She felt the surge of emotion rise up, closing her eyes as the power of it reached her heart, confirming what she already knew, that this was love, no less. To live without him, after this, would break her heart.

His lovemaking took her by storm, matching her mood with every vigorous thrust, timed to her timing, aware of her pulsating hunger, filling her with his completeness. Hardly expecting that she might achieve a climax again, as she had yesterday, he was jubilant when her cries of encouragement told him otherwise and, as he responded, their fervour rose to heights he had never experienced before with any woman, intoxicating and rapturous, utterly fulfilled.

'Quintus?' she said, stroking the thick hair above his ear.

'Mmm?'

'Are you alive?'

'More than alive. I'm with the gods.'

'Can you return, please? I need you.'

He turned his head to look at her in the first light of dawn that washed across the room. 'Do you, Princess? For what?'

'To tell me why you came back.'

Laughing quietly, he rolled with her in his arms, raking his hand through the mane of her hair that lay in tatters over her face, recognising the barely disguised need in her question to which a teasing answer would not suffice. 'I came back…' he said, kissing her damp throat. *Because I could not stand that bogus nonsense a moment longer, because I don't have time to discuss non-existent dreams all morning, because I need to find Math and Alexius, and because I need to speak with Valens, and possibly to arrest Helm, too.* 'Because,' he said, 'the thought of you being here alone, naked and desirable, was more than I could bear, little savage. And you would have torn me to shreds for my pains. Wouldn't you?'

'Brigantian women are taught to fight, my lord.'

'Yes, well, it's time Brigantian women were taught to distinguish between friend and foe, or they might all kill their husbands.'

'It was dark and I didn't expect you.'

'Obviously not. Who else did you think would get past the guard?'

'Valens.'

He sat up, looking down at her. 'Tell me what you're talking about,' he said, suddenly very grim.

So she did, then wished she had not for, by the time she had finished, he was washing himself down and, if she had hoped for some reassurance from him of a very specific nature, she saw that he had other matters on his mind that claimed priority. Guiltily, she admitted that to find her brother was one of them.

He had, in fact, been more angry than solicitous, having just experienced how well she could make her displeasure known. Unfortunately, until they had Math, they could not leave the place. And until he had found out exactly where Alexius was, he could hardly go and strangle Valens, which is what he'd like to have done.

A solution to one of these problems came unexpectedly at dawn soon after the arrival of the two young men whose task it was to prepare their master's clothes and to see him dressed presentably, to tidy the room and to collect food from the kitchen. Assuming that the shadowy figures in the doorway to the rear corridor brought the food for which he had been longing, Quintus became impatient with their delay. 'Come on!' he yelled.

'Bring it in, for pity's sake!' Then he looked more closely, recognising Florian with an attractive fair-haired girl who, between them, supported the drooping form of a young man as far as the nearest chair before lowering him carefully into it.

With a cry, Brighid flew to his side, kneeling at his feet and gathering him into her arms. 'Oh, my dearest! Oh, you're safe! Thank the gods. Where have you been? What happened? Who did this? Oh…your head.'

Math's dark hair was matted with blood on one side, and one eye had swollen too much to be of any use. He was covered, however, with a thick layer of dust, and the girl explained that she had found him tied up in a sack near the furnace that fed the hypercaust, the system of flues underneath the floors of the bath-house.

Quintus was intrigued, but suspicious. 'How did you know to look there?' he said, thinking that he might know the answer.

'It's warm down there.' She grinned. 'They take wood down there from the estate and there are sacks to sit on. And nobody looks there at night.' She glanced meaningfully at Math. 'But there was another young man down there with him, and he's only just waking up in my room.'

The young man in the Temple of Dreams being carried out, last night.

'You know it well, do you?' said Quintus.

'Oh, yes, sir. I know the whole place well by now. I can show it to you.'

They had been shown the furnaces and the hypercaust during their tour, but there had been no sacks of wood there then, only piles of it. 'Well done,' he said. 'Thank you. We are in your debt.' He gave orders, and soon Math's poor cramped body was being stripped and washed, his head cleaned, salved and bandaged, his hunger and thirst lessened by his sister's motherly feeding and Florian's tenderness. Tidied up, he began to look more like the Math they knew, though what he had to tell them gave him centre stage for longer than he'd ever had before.

Producing the evidence as they pulled off his sweaty tunic, he did his best to smile. 'Here it is, look! Bridie's bracelet.'

'But that's the one I offered to Brigantia at the sacred well,' she cried.

'Yes, love. And somebody retrieved it and brought it here. It was in a basket full of gold jewellery, still wet with the water caught in the cavities.'

'*Is* it yours?' said Quintus.

'Certainly it is. There's no mistake. But *why*? And how?'

To have one's valuable offering removed from a sacred well, the contents of which belonged to the goddess alone, was an act of abomination. Anyone who stole objects bearing the prayers of the supplicant would be fortunate to stay alive, if he were discovered. Brighid was shocked and sickened. The goddess would be very angry about it.

Quintus had a theory with which Tullus and Lucan, nodding their heads, agreed. 'Valens has the contract to service the baths,' he said, 'so it looks as if he's been sending his men in there at night with their toolkits and brushes, and no one ever asks what they get up to. It must be the easiest thing in the world to sift through the votive offerings and pick out the best gold pieces, leaving a few coins in place along with the pewter and silver. Once he's got them back here, they can be reworked into bullion.'

'What?' asked the girl.

'Coins,' Tullus said, 'to pay taxes with.'

'Oh, you found some of those, too, didn't you, Math?'

'Plenty,' he said. 'But wasn't the Lady Helena

there at the shrine too, Bridie? Did she offer something?'

Brighid nodded. 'I believe she did. So if what she offered was brought here with my bracelet, and Valens sees it, he'll know she's been there. And she didn't want him to. Remember, Tullus?'

'Don't worry,' he said. 'He's not likely to recognise his wife's jewellery.'

'All the same, didn't we ought to warn her? She might wish to retrieve it.'

'That's a tricky one,' he said. 'Telling a woman what her husband is up to is rarely a good idea. It's obvious she doesn't know about his thefts or she'd not have gone there, would she? But what I want to know is whether Valens is using forged coin to pay his taxes, or is he using it for some other purpose?'

'Ahem!' said Quintus. 'I think it's time we allowed our young friend to return to her mistress.'

'Yes, I'd better go. She'll be asking for me.'

'Then listen to me, young lady. What you have done for us was extremely courageous, but it was also dangerous. And you have a young man in your room about whom questions will be asked.'

The girl smiled, shyly. 'Not for the first time, sir.'

'Nevertheless, I shall have two of my men escort

you back to your mistress and they will take him away. I cannot have her chastising you over this.' What he meant, but did not say, was that he didn't want Valens to make enquiries about her or the young man.

'Thank you, sir. My mistress intends us to return home tomorrow.'

It was as if she'd read his mind. 'I'm relieved to hear it. We are all in your debt. Will you accept a small gift from me, as thanks?'

'Indeed, sir. Thank you.'

Florian, Math and Brighid hugged her, asking her name, thanking her, and Quintus gave her two silver *denarii*, which, he told her, was bullion. He commanded an escort for the young lady, which pleased her just as much as the money.

'Other purposes?' said Quintus, resuming the conversation.

'Well,' said Tullus, holding out his beaker for more wine, 'what he gleans from the shrine would hardly be enough to fill several chests with coin, would it? Maybe this has nothing to do with taxes. Maybe it's more to do with payment for our friend Helm's shady ventures, for instance.'

'If that's the case,' said Quintus, 'what does he offer Valens in return?'

'Protection?' said Math.

The others shrugged. It was hard to know what Helm had that Valens did not already have. 'Have you no idea who attacked you at the goldsmith's workshop?' said Brighid. 'Didn't you see anything?'

'Not a thing,' said Math, touching his bandage. 'but whoever it was knows how to take a man by surprise and to hit where it matters.'

'And was strong enough,' said Lucan, 'to carry you all the way to the bath-house and put you in a sack. Could be anybody.'

'Then perhaps it's time we took another look,' said Quintus. 'If there was another man imprisoned there, who knows what else is there besides.'

Overwhelmed with relief at Math's reappearance, alive and well, Brighid could see no reason why they need stay any longer in this dangerous place where the owner committed such terrible crimes. Understanding the message of her own intuition, its warnings and black-shadowed predictions, she knew that to stay would be to invite more trouble. Her time spent alone with Quintus had brought an unimaginable joy that had begun to fill her life with new emotions, new sensations and longings for more time with him, away from talk of taxes and abductions, thefts and murdered infants. But now the Tribune had placed her well down on his list of prime concerns, as men can do, and when they were alone she put it to him that they might return to Aquae Sulis. His reply was predictable. 'No, Princess. Not yet. There are things I have to pursue.'

'But it's dangerous here. For all of us.'

'Then perhaps I should send you back, until I've done.'

'No! No, forget it. I shall stay as long as you're here. We ought to hide Math, shouldn't we? They must not know he's been returned to us.'

'I shall arrange for him to stay in Tullus and Lucan's room. It's plenty big enough and he'll be guarded well. Florian will go with you to the baths.'

'Can I come with you, my lord? To your treatment?' she asked.

'I think that would be appropriate.'

So, she thought, we have come to being appropriate now, after a night of fierce loving and not a wink of sleep. What am I doing here, exactly? Like a spark to dry brushwood, her indignation flared out of hand by his lordly attitude towards her offer.

'Do you *really*?' she cried, loudly. 'Well, let me tell you, my lord, that if a Brigantian Princess had offered to accompany *me* to watch with bated breath while I perform some stupid exercises that I don't need, I would do more than think it was *appropriate*, I would consider myself honoured. I don't make offers of that sort too often. On reflection, I think I shall go out and count the carp in the pools. That *must* be marginally more interest—' The tirade had taken her as far as the door, but she was caught before her hand could reach the latch, and the word 'interesting' was cut off by the whoosh of air from her lungs as Quintus closed in on her, more like an antagonist than a lover.

He turned her to face him. It had not been her intention to anger him, but to shame him into admitting her value. It was, after all, what her father had drummed into her since she could remember. She raised a hand to push at him, but he took her wrist and pushed it back against the door, his face towering above her, dark eyes narrowed, commanding her attention. 'Enough!' he growled. 'Simmer down, woman. Jove's balls, but you fly off the handle faster than a flea. Listen to me. I *know* this business has unsettled you. It's all happened faster than any of us expected, even me. But if you want to stay here, you're going to have to calm down and do as I say. The last thing I need at the moment is a woman to—'

'You needed a woman last night, Roman. *And* yesterday, too.' Her voice shook as a tear forced its way from one eye.

He drew a deep breath, remembering. Then his tone softened and the grip upon her relaxed, his hand sliding to brush away the offending tear. 'Don't weep, lass,' he said. 'That's not what I meant. You know it isn't.'

'I'm *not* weeping,' she croaked. 'You're hurting me, that's all.'

'And you think I'd forgotten your worth. Well, I haven't. You led us to Watercombe, didn't you? That's been worth weeks of searching.'

'*Thank you.* I'm relieved to know I've saved you some time, my lord. You've already shown me how important that is to you.'

He knew from the bold stare of her eyes exactly what she referred to, but he would not be drawn into that discussion, seeing how they could both be wounded by it. He also saw that she was not inclined to be mollified, for he had not been able to conceal his natural urgency to move things on. 'We shall not spend a moment longer in this place than we have to,' he said. 'And you will obey me as the others do, Princess, or be sent back to town.' He must have guessed at the disobedient retort behind her stony expression, his next move being to prevent it with a gagging kiss that left her gasping for breath, meant to reinforce his mastery over her as much as to curb her retaliation. He could not have known how he had merely fuelled her resentment by his high-handedness which, although appropriate in his dealings with subordinates, was hardly consistent with the equality they had shared so recently.

It was unfortunate that Quintus expected her to understand his methods, and equally unfortunate that, having lived until now the life of a sheltered aristocrat, Brighid was still sadly innocent of the ways of men like him. 'You will accompany me to the gymnasium,' he told her, watching the violet-tinged eyelids slowly open, 'and let's have an end to this nonsense.'

She glared without deigning to answer.

Oh, yes, Tribune. Do let's have an end to this nonsense.

But before they could reach the gymnasium where, he assumed, the next phase of his healing would begin, they were intercepted by Helena Coronis bringing with her a whiff of perfume on the hem of her flowing linen chiton. A long scarf swathed her head and neck and hung almost to the ground, its folds not quite covering the glossy brown hair above her brow and the gold pendant earrings. A large golden brooch shaped like a crescent moon sat upon one shoulder, making Brighid wonder if this was a good time to tell her about the item she might have lost.

She was forestalled by the Lady Helena's greeting and by her immediate revelation that the temple priest had been to see her concerning the sudden disappearance of the Tribune last night. And while she was relieved to see that he was still with them, she thought that the priest would appreciate an explanation. If the Tribune would be so kind.

They strolled along to the spacious atrium while Quintus made out a convincing excuse concerning the unhygenic conditions that were some way from what he was expecting. Did the Lady Helena *know* of the state of the beds they were supposed to sleep in? The bed linen? The filth? He had no wish to make a fuss, but he had been forced to abandon that particular treatment. He could show her the dust-covered boot, now in his possession, if she required evidence. And before she could demur, he had sent Florian off to get it and bring it back, not thinking, as Brighid did, that this was not the best time to launch, however politely, into a criticsm of the lady's business.

She saw the deep flush of embarrassment that came only moments before the beautiful sorrowful eyes began to swim in tears, the head turned away, the trembling hand that came up to hold her scarf. When no response came from that direction, Quintus turned to look and was met with Brighid's accusing green eyes daring him to say one more word.

He blinked, then led the way to a long marble bench set into a corner beneath the projecting roof where the rattle of a fountain in the centre of the pool would conceal their discussion. Chivalrously, he held out a hand to her as she sat, beckoning to a nearby slave to bring water and beakers, arranging himself on the bench at an angle to hers.

From the lady's other side, Brighid attempted to comfort her, understanding only too well how close to desperation she was. 'It's nothing,' she whispered. 'As a soldier, the Tribune must have slept in some...' She stopped with a sigh. That analogy was not going to help. Brighid poured the water when it arrived, handing a beaker to their hostess first, making the most of the respite as they sipped.

Florian returned, dangling the disgusting boot

by one of its leather thongs before placing it directly in front of Helena Coronis, quite unprepared for his master's displeasure. 'Pick it up, *imbecillus*!' he snapped. 'Bring it here.'

'Is that it?' whispered Helena Coronis, following its progress with her eyes. 'Where did you find it, Tribune?'

With a quick glance at Brighid for approval, he turned it over to look at the sole. 'I found it beneath the bed in my cubicle. I wonder if anyone might know the whereabouts of the owner who must have walked off wearing only one boot.'

'I presume,' she said, 'that you did not accept the drink you were offered. There is a limit, you see, to the help I can give you. I would have warned you not to, but my husband made it impossible for me to reach you, or even send a message.'

Quintus glanced about him before answering. 'Is Valens likely to see us in conversation, my lady?'

'Not today. He went out on business early this morning. I never know when he'll return. Tonight? Tomorrow?'

'And your steward?'

'He's a good man. He's been with me since my first marriage.'

'And the priests?'

'Are my husband's men. They're nothing to do with me, Tribune.'

'Yet I seem to remember, my lady, that you recommended the temple and the dream-interpreters to us when you showed us round.'

'Then you will also remember that my youngest daughter Carina was with us at the time. She tells my husband everything.'

'Because he asks her?'

'Yes, because her asks her. They're very close.' She had said nothing so far that was directly critical of her husband, yet Quintus and Brighid were in no doubt that she was telling them as clearly as she dared that all was not well at Watercombe under Valens's supervision. That she was deeply afraid of him was also very obvious. Less apparent was the notion that she was letting slip information that could damage him although, as she had said, there was a limit.

Quintus thought, however, that she might be persuaded to show a more positive disloyalty. 'Am I correct in thinking that you've seen this boot before, my lady?' he said. 'On one of your guests, perhaps?'

She needed no second look at it. 'Yes,' she whispered. Her hand still shook as she sipped at the water, showing him the purple bruises on her wrist as the fabric fell away. 'Yes, I know who it belongs to, Tribune. The man wore them under his toga, and I remember thinking how unusual, though I think he might have been the kind of man who lived by his own rules.'

'His name, lady? Do you remember?'

'Alex, was it?'

'Alexius?'

'Yes...*yes*, that's it! A year ago, it was.'

'And did you warn *him* not to drink the priest's brew?'

The deep breath she took emerged as a sigh that could be heard above the noisy fountain, and her reply was slow to follow as if the words needed preparing. If the answer had been yes, they knew it would have come immediately. 'It's not as you think, Tribune,' she said, still guarded.

'Lady, you may already have guessed why I am here with my two assistants,' Quintus said, leaning forwards to rest his arms along his thighs. 'It would assist us greatly if you could tell us what is going on here at this beautiful place. It once belonged to you and your first husband, but now it appears to have grown out of your control, and beyond your wishes. We have already discovered things about Valens that are highly illegal, enough to remove him from your life for ever. For your co-operation in providing us with more evidence of his activities, I can guarantee that you would not be prosecuted. Now is your chance to put matters straight. Think of the safety of your daughters, too.'

He had touched a raw nerve there. Fortunately, there were few guests about and no one except them to hear the sob of anguish or to see the shaking of her shoulders. 'You saw,' she said, gulping back the tears, 'how he looks at her, my darling Clodia, and what he threatens to do when he wishes to hurt me. A gladiatrix, of all things, for my lovely girl…and he *could* do it, too. She would do whatever he wanted. She worships him, and he knows it, and plays upon it. I'm so afraid for her.'

'Then you must do something to help matters,' he insisted, gently. 'Will you tell me about the young men who disappear from Watercombe? About Alexius?'

'A year ago, Tribune, I knew nothing about that business. If I'd known the priests were to be men chosen by my husband, I would not have approved of them working here, but he assured me they were honest and reputable and I was stupid enough to let it go, because I could not contend with his bullying. Then I found out that men were regularly disappearing. I knew my husband was involved in this, but it's of no use to ask me why he needs them, or what he does with them, or where they go. I don't ask. It's safer for me that way. All I know for sure is that his friend Helm is also somehow involved. He comes to stay here for a few nights, then goes again.' She looked at Brighid. 'And when you appeared, Princess, I knew somehow that you must be the one he met when he went north a few weeks ago. He didn't tell me what his business was up there, only that he'd seen a lovely woman with hair like fire.'

'But he's married to Dora,' said Brighid, puzzled.

'Yes, to please me. Dora is expecting my husband's child. Helm has assured me that he will accept it, whatever sex it is.'

'Why, lady?' said Quintus.

'As a favour to me,' she said, looking down at her hands.

He did not press her further on that, though he could not imagine why a rough specimen like Helm would owe the Lady Helena a favour. As for not knowing the reason behind the abductions, he did not quite believe that either, for he knew she might have guessed, even if she had not asked. 'And your husband's friends at the tax office, my lady? Apart from Nonius, do you know who the others are?'

'Then you'll not have heard the news, Tribune,' she said.

'What news?'

'About Nonius. My husband was told late last night that Nonius was pulled out of the river at Aquae Sulis. He'd died of stab wounds.'

'Murdered?' Quintus paused, watching her face. 'Was your husband surprised?'

'He hides his feelings when it's convenient,' she whispered.

He hoped she would say more, but her attention was caught by the figure of her elder daughter, whose arms were waving in excitement as she ran across the atrium. She stood up to meet her so that her message would not be shouted for all to hear. 'Mama…Mama! It's Dora! She's started.'

'Yes, I'll come. Where is she? Please excuse me, Tribune. I think we may be occupied for the rest of the day. Princess, if you would…'

'I'll come, too, shall I?'

'Er…would you allow me to send for you, when we need help?'

'I shall be in the gymnasium with the Tribune.'

'Oh…er, my lord, if I might suggest…?'

'Yes?'

She turned back, away from her daughter's hearing. 'That you may be interested in seeing our workshops, after your treatment. Take your guards with you.' Giving him no time to ask why he would need guards, she strode off to catch up with Clodia, her pale blue gown billowing out behind her.

'Murdered? Nonius?' Quintus murmured. 'Well, we should be able to guess the reasoning behind that, I think. Come on, Princess. I'd better be seen to be sticking to my timetable before we go off investigating. Bring that boot, Florian. And take that rotten-vegetable look off your face. It's only a boot.'

There had been no chance to mention the possible fate of the Lady Helena's offering, but Brighid had a question to ask. 'Who is this Alexius you're so concerned about?' she said as they left the cool atrium now thronging with departures and arrivals. 'Is he one of your men?'

'A very close friend,' he said. 'I intend to find him.'

'Ah. Things you have to pursue. You believe he was here?'

'That's his boot. He *was* here, Princess.'

'So you think the thefts of gold, and the making of coins, and the disappearance of men from the temple are somehow linked, do you? And where does Helm come into all this?'

'He needs men and money, lass. It's obvious. He's involved, and I have to find out exactly how before I take him.'

'But surely you realise, my lord, that now he and Valens know who you are and why you're here, your life is in grave danger? And Tullus and Lucan, too? And me? If Valens can get rid of his friend Nonius simply for suggesting we ought to come here, then…'

Quintus stopped on the pathway and took her by the shoulders, halting her rhetoric in mid-flow. 'Yes, I *do* realise that. That's why I have to work fast before Valens returns. But Nonius did *not* recommend Watercombe to me, remember, it was one of the young clerks who did that. Valens was made to believe it was his friend who sent us here, knowing what we might uncover, but it was Helena Coronis who's responsible for that little mix-up. She's scared of what her husband might do to her and her daughters, but she's also trying to give us some leads. And you must take extra care not to be alone. Do you hear?'

'Yes, I hear. But surely I can be of some help, can't I?'

'I told you, you already have been. You've got Helm worried enough to do something desperate.'

'He'd have gone straight back home if his wife had not gone into labour,' she mused, looking across at the building that housed the birthing room and the gymnasium, 'but now he'll wait to see how big a favour he has to repay. Boy or girl.'

His hands dropped from her shoulders, his gaze following hers. 'Well, I think,' he said, quietly, 'that Helena Coronis is being rather optimistic.'

'What do you mean by that?'

'I mean, Princess, that if I were a man of Valens's sort with a daughter and a stepdaughter, I would certainly not be giving my newborn son away to a man like Helm, favour or not. If Helm is dependent on Valens for something, he's not in a position to object, is he? Perhaps that's why he was so eager to forge a tie with your father, chieftain of a powerful tribe. He needs all the friends he can get. And all Valens needs is another twenty years or so for his son to inherit Watercombe. If he gets a son, that is.'

'That's a bleak picture, my lord. Where will I be in twenty years' time, I wonder?' She hoped her rhetorical question might prompt a more considered reply, but the one he gave her was as ambiguous as ever.

'We'll deal with that problem when it comes,' he said, dismissively, starting off down the slope to the white-plastered porch.

Stung, she felt her anger rise yet again. 'The problem is in the present, my lord, in case you were not aware of it, and if you do not deal with it soon, I shall have to deal with it myself.'

His sandals scrunched on the gravel as he slewed round to face her so abruptly that she almost cannoned into him. 'And what exactly do you mean by that? What is this problem that cannot wait, that you'll have to deal with alone?'

She wanted to take the rash words back, but it was too late. This was not a discussion one could have in the middle of the pathway in someone else's garden with Florian standing by. 'Nothing,' she whispered. 'Nothing you'd understand. Please, let us go on.'

'You credit me with a lack of understanding I'm unaware of having done anything to deserve, Princess. I understand that your future has not been fully discussed, so far, but that's because the time and place for deciding it has not presented itself. It's enough for me that you're here. It should be enough for you, too, while there's so much else to think about.'

'So much else for *you* to think about,' she retorted. 'My experience of men is limited, I agree, but I *do* know how their minds run along only one track at a time, and that women are capable of handling myriad problems at once, especially when their own future is one of them. Don't concern yourself, Tribune. I'm not as helpless as I've led you to believe. Carry on with your important task, but don't be surprised if, when next you turn round, I'm not following in your footprints.'

'Ah!' he groaned. 'You talk in riddles, woman. Have I not told you that you're mine? Have my kisses not convinced you?' Impatiently, he took her again by the shoulders, pulling her roughly towards him before she could dodge his embrace. His kiss was not the quelling kind she anticipated, but soft and beguiling, and against all her pent-up emotions and confused plans to go her own way, she found that her mind was blotting out everything but the security of his arms and the need within her heart to become his for ever, as she might once have been Helm's.

'Wait a while longer, lass,' he whispered so that Florian could not hear. 'I shall take you to bed as soon as we're back in the room, and I'll leave you in no doubt then what your future will be. Can you wait that long, or shall we go now? Eh?'

With dignity, she removed herself from his arms

and brushed a hand down her gown to smooth it. 'I can wait indefinitely, Tribune, I thank you. Shall we go on?' He had not understood, as she had known he would not. She would have to make her own way, once this business was cleared up. Her heart ached, sending a hard ball of pain into the base of her throat. If only she had not loved him so desperately, her path would have been much smoother, she thought, holding back a sudden rush of tears.

Chapter Twelve

The message that she was needed in the birthing room did not come, yet Brighid could not help but assume that, if she were to appear uninvited, they would hardly refuse her offer of support. It was the thought of being no help to anyone that she found hard to bear. So when the sight of Quintus heaving at a pulley began to pall, she quietly excused herself and slipped further along the building, expecting to discover the right door by sound, if not by sight. She stood still to listen.

'Princess?'

She jumped, hand over heart. She had heard no one approach, but then saw that, in a deep alcove near the door, a man had just risen from a footstool. Behind him, a lamp burned before a shrine to the goddess of childbirth, and Brighid guessed he had been communing with her, Sulis-Minerva.

'Helm!' she whispered. 'What…?'

Out of the sun, he appeared smoother and less grizzled, his sandy hair brushed straight, his beard trimmed. The white tunic had been exchanged for brown plaid trousers, an undyed linen shirt and a leather belt from which hung his scabbard, tribal-style. It was how she had first seen him, weeks ago in her father's hall, wearing a heavy gold torque around his neck. 'I hoped you might be here,' he said, glancing at one of the doors. 'We should talk in private, Princess, before Valens returns.'

Brighid drew her woollen scarf around her shoulders, though not against the kind of stare to which Valens had subjected her, even though he was clearly appreciative. 'Should we?' she said. 'I don't think it matters now, does it? You've made a choice and you must stick to it, though I'm not at all impressed by your negotiating skills, sir.'

'Neither am I. Your father was a hard man, Princess. I was getting nowhere. Then it went badly wrong, didn't it? It would have been foolish for me to stay any longer, once they'd taken you.'

'It was foolish of you to go there in the first place.'

'My father sent me. But now I've found you again…'

'Er…no, sir. You did not find me. I was not lost.

And when I gave you the chance, you preferred to deny you'd ever visited my home. You can hardly expect me to show any interest in you now, especially as you already have a wife. We really don't have anything to discuss.'

'We have your brother to discuss. If you want him returned to you alive, you'd do well to grant me a few moments of your time, I think.'

'My…my *brother*?'

'I knew that would change your tune.'

'You have him? Is he safe? Where?' This was something she could never have expected, that Helm still believed Math was a captive. Could she find out more? Could she act her way through this giant misconception? She saw his eyes light up at her concern, and she thought she knew what he was about to offer her in return for Math, who was hiding in Lucan's room.

'He's safe enough, at the moment,' he said, smiling in satisfaction. 'Hungry, I expect, but he'll live. Look here, I have his dagger.' He drew the hilt up out of the scabbard and lay the weapon across his palm, the pommel decorated with gold and enamel, the blade a piece of the swordsmith's art. Brighid recognised it.

'I hope he injured you with it, sir, before you stole it from him.'

'He did. That's why I'm wearing my trews. Now, shall we talk?'

She glanced along the corridor. 'Make it quick.'

'My plan is to take your brother to join my tribe, the Dobunni, if you agree to come too. If you should decide not to, your brother will belong to Valens to do with as he does to other healthy young males.'

'Which is?'

'Ah, that's for him to tell you, not me. Your brother would join my forces, be trained with my men, toughen up, fight for Britain, eventually. A good life for any man, Princess, but I would want you to come, too. You could keep an eye on him.'

'May I remind you once again, sir, that you have a wife?'

'But my father does not.'

'Your…your *father*? What does *he* have to do with it?'

'What do you think I went to see your father about? Did you think it was…oh…hah! You *did*, didn't you?' Hands on hips, he grinned broadly with white even teeth, showing his pink tongue. 'You thought *I* was bidding for you…nay, lass, you were intended for the *chief*, my father, not for his married son. Think of that. You have a second chance now, to be the Dubonni chief's wife and live in style. We don't live in wooden huts as your people do, Princess. We live in a villa as big as Watercombe. Your father appears not to have kept you informed about your future.'

No one keeps me informed about my future.

'I was not the only one to misread the situation,' she said. 'My brothers, too. They would not have agreed to your proposal.'

'They don't have a say in it now, do they? You can make your own decisions. Valens believes you're the Tribune's slave, but I know different. A tribal woman like you will never be anyone's slave. Think about it, Princess. Is it better to follow him around to catch the crumbs he throws your way, or to be the chief woman of our tribe, revered and honoured, able to sit at her husband's side and advise him? That's what I call a future.'

'Are you speaking the truth?' Guiltily, she savoured his proposal in an attempt to be realistic, self-seeking. Surely this would answer at least one of her problems.

'I swear it, before Sulis-Minerva. I shall take my wife home as soon as she's ready to move, and I urge you to come, too, or you and your brother will belong to Valens.'

'That's not likely, Helm. The Tribune is aware of

the danger we're in and he's prepared. He protects me well.'

'Really?' he scoffed, smiling over his shoulder into the empty corridor. 'He didn't manage to protect your brother either, did he? I, however, know how to keep a woman safe. I shall get my wife away from Valens; I could get you away too. Believe me, he uses his women hard and has his sights on you, Princess.'

'Thank you for the warning. I thought you and he were bosom friends.'

'We have the same political interests, that's all.'

'But not the same scruples?'

'Let's just say that my scruples are more transparent than his. He's a very clever man, but he needs my help. It won't last for ever.'

'I need some time,' she whispered. 'Give me more time. Another day.'

'It's running out. Valens moves fast. As soon as—'

A sound from behind the nearest door flattened Helm like a shadow into the recess from where, as the door opened, he became invisible.

'Ah, Princess,' came the voice of Helena Coronis. 'I was just about to come for you. Would you care to add your opinion to ours? She's getting close.'

The door closed behind them, and the shadow slipped along the wall, unseen.

The birthing room was stark, functional and not large enough for the three midwives, Helena Coronis, Brighid, and the long table upon which Dora lay to be examined. There was also an unusual chair with a cutaway seat on which the mother would sit to give birth, gravity being the obvious accomplice. Piles of towels and bedding were stacked on shelves next to bottles and jars, metal instruments, bowls and beakers. The scent of lavender and mint mingled with the tang of body odours. A perfumed candle burned on the window-sill to keep the air sweet and, from the table, Dora's cry rose to a crescendo with her latest contraction.

The hum of chatter stopped as Brighid's hand was caught in a painful grip that she bore without flinching, keeping hold of the hand as the contraction passed. Dora seemed not to mind whose hand she held, simply nodding when Brighid asked if she might take a look. She had not expected the birth to be imminent. In her experience, first babies usually took their time to arrive, but Dora's infant was not inclined to wait, and Brighid could see that it would not be long before it made an appearance. Between contractions, there was little for her to do but help Dora onto the birthing stool, massage her back, and keep her feet warm.

If Brighid's head had not been teeming with the information Helm had just passed on to her, and with the critical situation she was witnessing, she might have found a convenient time to take Helena Coronis to one side and warn her to go and retrieve the piece of jewellery that might still be in the workshop, the one she had offered to the shrine. But the thought went from her mind as Dora's infant slid into the world, and in the rejoicing at the birth of a lusty boy, all other matters faded into insignificance. Then, there was much to be done for mother and child, and Brighid's exit went unnoticed by anyone.

Pausing at the small shrine to give thanks, she leaned against the wall to think. It would have been easy to dismiss Helm's unexpected offer as absurd, but the growing concerns about her future had left an empty space where any offer, however extraordinary, could take root and live, if only for a short time. It was not, as it happened, as extraordinary as all that for, if her father had decided that this was to be her future instead of playing cat and mouse with them all, she might by now have been installed as the wife of the Dobunni chief, Helm's stepmother. Such things could and did happen. And whether she liked the idea or not, it *was* a viable alternative to an uncertain future as the Tribune's 'healer'. The issue of her virginity had not been raised, so she could only assume that Helm and his father cared little one way or the other, as long as she was not already pregnant, as his wife Dora had been. There would, however, be a brutal solution to that problem which she knew these men would have no qualms about putting into practice. She had seen a dozen or so tiny graves to prove it.

Much as she disliked the idea of leaving the Tribune, the facts were not far from the way Helm had described them, and no matter how hard she tried to be optimistic about her chances of remaining with the one she had grown to love, the stark truth was that he had not taken her out of love, but as a shrewd calculated move against her marriage to the Dobunni man they were both pursuing. The Tribune would not even consider her future, but was more concerned with finding the friend who had been one of the prime causes of this journey to Aquae Sulis. She herself was no more than an appendage, as she'd been from the outset. Better to take matters into her own hands now, she thought, than leave it until it was too late. Time was running out, for when Helm discovered that he had no Math to bargain with, he might withdraw his offer. What was equally interesting, though, was that Helm needed young men for his revolt against the Roman occupation, and Valens needed them for something else, as yet unspecified.

Peeping into the gymnasium, she saw that Quintus had left, probably assuming that she was still helping with Dora's birthing. This was her chance to go up to the workshops to find the one where Math had discovered her bracelet. If she could find the Lady Helena's piece and return it to her, it might encourage her to co-operate in the exposure of her husband. She did not agree with Tullus that a woman should not be told what her husband gets up to. The Lady Helena had a right to know.

From the garden, her route up the rough slope was unobserved by those on the pathways below, their heads covered against the drizzle and the cool breeze that bent the spray from the fountains. She intended to follow the path that Math had described, but behind the thick screen of trees, the nearest hut clattered to the sound of a potter's wheel. She passed on, unseen.

The next workshop was busy with men sitting on the floor where a mosaic was being assembled on a wooden pallet, their concentration too intent to notice her progress. Next door to the mosaicists was a weaver and his wife, standing at a massive upright loom with baskets of coloured wool beside them. Beyond their hut was an open door where a white-bearded man sat at a bench, carefully filing at some small object held in a vice. Could this be the goldsmith?'

He looked up as she hesitated, clearly intrigued by the sight of a lovely red-haired woman decked with gold ornaments worth a fortune. *'Domina,'* he said.

'Good morning. Will you show me your work?' she said, drawing closer.

Putting down his file, he unclamped the tiny pewter thing and held it out for her to see. It was a miniature leg no longer than her middle finger, exactly like the ones she'd seen being sold near the shrine at Aquae Sulis. Beside the old man was a tray of amulets and charms made of pewter, tin and silver, with flat pieces of metal on which messages could be written. All kinds of body parts were represented: arms and breasts, hearts and feet, ears and eyes, even small pans for pouring liquid offerings, covering every kind of need. 'It's beautifully made,' she said, 'like those I saw a man selling at the shrine of Sulis-Minerva in town. He said he made them here, too.'

The man nodded, tossing the leg into the tray. 'My assistant,' he said. 'Did you want me to make something especially for you, *domina*? You're one of the guests?'

'No thank you. I was hoping to find the goldsmith's workshop.'

'You won't. He's locked up for the day.'

'Oh. When will your assistant be back?'

A knowing smile lit his blue eyes. 'Ah, it's Gaditanus you came to see, is it? He's only been here three moons, and already he's got the ladies asking for him. He'll be back from Aquae Sulis before long. Do you want to wait?'

Smiling back, she shook her head. 'You've got it wrong. Your Gaditanus doesn't know me. Good day to you. Your amulets are beautiful. If I'd brought some money with me, I'd buy one.'

'Then take one as a gift from me. Which shall it be, a heart? Not as valuable as your ornaments, *domina*, but they seem to be effective. Here you are. Take it.'

Her fingers closed round the smooth cool silver

heart that fitted so comfortably into the palm of her hand. 'I shall keep it,' she said. 'Thank you.'

In the suite assigned to Quintus and his assistants, doors slammed and voices shouted. 'Not here, either. No, not here.'

'She's not been in here, sir,' said Math.

Another door slammed. 'Where *is* she, then?'

'The workshops? Would she have gone…?'

'Come with me,' said Quintus. 'I was going to look there anyway. Bring one of the guards. The other had better stay here.'

Like a flock of flustered white-and-grey pigeons, they flapped off into the gardens and on up the hillside, stopping with a concertina-like squeeze as the figure of Brighid tripped towards them, still smiling at the old smith's kindness. 'If you're off to find the goldsmith's workshop,' she called, 'it's closed for the day. Plenty of others are open, though.'

'I *told* you,' Quintus said, unsmiling, 'not to go out alone.'

Feeling four pairs of eyes upon her, Brighid bristled. 'Oh, my mistake, my lord. I thought you *asked* me. Well, here I am. Quite unharmed.'

'For which we have good fortune to thank rather than a sudden rush of common sense,' he muttered, exasperated. 'I wonder if you would be so good, Princess, as to remain *at all times* with at *least* one of us. Preferably myself. I do not have time to add *you* to my list of searches.' His request was a lightly veiled command.

'I shall give your request my due consideration, my lord.'

'Yes, do. Now, if you will be pleased to follow me?'

'But I've told you, the goldsmith's place is locked up.'

Tullus and Lucan exchanged the lift of an eyebrow as Quintus set off once more, sweeping Brighid along with him like an autumn leaf. 'That will not prevent us from taking a look, however,' he said sharply.

Brighid thought he must be mistaken, but she had not bargained for the guard's mighty shoulder that crashed the locked door open at only the second try, leaving the place wide open for their search. It revealed all they had hoped to find: chests of newly cut and stamped gold coin, the dies and tools used for the forgeries, and the latest basketful of thefts from the shrine, from which the bullion was manufactured. It was the answer to the riddle of who was paying his considerable taxes in new coinage.

Leaving the workshop intact, they posted the guard outside until they could return with reinforcements. Meanwhile, Brighid stood apart, silently fuming, turning the heart over and over in her hands.

'What is it?' said Tullus, politely.

Wordlessly, she showed him.

'That's nice. Where did you pick it up? At the shrine?'

'Over at the amulet maker's workshop. The old man gave it to me. He thought I was looking for his assistant, Gaditanus.'

'Who?' His voice went up at the end, in disbelief.

'Gaditanus. He was not there. He sells these at the…what's the matter?'

'Will you tell the Tribune, *domina*? I think he might be interested.'

'No, I shall not tell the Tribune anything until he finds a civil tongue in his head. I am a Brigant—'

'Yes, a Brigantian Princess, I know, but I think you should. Quintus! Come here, man. What does the name Gaditanus mean to you? Isn't that what you Cadiz men call yourselves?'

'From Cadiz. Yes. Why?' Quintus frowned at Tullus, then at Brighid's tight-lipped mouth.

'Princess,' he said, '*tell me*, if you please. It's important.'

There was no mistaking his commanding voice, though the urge to make him wait was very strong. 'A man called Gaditanus helps the old man to make and sell his votive offerings at the sacred shrine. I met him when I was there; he told me he works here. The old man gave me this.' She held out her silver heart to show him, but he was staring at Tullus as if he'd seen an apparition.

'How long has this man been working here? Not the old one. The other.'

'He said about three moons.'

A breath went out of Quintus that trembled and was sucked in again, sharply. 'It's worth taking a look,' he said. 'Which way?'

'But he's not there,' Brighid said. 'He's on his way back...'

But Quintus had already set off along the track, and she had no choice but to follow him to the amulet maker, who showed some concern at the sight of the red-haired woman with three burly men. Respectfully, he answered the Tribune's questions, which he at first assumed were to do with the legality of his trade and his employing of an assistant without the permission of Watercombe's owners. They had never seen Gaditanus, he told them, but he'd been taken on during the winter months when the trek to Aquae Sulis with a heavy basket had been too much for him personally. Gaditanus was strong, honest, and willing, once he had recovered.

'Describe him to me, old man, if you will,' said Quintus.

'Tall. About your own age, I should think, and dark like yourself. He has a fresh scar on his brow, up here…' he touched his white hairline '…but he's said nothing about himself to me, and I've never asked. Do you think you might know him, my lord? He's not in some kind of trouble, is he?'

'No trouble, but, yes, I think I might know him. Would you tell him that Tribune Quintus Tiberius Martial has been asking after him? He may recall my name.'

'Indeed, sir. My lords. *Domina*.' He returned Brighid's smile and picked up another leg to clamp into his vice.

Brighid would rather have gone back to the room to change into dry clothes, but the hold on her hand was relentless, and she was not surprised that Quintus offered her no thanks for giving him the lead he'd been so desperate for. Apart from his hand clasped around hers, she had ceased to exist except as someone who irked him. It was not the way for a chieftain's daughter to be appreciated, she told herself, angrily.

Yet her sideways glances at his set expression, his strong determined jaw, his alert brown eyes that scanned the buildings as they approached, made her heart leap with love, aching for a gentle word from him, a look of tenderness. The pain in her heart became almost unbearable when the terrible alternative came back for review: Helm's offer of security and status, her own identity valued for what it was, and a life lived in pride instead of slavery. She could do it. Yes, she *could* do it. She must not credit the Tribune with any finer feelings that would set her apart from other women he'd known. Helm's father needed a wife and the Tribune would marry a woman of his own kind. She must stop trying to make her dreams into reality, for that was not how things worked. The Brigantes were realists, not dreamers.

She pulled back on his hand as they entered the men's part of the bath-house, but Quintus kept hold of her, making a signal for silence. She thought he was about to take the steps down to the furnace room on the lower level but, on hearing the distant sound of voices raised in anger, he slipped off his sandals and motioned for her and the others to do the same.

'That's Valens's voice,' Lucan whispered. 'He's supposed to be away.'

'And that's Helm's,' Brighid said.

Tullus had crossed to the half-open door that led directly to the tepidarium and from there to the next room where the space was taken up almost completely by a circular pool of cold water across which the two men's voices echoed. Venturing further, Tullus waved them on, holding a hand up to warn them.

The owner of Watercombe and his friend had obviously not gone there to bathe, for both were fully clothed, but to find shelter and privacy at a time when the bath-house was deserted. Valens was leaning against one red-painted wall, his arms folded across his chest, his attitude contemptuous. On the other side of the pool stood Helm, whose belligerent stance was meant to show that he had the advantage, borne out by his words of defiance. 'It was agreed months ago, Valens, as you well know, and there's nothing you can do to change it. It's a boy and he's mine.'

'Wrong, my friend. I sired him. He'll stay here with me.'

Quintus frowned at Brighid, her hand still in his grasp. 'You didn't tell me,' he mouthed at her.

She glared back. 'You didn't ask.'

Again, Tullus held up a warning hand. The men had only to turn towards the doorway to see the four figures listening to the quarrel. Helm was shaking his head. 'You're not up to it, man. You're slipping. You can't even keep your captives secure any more, can you? The lad I brought in on the night I arrived you've already let slip. I could have had him halfway there by now if you'd had your wits about you. Now we've lost him.'

'No, you couldn't,' said Valens. 'You'd have been here waiting for your wife to perform, and that lad would be of no use to you half-dead from suffocation, would he? And how much help are you to me anyway, my bearded friend? Whenever I need you to take men to the mines you've been away on some wild goose chase. What good was your trip up north when you came back empty-handed? We're never going to get paid if you're diverting the work-force to your useless recruitment camp. It's Cambrian mines where they're needed, man, not your training grounds. The gold is split between us, remember, for my tax dues and your rebel causes, but we've seen nothing to show for it from your side yet, have we, fool?'

'Then supply me with more men, Valens. Last time I was in Cambria they told me that one from here had got away, so how long will it be before he returns to spill the beans? It won't last for ever, you know, and if you can't get me the workers, I can't get them to the mines and neither of us will get what we need to operate. Any dimwit can see that.'

'Insult me at your peril, man,' said Valens, placing his hands on his hips. 'And if you want gold faster than you can get it from Cambria, then take it off the red-head when you get her back to your place. That should keep you going for a year or two. I still can't believe she's willing.'

'She is,' said Helm, his voice ringing out across the water.

'Has she said so?'

'Yes, only an hour ago. I made her a better offer than the clever Tribune's, and she knows it. I may not get the brother now, but she'll come.'

Brighid felt the hand tighten over hers, pulling her to make her look at him; when she refused, he took her chin in his grip, turning her face to his. 'You didn't tell me,' he mouthed.

She met his eyes, stubbornly. *You didn't ask me.*

'Don't even *think* it,' he snarled, his eyes burning into hers.

Tullus's hand moved, flapping a warning. But it was too late.

'What was that?' said Helm, already whirling on the balls of his feet.

Still holding Brighid, Quintus stepped forwards. 'It's me,' he said, 'come to contribute a few facts to your discussion. It's been most entertaining, so far.'

Valens appeared unflustered, even amused. 'Well, if it's not our clever Tribune and his side-kicks. And the beautiful slave. Helm, my friend,' he said without looking at him, 'while our busy-bodys are here in force, I suggest you go and help yourself to that strongbox in the Tribune's room. You should be able to manage the guard. There's only one of him.'

'Yes,' said Helm, 'while you help yourself to my son, Valens. I think not. I know which I'd rather have, I thank you. Something that you'll never have, for all your connections. A loyal wife and a son.'

That stirred Valens as nothing else could. Enraged by those two home truths, he let out a roar of rage that resonated round the cavernous room, followed by a volley of oaths that called into question Helm's birth, his parents' birth and, naturally, Helm's inability to father a child. And while this explained to the audience why he had agreed to marry the Lady Helena's pregnant slave, it did not explain, except to the two people involved, his reasons for negotiating with Brighid's father.

'So while we're on the subject of wives, sons and impotence,' said Quintus, 'let me put one other matter straight. I used the Princess to lead me to the man who is acting against the Emperor Septimus Severus. At the time, I did not intend her for anything beyond that. So if you have some grand idea that the lady will choose stability with you, Helm, rather than remain for the rest of her life in my protection, then I advise you to forget it. You have a son and a wife, but you do not have the woman who will be *my* wife. As for you, Publius Cato Valens…'

My wife. My wife? Was that what he'd said?

Brighid stared up at him, then beyond him to Lucan and Tullus, whose faces told her nothing they'd not expected, then at Helm, whose accusing eyes seemed to imply that she had deceived him. Quintus had not looked at her directly, and even now she thought she might be dreaming, while his voice boomed across the water on matters to do with tax evasion, forgery, murder, and the abduction of men into slave labour.

Only half-listening, she could not tell what triggered the sudden explosion of activity, men running and chasing, roars of fury as Valens and

Helm leapt into the pool to get at each other faster than running round it. Surges of water frothed over them as they heaved and ducked, wrestling and throwing each other while spitting out insults with the water. Shouts at them to stop were heard in the commotion, and would not have been heeded, but Helm's dagger flashed, and Valen's struggles became more desperate, for he was unarmed. A cloud of pink swirled through the foam and then, as Valens roared, twisting away, Helm dived like a dolphin, swimming underwater to the far end where Brighid had been told to stay by the door. The men lined the edge, ready to heave the wounded Valens out.

But Helm did not wait to see. With water pouring off him in torrents, he headed straight for the door. Brighid could have tripped him, slammed the door shut, slowed his exit somehow, but she stood aside and allowed him to pass. He staggered back instead, bowled off his feet by a man who hurled himself headfirst like a demon into Helm's body, ignoring the dagger, roaring with fury and all the impetus of a year-old rage. It was Alexius Tito Gaditanus, Quintus's lost friend, now transformed from the smiling man who had sold offerings at Aquae Sulis to this raging fighting machine, rolling on the floor with murder in his heart and his hands clamped round Helm's thick neck.

The heavy gold torque at Helm's throat, however, protected him from the full force of Alexius's stranglehold and, as Helm heaved his assailant off, a gap appeared between them into which Brighid threw herself like an enraged mother breaking up a fight between her sons, knocking the astonished men apart just long enough for Helm to roll away and scramble to his feet. And before Alexius could shake off her clinging, clawing hands, Helm had gone, slamming the door behind him.

Lightning fast, Brighid hurled herself at the door and pressed her back against it, legs apart, head down, pointing the wet dagger directly at Alexius. It was her brother's, stolen by Helm and already put to good use. She knew how to wield it, but never in cold blood, as a man could. A woman's defence was tied to her emotions, and already her voice was husky and broken by the last few turbulent moments, her free hand pushing against one breast that burned with the pain of a blow from someone's elbow. She could control neither pain, nor tears, nor rage.

'Leave him!' she panted. 'Let him go! Let him *go*, I say!'

'Domina,' Alexius whispered, pointing at the

door. 'He's mine. I've waited long for this chance. Let me get at him.'

'No!' she screamed, hoarsely. *'No!'*

Quintus and Tullus were already at his back, but Brighid misjudged their intentions, swinging the dagger point at them, too, preparing to launch herself in Helm's defence. 'Lass,' Quintus said, gently.

Hot tears filled her eyes, blinding her. 'He has a *wife*,' she gasped, 'and a new son…and you *cannot* deprive her of his protection when she… she most…needs it. I don't…*care*…what he's done…but I had a maid once…who'd done nothing…to deserve…' The memory of it, so recent, overwhelmed her as the dagger wavered and clattered to the floor, turning her away from their stares of masculine bafflement towards the door upon which she poured out tears of grief and doubt and hope.

Hands caught her before she slid to the floor, contorted by her emotions, and she was lifted, sobbing, into the arms of the man she loved, the one whose throw-away words she still could not quite endow with the sincerity they ought to have. Carried away out of that dreadful place to the warm tepidarium, Quintus sat with her on the massage table in a tangle of arms and legs, soothing her with his hands and lips, and with the deep velvet voice that could change, too abruptly, to an officer's command. He was, he admitted, sadly out of practice, a fault he intended to work on in the future.

'Whose future?' she sniffed, wiping her tears on his tunic.

Through the closed door, shouts reached them, but his attention did not waver from the woman in his arms, which amazed and delighted her, having assumed that the first sighting of his friend would take priority over everything. 'Whose future, sweetheart? Well, ours, of course. Yours and mine. I really cannot let you go to that thick Dobunni barbarian with the beard. Once I've set my mind on something, I don't easily let it go, particularly when that something is a woman of such quality. Brigantian Princesses are not exactly two for a *denari*, you know, and once a man has one in his clutches, he doesn't let her go, he marries her.'

'Marries her? But senators are not allowed to—'

'You've been listening to the enemy, my little hot-headed beauty. I have no intention of becoming a senator. I shall be doing this job for no more than another year or two and then, when we have a family in the making, I shall take you back to Cadiz to breed horses on my father's farm at

Jerez. They'll be very impressed by my wife's status, and I shall milk it for all it's worth. Shall you mind that, sweetheart?'

'Is it true, Quintus? Am I dreaming it? Before I wake, can I tell you that I love you? Does a soldier-turned-tax-collector wish to know about such things?'

'This one does,' he whispered. His kiss roamed over her face and lingered tenderly over her lips, taking into account her recent weeping. 'This particular one has found the woman of *his* dreams, intelligent and incredibly beautiful, caring, fierce and loving, too honest for words and generous even to her enemies. You are my heart's desire, and I want you as I've never wanted a woman in my life, my darling. I cannot let you go, for I love you too much. I know you had thoughts of being Helm's wife, but I would not have allowed it. You're mine. You have always been mine, right from the beginning. I used you badly and kept you in fear of being sold, but I had to make my ownership marginally more attractive than thoughts of escape. Did I hurt you badly, sweetheart? It was never my intention.'

'My pride,' she said, tasting his lips. 'But I have plenty left, still in good order. But, Quintus, I longed to know…'

'What my plans are for you?'

'Yes. It was like being cast adrift without an anchor or a sail. For a woman brought up the way I've been, it's hardly possible to survive without a home or a protector, even one she doesn't love. And yet slavery was never an option, for me. Not even yours, Quintus.'

'I can understand that. You're not slave material. You let me know it, too, didn't you, lass? Daily, almost.'

'Blame my father. For all his faults, he was a proud man.'

'Yes, and he would also have sold you to the Dobunnii, if they'd offered him enough. You might now have been Helm's other wife. You have your father to thank for that.'

'I do,' she whispered, smiling. 'I do indeed.'

The sounds from the distant room had died down, and for the time they had in private, Quintus comforted her bruised breast with a gentle hand until it could be attended to, taking her mind off its pain with his kisses and the tender words she had sorely missed while his mind was so preoccupied. 'But now, my love,' he said, 'I want you to be patient while I attend to business here at Watercombe. I have to do what I was sent here for, or my next interview with Severus will be even more uncomfortable than the last. We shall have to spend another day or two here, before we return to Aquae Sulis, and then home. I promise I shall not neglect you, my love.'

'You'll not go after Helm and his wife, will you?'

'No, we can stop his recruitment activities, now we know who we're dealing with and how he's been funded all these years. Go back to the apartment, my little love, and get Florian to tend you. Then we'll have something to eat. A celebration feast.'

He escorted her to the door and watched her reach the guard waiting by the room before turning back to the bath-house where his three colleagues had already begun to attend to the very limited future of the owner of Watercombe.

'Will somebody please tell me what's going on?'

The voice of Helena Coronis reached the four men who stood at the outer door of the bath-house, still talking. The rain had stopped and the path shone with wet, reflecting the lady's pale blue chiton that billowed behind her rather like, Tullus thought, one of those statuettes of Astrae, goddess of justice. Instantly, they stood to attention, blocking the access to the door.

'Where is my husband?' she said, looking in turn from one man to the other. 'Helm has just stormed into the infirmary, scooped up his wife and infant, *wet through*, I might add, and carried them off without a word of explanation. What on earth is the matter with the man? Have they had words? Is that it?'

Quintus went forwards to meet her. 'Yes, my lady. I think one could say they've had words, and more besides.'

'What do you mean, Tribune? What's happened?'

Tullus strode past him, courteously holding out an arm to steer her back up the path towards the atrium, the way she had come. 'I think, my lady, that we need to find a quiet corner somewhere. That would be best. Somewhere private where we can talk. Will you come?'

With a glance at the row of sombre faces, and a lingering look of surprise at one of them, she found something in the deep appreciative eyes of her escort that informed her here, at last, was a man she could trust. 'Yes,' she whispered. 'I'll come.'

Their rejoicing had been done privately where guests could not hear them, for by now the news had spread through the whole estate that the owner, Valens, had been overtaken by fumes in the caldarium, the hottest and steamiest of all the bath-house rooms. It was no more, they said, than a risk run by anyone in his profession who took such care that the pool was clean and in good working order. A terrible loss to the Lady Helena and her two daughters, they murmured, unaware that the furnace had been fed only recently with clippings from the gardens gathered especially for the half-yearly fumigation. Poisonous, of course. His wife was keeping to her rooms. Distraught, they said, lacking any evidence to the contrary.

After a dark and dismally damp morning, the sun had now set leaves sparkling, its beams bouncing off the pools, diamond-bright and mirroring the hands of those who sat on the edges to talk about the year that Alexius had missed, somehow. Passing food and balancing glasses of red wine, they heard how, after unwisely sampling the priest's dream-inducing potion, he had found himself bumping along in a covered wagon, tied up and aching in every limb.

By now, the men knew that Valens had been supplying young fit men to work the gold mines in Cambria in which Helm and his father had shares. 'So it's not state run, then?' said Lucan.

'Only partly,' said Alexius. 'Our men are there to guard it, but only half of the slave miners are civilians stolen from somewhere. Like me. Those who supply slaves are paid in gold. Helm was responsible for getting them there because it's not far from his territory and he travels that route regularly.'

'So,' said Quintus, 'he syphoned a few of them off to his own place. It fell apart, didn't it? Valens suspected.'

'Neither of them trusted the other,' said Alexius. 'But a few months of mining and I'd had enough. The work is killing men faster than they can be replaced.'

'Is that how you got your injury?' said Brighid. She nestled cosily in the crook of Quintus's arm, her bruises salved and bandaged by Florian, her earlier tempestuous challenge now explained by her lover and fully understood by her three admiring friends.

'Yes, Princess. The tunnels are airless and hot, and the work is back-breaking. But I managed to escape one night, and make my way back to Aquae Sulis with the intention of finding out who exactly was responsible, and whether, as I suspected, it was how Valens was able to mint his own coin. I was picked up off the roadside by the old man you met; he brought me here and nursed me till I recovered.'

'Wait,' said Brighid. 'The old man said that Valens and Lady Helena didn't know you were here, but that's not so, is it? She must have suspected, because it was she who suggested that Quintus should go up to see the workshops, after she'd seen your boot. She hoped he'd find you, even though she pretended not to know.'

'One can hardly blame her,' said Quintus. 'Valens would have revenged himself in some unspeakable way if she'd ever involved herself with what he was doing.'

'Yet she did,' said Tullus, quietly. 'As soon as she realised who we were, she saw a way to show us what they were up to. I'll tell you something else, too, about our friend Helm who's disappeared with his wife and son.'

'Go on,' said Lucan. 'You are obviously in the lady's confidence.'

Tullus sent him a withering look. 'The favour that Helm was doing the lady by marrying her pregnant slave Dora was nothing of the kind. That was *his* version. In fact, the Lady Helena insisted on it, threatening him with the complete exposure of the whole sordid business if he didn't agree, even if it lost *her* everything in the process. She expected him to take Dora away much earlier, out of Valens's control, but Valens wouldn't let him. He said she had to stay until the child was born.'

'So that he could claim it, if it was a boy,' said Brighid. 'Which he did.'

'One step too far,' said Tullus. 'But Dora and Helm were always very fond of each other, so the Lady Helena tells me, and Helm was naturally furious when Valens took advantage of her.'

'Hah!' grunted Alexius, sourly. 'I'm glad to hear somebody's fond of him. I'd like to have strangled the murderous little... Sorry, Princess. I shall have to be satisfied with my revenge on one, rather than both, I suppose.'

'Yes,' she said. 'Think of what you've gained, not lost.'

'He's gained a *boot*,' said Quintus, caustically, 'and lost the other one. Serves you right, man. I've told you before about leaving them under people's beds.'

The men would have talked until dawn, but Quintus had other more important things on his mind, now he could see past the dangers that demanded prompt dealings. If Brighid suspected that men's minds were, on the whole, less flexible than women's, she had not applied that knowledge to their relationship which, to her, came before anything else. It ought, she believed, to have been dealt with immediately, not put on hold until it was convenient, not when he had taken her to the peak of ecstasy and left her to find her own way down, as it were.

Nevertheless, there was some guilt to their first embrace of the night, for she had discovered that he was no ordinary man with an ordinary man's job, and this was no holiday villa she had brought him to. It had been, he told her, one of the most dangerous situations he'd faced since leaving the army, for they had walked straight into the hornets' nest without knowing what to look for.

'I'm sorry,' she whispered, snuggling deeper into his arms. 'Can you forgive me for behaving so badly, at times? I was jealous of your involvement and needed you all to myself. You are the first man I've ever loved, you see.'

'Nothing to forgive,' he said into her hair. 'I turned your ordered life upside down, beloved, and I expected you to take it in your stride. It was unreasonable of me, but you did it. Magnificently.'

'Up to a point.'

'You were entitled to object. Any proud woman would. I would not change any part of you. Will you stay by my side now, for ever? Will you be my wife, sweetheart? As my very own Brigantian Princess?'

'For ever, my lord, as whatever you want me to be.'

'Except a slave, lass. There'll be no more talk of slaves, I promise.'

'You said I was not slave material. Is that the reason?'

'Well, partly. But you'd have to cut your hair off and we couldn't have that.'

Laughing, he caught her fist before it fell, holding it upon the pillow while he kissed her to silence. Then, as she moaned and responded to him, her palms smoothed over the ripples of muscle and her body was set alight by the feel of his long hard limbs over hers. His sculpted chest pressed tenderly upon her breasts, replacing the cares and heartaches of the past weeks with the love that had waited impatiently, disguised as protection, obligation and the mending of minds and bodies, hers as well as his. 'I adore you, my lord,' she whispered. 'I sent a message to Brigantia at the shrine, asking her for your love. She returned my gift and I thought she meant it not to be, but then she gave it to me free of charge. How blessed am I?'

'Perhaps, my darling, she knew you already had it.'

Brighid smiled. She had shown him the little silver heart that Alexius had made that now lay safely under their pillow. It was very strange, he had said, how love can sometimes travel such a roundabout route to reach its destination.

Epilogue

The one who stayed on at Watercombe to help Helena Coronis with the aftermath of her husband's demise was, predictably, Tullus, although he was a few years younger than her. The bond they had forged at the outset was strong enough for Helena to recognise a good man, at last, who would give her the love and respect she desired. The estate owed taxes amounting to a fortune, so she sold Watercombe and bought a more modest villa, with Tullus's help, and with Clodia and Carina lived a peaceful, busy and happy life in the town of Aquae Sulis. They had two sons. Twins.

Alexius returned to Eboracum with Quintus, Brighid and Lucan, to explain his long absence from duties. The Emperor Septimus Severus and his wife, Julia Domna, attended the wedding of Quintus and Brighid only a few weeks after their return, when it occurred to the bride that the family they hoped for might already have commenced. A month later, she was sure of it. It was a boy, born in Brigantia. Two daughters followed, both born in Cadiz.

Math and Florian were inseparable and so, since Florian belonged to Quintus, the brother and sister stayed together as they had been destined to do from the start. Neither of them particularly missed their former life, their new one being much more to their liking. Lucan lived with them, too, when they eventually moved to Cadiz, remaining as an adopted uncle and close friend, never marrying, but never short of female companionship, either. Together, he and Alexius directed a mercantile business in Cadiz, trading in luxury goods from Byzantium and the Levant, which the sons of Alexius eventually inherited.

After Helm's narrow escape from capture, no more was heard of him or his planned revolt against the state, probably because the Emperor remained successfully in Britain until his death three years later in Eboracum in the year 211. I can disclose, however, that the insult Valens threw at Helm during their fatal quarrel was untrue. Helm and Dora went on to raise three beautiful daughters, and Quintus remained for several years in blissful ignorance about the true nature of Helm's offer for Brighid's hand. When Brighid told him about it, during his daily massage, adding that she might have been a Dobunni chief's wife by now, she knew by the way his shoulders were shaking that it was nothing Florian was doing. But by now Brighid had learnt almost as many massage techniques as Florian, as well as some less familiar to him, and when she nudged him out of the way, he knew to leave the two of them alone while she took her own kind of sweet revenge for a wholly inappropriate moment of amusement. Predictably, Quintus was not in the least chastened by his treatment.

End Note

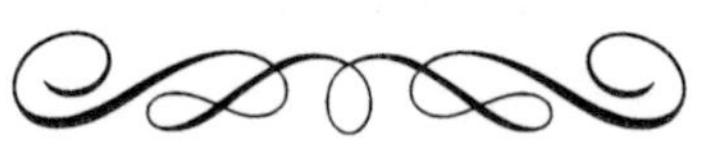

Cambria was the Roman name for Wales where the gold mine at Dolaucothi still exists for visitors to see. It is owned by the National Trust whose guided tours take you back to Roman times, as well as more recent eras. There are practical experiences and exhibitions, rare Welsh gold for sale, walks to take and a nearby castle to explore. The address is: Dolaucothi Gold Mines, Pumsaint, Llanwrda, Carmarthenshire. SA19 8US.

Roman engineers discovered the most efficient way to remove the gold from vertical veins of white quartz, blasting it out by powerful jets of water brought across the valley via aqueducts. This is how our story character Valens became involved, for his local knowledge, his supply of workers, and his water-engineering, not to mention his greed for gold. Across the Severn estuary and over the Brecon Beacons, the journey from

Bath might have taken two or more days; today it would take only a few hours.

Watercombe itself is entirely fictitious but is closely modeled on other healing shrines and centres known to exist in that area. The standard of living at such places was very high indeed, though the medical care was high-risk, to say the least.

HISTORICAL

Large Print

GLORY AND THE RAKE

Deborah Simmons

As if the continual vandalism of the spa she's renovating weren't enough for Glory Sutton, she also has to deal with the enigmatic Duke of Westfield! As they get drawn into the mystery, they must reveal their own secrets in order to uncover the truth…

LADY DRUSILLA'S ROAD TO RUIN

Christine Merrill

When her flighty sister elopes, Lady Drusilla Rudney knows she has to stop her! She employs the help of ex-army captain John Hendricks. Drusilla's unconventional ways make him want to forget his gentlemanly conduct…and create a scandal of their own!

TO MARRY A MATCHMAKER

Michelle Styles

Lady Henrietta Thorndike hides her lonely heart behind playing Cupid—but Robert Montemorcy knows it has to stop! He bets Henri that she won't be able to resist meddling…only to lose his own heart into the bargain!

THE MERCENARY'S BRIDE

Terri Brisbin

Awarded the title and lands of Thaxted, Brice Fitzwilliam waits to claim his promised bride, but Gillian of Thaxted will *not* submit to the conquering knight! Will Brice risk exposing the chink in his armour by succumbing to the charms of his new wife?